Cali Boy

THE LOYAL BOYS BOOK ONE

CHARLI MEADOWS

Editing by Novel Mechanic
Special Edition Cover by Tal Lewin - Instagram @caravaggia13
Formatting by Elizabeth Dear and Silver at Bitter Sage Designs

SYNOPSIS

Finn

One devastating night. One tragic accident.

I survived, but the boy I used to be didn't.

And I've been on a downward spiral of anger and resentment ever since. That is until my father makes a selfish decision that changes the course of my life and my future.

It brings *him* into it.

Golden-haired surfer boy, Oliver Chase.

Sunshine personified and my new stepbrother.

I want to hate him, but his shy smiles and endearing dimples have me questioning everything I thought I knew about myself. I definitely don't deserve him, and I'll probably hurt him, but the ease with which he breaks down the walls surrounding my battered heart might not leave me with a choice.

Oliver

I don't look back when Mom moves us from our sleepy California beach town to the wealthy suburbs of Chicago. I need a fresh start, to leave all the negativity and hate behind me, and I'm taking it.

But I wasn't expecting the grumpy, brooding, hurt boy that bangs on my bedroom door. Nor was I expecting the toxic relationship he has with his dad, my mom's new husband.

With mounting tensions at school and home, I'm not sure how to feel about this fresh start anymore. But what I do know is that Finn's tender touches and growly commands make me want him. And you should never lust after a straight boy... especially your new stepbrother.

Cali Boy is an 86,000-word M/M stepbrother romance. It is book one in The Loyal Boys Series, a collection of standalone contemporary gay romances. You can expect grumpy/sunshine, hurt/comfort, and steamy first times. This novel is intended for 18+ readers and touches on some sensitive subjects.

Content Warnings: Language, explicit sexual scenes (both MCs are eighteen), parental death, grief, brief homophobia, bullying (outside of the MCs).

PLAYLIST

Available on Spotify

chance with you by mehro
Backseat (Kiss Me) by Jutes
Mr. Rager by Kid Cudi
Kiss My Scars by August Royals
California Down The Road by Elvis Drew, Avivian
I Need U by yaeow
Ghost by Justin Bieber
I Think I'm OKAY by Machine Gun Kelly with YUNGBLUD & Travis Barker
Sad People by Kid Cudi
Slip by Elliot Moss
Sexy MF by Labrinth
Where Are You? by Elvis Drew, Avivian
Fade Away by Rebelution
Slow Motion by Charlotte Lawrence
*Out of Touch by CUT_*
Boyfriend by Dove Cameron

Wait 2.0 by NoMBe, Skott
Moonlight by Chase Atlantic
heaven come by Josh Golden

DEDICATION

This book is dedicated to the first two people to ever read my words. Elizabeth and Morgan, thank you for your constant support and encouragement. It means everything. And your friendship is pretty fucking awesome, too.

CHAPTER ONE
FINN

Consciousness hovers within my grasp, and I reach for it, my eyes slowly fluttering open. There's something warm and wet oozing into them and trickling down my forehead. I try to make sense of my surroundings and blink the dark, hazy world around me into focus, but the potent smell of gasoline and the coppery scent of blood is overpowering, and I dry heave. I immediately regret it as I clutch at the excruciating pain in my side. A violent cough racks my chest, and a strong metallic taste fills my mouth, making me gag even more.

An odd pressure starts to build in my skull as I realize I'm hanging upside down, still strapped into the front passenger seat of my mom's car. The vein in my forehead pulses as all the blood rushes to my head.

Oh fuck. Fuck. Fuck. Fuck. We're trapped.

My whole body starts to shake. My chest pounds angrily, and my heartbeat thrashes in my ears. "*Mom?*" I croak, but it's barely even a whisper. I feel like I've swallowed razor blades.

I gingerly turn my head, groaning when I feel the

tendons in my neck protest. I grit my teeth and push through the pain while black spots flash across my vision. "Mom? *Pleeease*, answer me," I sob in a choked, raspy voice. I wipe at my eyes, trying to see through the blood that won't stop dripping into them. I squint through the red haze and thick smoke starting to fill the cabin, and my world shatters into a million pieces. Her arms hang limp below her, bent wrists resting on the crushed roof.

My lip trembles, and I scream louder. "*Mom!*" I jerk and wrench at the seatbelt, desperate for it to release me from its hold as a primal scream tears from my throat, stripping it raw. My struggle is quickly reduced to a whimper. I grasp the sides of my head, hopelessly trying to keep a grip on my sanity and consciousness.

I whisper a prayer to someone, anyone, but I don't even know who.

"Wake up."

"Please. I still need you. . ."

The only reply is the wail of sirens in the distance and my own strained breathing.

A guttural moan escapes my lips, and the despair is heavy and devastating. My chest heaves, and my breath becomes a syrupy sludge trapped in my lungs. Blackness starts to creep in along the edges of my eyesight as I desperately attempt to suck in air, but my lungs won't obey. The hysteria bubbling inside me causes my heart to palpitate wildly and the spots dotting my vision coalesce and converge until the darkness fully takes me.

I wake with a gasp, my T-shirt drenched in sweat and clinging to my body. Sitting up, I rake my hands through my shaggy, dark brown hair, peeling the sweaty strands from my forehead. Nausea churns in my stomach, so I take a few deep breaths, trying to calm my rising panic.

Fuck. I haven't had a nightmare that bad in months.

I knead the heel of my palm into my chest to slow my pounding heart and ease the sharp pain attempting to burrow its way out. I've locked that shit down tight. The grief, the devastation, the bitterness, the *guilt.* I don't feel these things anymore. I *refuse* to feel them.

There's an angry, volatile beast living inside of me. It feeds on pain and despair, and I let it. I let it consume all the anguish, the pure agony left behind after having your heart ripped out of your chest right in front of your eyes. I keep the monster fed and locked up deep down, leaving me with all the anger and resentment bubbling under the surface like a toxic stew.

I'm not the same boy I used to be.

Fourteen months since that horrible night, and most people have moved on. It's just a tragic accident that happened to someone they know. They say, "Aw, that's so sad," bake a casserole or send flowers and move on. I mean, my own father clearly has. It's barely been a year since we buried my mother, his wife, yet he's already remarried and moved his new, perfect family in. But he's still the same old prick to me. I know he blames me for her death. How could he not when I blame myself. We were on the way home from *my* championship football game, after all.

But I don't give a fuck what he or anyone else thinks. Not anymore. There's less than one semester of school left, and then I'm getting the fuck out of here. Out of Chicago, out of Illinois, maybe even out of the fucking country. I gained access to my trust fund when I turned eighteen last month, so I don't need to stay for anything or anyone. The only condition to keeping full control of my money is to graduate from Lake View Preparatory Academy—Mom's alma mater. It was supposed to be a given, automatic. But no one could have expected the events that led us to where we are today. It's a lot harder now. And I'm counting down the days.

At least it's still the weekend, which means I finally get to play some flag football. The thought of my favorite sport gives me the boost of energy I need to get out of my cozy bed. Goosebumps pebble across my bare skin as I whip my fluffy comforter back and hurry to my en-suite in just my boxers. January in Chicago is fucking brutal.

I turn the towel warmer on and twist the shower handle to hot until the bathroom billows with steam. Stepping under the massive rainfall showerhead, I let the scalding water melt away any traces of the nightmare I just had. I can't afford to let my mask slip. I have a new stepmom and stepbrother to meet today.

After my shower, I amble downstairs toward the kitchen for breakfast. The rich, smoky aroma of my father's expensive ass dark roast lures me in. He's perched at the massive black marble island, reading the newspaper and sipping his coffee. Yes, *an actual physical paper.* It's been his morning routine for as long as I can remember.

Dr. Gabriel Finnegan is a handsome man, I can admit that. I mean, I look a lot like him, except he wears his dark hair slicked back, and it's starting to gray at the temples. He also has brown eyes, whereas I have midnight blue like Mom. His irises are so dark, they're practically indistinguishable from his pupils, and it always freaked me out as a kid.

Black, fathomless eyes like the soulless bastard he is.

I mumble out a "Morning," knowing better than to not acknowledge him.

"Good morning, Son."

And there it is. The instant annoyance I feel whenever I hear his deep, raspy voice. I clench my jaw and flare my nostrils while my back is turned to him, grabbing my favorite sugary cereal from the walk-in pantry and trying not to crush the box in my grip.

There's been this unspoken tension between us ever since Mom died, but neither of us has tried to fix it. I turn around and face him again, and he drags a full-width smile up from the bowels of Hell itself and pastes it across his smarmy face. His perfectly straight, white teeth are on full display. It's weird and fucking creepy. I don't like it.

What the fuck is he so happy about, anyway?

Oh yeah.

New wife. New son. *New family.*

How could I forget?

"You should take your brother with you today, Wyatt." His gravelly voice grates on my fucking nerves, and I grind my molars in irritation, hating it every time he uses my first name. This fucker thinks he has the right to tell me what to do. Just because he wants to play house and get a new family doesn't mean I do.

"I'm leaving in fifteen minutes," I bite back with a tight jaw.

"I said go ask your brother," he counters, more firmly this time, shaking his newspaper to make it stand up stiffly. "He was in his room all night. . . painting," Dad sneers dismissively. He clearly only wants to please his new wife and doesn't actually care about her son. Typical. Why would he care about someone else's kid when he can't even stand the sight of his own?

"He didn't show up for dinner or breakfast," he says as he eyes me critically over the top of the paper when he knows damn well I didn't show up to his bullshit family meals either. I purposely stayed out late last night to avoid, or at least delay, meeting Vivian and Oliver.

"It'll be good for him to get out and meet boys his own age before school starts, so take him with you, or you're not going."

My posture instantly stiffens. "I'm eighteen," I state simply, trying not to shake from the pent-up rage boiling inside me. I really don't feel like fighting with him right now. He knows I play flag football at the park with my friends every Sunday the weather allows, and we finally have a day above freezing, with no snow on the ground. Why is he trying to force this *brother* bullshit on me?

"And you still live under my roof, so you will obey my rules." He tosses his paper down on the marble countertop with a smack. Grabbing his coffee thermos and an apple from the fruit bowl in the middle of the island, he stalks out of the kitchen, leaving no more room to argue.

Son of a bitch.

It's not like he would deign to introduce us or anything. I slam the silverware drawer shut after grabbing a spoon and cringe at the sound of metal clanging against metal. *Fine.* He wants me to take my new stepbrother with me? Then he can come right the fuck now. When *I'm* ready.

I toss my spoon onto the counter and turn to head back upstairs, taking them two at a time in my haste. Oliver's bedroom is across the hall from mine, so I march right up to his door and bang none too gently.

Fabric shuffles, and a bleary-eyed blond kid opens the door, scratching his head and yawning so big I hear his jaw tick. I stand tall and imposing in the door frame, arms crossed, legs slightly spread in a *don't fuck with me* kind of pose. If I had to guess, he seems to be about five feet ten inches, so I have a good four inches on him. I don't care if I have to intimidate the little shit; he's coming with me. I *never* miss Sunday flag football.

When he realizes who's standing in front of him, he immediately straightens up and opens his eyes a little wider. Holy shit, they're vibrant, like the bluest sky on a cloudless day.

"Oh. Hey, Wyatt," he chirps, smiling politely and holding out his hand to shake. "I'm Oliver."

"I know who you are." I ignore his hand and brush past him rudely, looking around his room. He's only been here a day and already has three canvases set up. Not much else, though, just a few unpacked boxes in the corner that my dad apparently had shipped here before they even arrived. Otherwise, it's the same boringly neutral guest room it's always been. "And it's Finn. Only my father calls me Wyatt."

"Oh, okay. Well, it's nice to meet you, Finn." He gives me such an authentic smile with deep, endearing dimples to top it off that I look away, feeling slightly guilty for barging into his bedroom at ten in the morning like an asshole.

"I'm going to the park to play flag football with my buddies. You should come."

He perks up even more at that. "Really?"

He seems genuinely thrilled that I would ask him, and *fuck*, it's proving impossible to be mean to this kid. He's just too damn nice. My eyes rove over his disheveled golden blond hair, silver nose ring, tight white T-shirt, and tiny black boxer briefs. *Shit.* Are his fingernails painted? The guys are going to eat him alive. Scratch that. The entire fucking academy will. "You should take that polish off first, though," I blurt out, sounding like an ignorant asshole and instantly hating myself for it.

His smile morphs into a frown, and a spark of defiance shines in his sunny blue depths. "I won't change who I am for anyone, Finn."

"Whatever," I say nonchalantly, brushing it off like I don't care. "I'm leaving in fifteen. Meet me in the kitchen if you wanna come." I leave his room and head back downstairs to eat my Cinnamon Toast Crunch, not waiting for his response.

Just over ten minutes later, Oliver strolls into the kitchen with his hair still damp and appearing darker than I know it to be. It's shaved on the sides and swoops back into one of those pompadour styles pretty boys like to wear, except it's messier and less refined. He's sporting black joggers and a matching black hoodie. And, as unassuming as that is, it only makes the neon green of his nail polish stand out even more.

Cali boys are weird.

I take the last bite of my breakfast and head to the sink to rinse out my bowl. "Grab some cereal, and let's bounce. There's still some coffee in the pot, too."

"Nah, I'm good."

I stare him down, crossing my thick arms across my chest. My dad said he didn't come down for dinner last night either. He won't make it very far today if he doesn't get something in his stomach.

"I don't normally eat breakfast, and I don't like coffee," he tries to clarify.

"Just grab a granola bar then. I'm not having you pass out on the field." I rummage in the pantry and toss him a peanut butter and chocolate chip protein bar. He catches it but looks down as his ears turn pink, awkwardly shuffling his socked feet.

"What?" I demand gruffly.

"Um. . . I'm allergic," he says quietly as he picks at the edge of the wrapper.

"Allergic?" I parrot.

He peers up at me from under his dark blond lashes, and our eyes connect. There's an innocent vulnerability sparkling in his bright blue irises, and I can't look away. "Yeah. To peanuts. Like, deathly allergic," he chuckles in a self-deprecating way. "I carry an EpiPen with me at all times, too," he says as he pats the pocket of his joggers. "It's pretty surprising what comes into contact with peanuts during processing."

"Fuck, sorry." I snatch the protein bar from his hands as if the peanuts can seep through the plastic wrapper and poison him right here and now. "Uh, I'm not sure what we have then," I say sheepishly, rubbing the back of my neck and feeling unsure. Now I'm a little freaked out that I'm going to feed him the wrong thing.

He laughs musically and strolls over to the refrigerator, stirring up a gust of air in his wake. I can't help but inhale deeply when I catch a whiff of fresh soap mixed with a woodsy aftershave. I've never liked the sickly sweet fragrance of women's perfume, and I've never worn cologne myself. But for some reason, Oliver's clean, earthy scent invites me in. It envelops me, tantalizing and heady, and I have to grip the edge of the counter to stop myself from stalking over there and burrowing my nose into the crook of his neck to breathe him in more completely.

Wait, what? Smell him? I must be losing my goddamn mind.

"Don't worry about it, Finn. I can just grab a yogurt."

I don't argue with him as he reaches into our industrial-sized, stainless steel refrigerator and pops the top of a blueberry yogurt, downing it in two bites. He tosses the container into the trash and rinses his spoon, placing it in the dishwasher. Damn, this guy is seriously fucking polite.

My Jeep keys clank against the hideous ceramic bowl I made Mom in third grade as I pluck them from the credenza table by the front door. I head to the mudroom, where Oliver already has his sneakers on and is casually leaning against the doorframe, scrolling through his phone. I slip my own shoes on and snatch my puffy winter coat from the row of hooks above the built-in bench seat. I glance at Oliver from the corner of my eye and notice that he's not wearing a jacket, just his hoodie. This Cali boy has no fucking clue.

I grab a spare and toss it to him. The dark blue coat smacks him in the face before he catches it, and I snort. "Put this on. It's fucking cold, and this isn't the beach." Oliver doesn't protest and slips his arms into the warm, down jacket. I take a couple of the hand towels I keep stashed in one of the wall cubbies and shove them into my gym bag next to the water and Gatorade I packed while waiting for him to shower.

I open the door to the garage and flip the lights on. A

low buzzing fills the air as the overhead fluorescent bulbs kick on, reflecting off the high gloss floors and illuminating the entire space. My gaze darts over to Oliver at his sharp intake of breath. His eyes flash wide, practically doubling in size, and he trips on the first step down to the garage. I stick my arm out on instinct to stop his fall as he steadies himself on my bicep.

"Thanks," he mumbles shyly and lets go. He looks at all the cars with a slack jaw and slumped shoulders, unabashedly gawking at our car collection. A grin tugs at my lips. I forgot what this can look like to outsiders. I've just become so accustomed to living like this. Our expansive garage has four doors and boasts nearly a dozen expensive, mainly foreign, vehicles.

"*Holy shit,*" he murmurs, mostly to himself. "This is fucking *insane*."

I shrug as if it's no big deal. "You can pretty much drive whatever you want. Except for the Aston Martin, that's Dad's. Oh, and the forest green Jeep. That one's mine."

"Yeah, not so sure I'm gonna take you up on that offer any time soon. It's a little intimidating," he chuckles.

"No biggie. I'll be driving us to and from school anyway." What I don't tell him is that I refuse to ride in a car that I'm not driving. Ever since the accident, I need complete control behind the wheel.

Our sneakers squeak as we cross the sterile white floors and climb into my Jeep. "So, where's your mom this morning? Vivian, right?" I change the subject as I pull out of the garage and head down the long, winding driveway to our front gate.

White powder usually blankets everything this time of year, but the trees lining the drive are barren of leaves and snow. The black, wrought-iron gate at the front of our property looms in front of me, boasting gold filigree embellishments and smugly reminding me that I am indeed trapped here for the next four and a half months. It's ornate, ostentatious, and completely unnecessary.

Why the hell does our house need to be gated when the entire neighborhood is?

I drum my fingers on the steering wheel as I wait for it to open, and Oliver informs me that his mom went to the salon to get her hair and nails done. I know she and my dad are getting ready to go on their honeymoon to Aruba, and I really hope she's not just using him for his money. Even though I don't get along with the bastard, he doesn't deserve to be used like that. No one does. Although, after meeting Oliver, I highly doubt his mom would be that type of person.

My father, Gabe, and Oliver's mom, Vivian, fell in love online in a whirlwind romance and got married at the courthouse downtown not even six months later. I've never even met her, and I didn't even know my dad was dating anyone. Imagine my surprise when he sat me down to tell me I have a new stepmom and stepbrother, and they were moving in with us the next day.

Thanks for the heads up, prick.

And now I'm sitting here in my Jeep, driving said brother to the park to meet my friends. I flick a lightning-fast glance at him out of the corner of my eye. He has his face plastered against the window, looking wide-eyed at everything we pass and fogging up my glass. A smile threatens to form on my lips. "I can't imagine the views of suburban Chicago are better than Cali."

He laughs lightly, clearly embarrassed over his enthusiasm, but I find it refreshing. I've become numb to all the jaded, cynical assholes I'm constantly surrounded by. Including myself.

"It's just different. I'm used to the sun, sand, and palm trees."

"Where exactly are you from, anyway?"

"A tiny beach town called Marlo Bay in Southern California."

I turn my head to look at him when I stop at a red light. "You miss it?"

He continues to peer out the passenger window, this time with a slightly vacant look. "I miss surfing every morning before school and watching the sunset on the bay. I can't even tell you how many canvases I left behind with the exact same sunset painted on them."

"So you're into art then? I saw some of the stuff in your room."

"Yep. It's just always been my thing. What are your hobbies?"

"Football. And cars."

"Guess I could have figured that one out on my own, huh?" He chuckles, and I toss him a smirk.

"Friends? Girlfriend?" I prod, trying to figure out more about who Oliver Chase is.

"Nah." He leaves it at that, not elaborating or explaining any further.

Hmm, okay then.

"What about you? Got a girlfriend?" he asks, and I just give him the same answer.

"Nah."

We're both silent for the rest of the drive to the park, and I don't ask him if he's actually ever played football before. Guess I'll find out soon enough.

CHAPTER TWO

OLIVER

Finn parks his Jeep in an area where the trees are thick and hang low, casting dark spindly shadows over the cars and trucks already parked there. I see a group of about six guys huddled by one of the picnic tables, laughing and goofing around.

I pick at my nail polish, feeling a little nervous about meeting them when I've only just met *him*. The fact that I've never even touched a football before doesn't help. My go-to outdoor activity has always been surfing, but I don't have that option anymore. Besides, I'm trying to bond with my new stepbrother. I've never had a family before. It's always just been my mom and me, so I really don't want to fuck this up and have his friends hate me.

We both hop out of the Jeep, and Finn swings his gym bag over his shoulder. "Ready?"

Shit, it's fucking cold out here.

I blow into my hands, attempting to warm them up, but it doesn't really help. There's a thin layer of frost covering the wide expanse of grass, and I really hope the sun comes out soon. I'm not used to overcast skies and frozen ground. I thrive on sun, sand, and the ocean.

"Yep." I stretch my arms above my head to loosen up, sounding way more confident than I feel. I'm still a little tired from the flight yesterday, too.

I see Finn's eyes dart down to the bit of flesh peeking out from under my hoodie when I lifted my arms. His Adam's apple bobs as he swallows hard, but he quickly looks away, pretending he wasn't just checking out my abs.

Interesting.

Finn abruptly turns and strides toward his friends while I follow behind like an obedient little puppy. He greets the first boy with one of those half-handshake, half-hug things where dudes thump each other on the back to show affection.

"Hey man, what's up?" the boy asks.

"Oh, you know, the usual. Just got a new stepmom and stepbrother, nothing too crazy."

"What?" The kid laughs in disbelief. He has dark buzzed hair and bright green eyes. He's pretty cute, actually, but I keep that part to myself.

Finn claps me on the back, and I stumble forward a bit from the force of it. "This is my new stepbrother, Oliver. Oliver, this is my best friend, Jared."

"Nice to meet you," we both say, and I grin.

"Hey, what about me, bro? I thought we were best friends, too?" A guy with auburn hair saunters over and grabs Finn in a headlock, catching him off guard. He can only do this because he's just about as tall and wide. Finn easily slips out of the hold.

"Har, har, har, asshole." He shoves the guy playfully, with no real animosity involved.

"Oliver, this ginger without a soul is Eric." Then he

points to the rest of his friends and names them. "Ethan, Danny, Trace, and T's little brother, Jayden." The kid on the end looks about fifteen with silver braces and goggles for glasses that magnify his brown eyes about five times.

"Guys, this is Oliver."

We all make small talk, and they ask me the usual questions. Where are you from? How old are you? What do you like to do for fun? Are you starting school on Monday? I've never been to private school before, so I'm feeling a little intimidated to start Lake View, but at least I'll know a few people now.

I wonder if Finn would show me to my classes if I asked?

"Alright, enough chit-chat, pussies." Eric laughs harshly and holds up his pointer finger, twirling it around in the air. "Let's fucking go!" He doesn't wait for anyone, just turns and struts toward the field with an arrogant swagger that I scrunch my nose at.

"Don't worry, he grows on you," Jared teases, but I'm not so sure that'll be true for me.

"Yeah! Like a toxic black mold that releases deadly spores into the environment, contaminating everything around him!" Jayden shouts out. We all chuckle at that because he could have just said fungus, but I like this kid. He's nerdy *and* feisty.

"I heard that dweeb!" Eric yells back like he's the schoolyard bully about to give the geek a wedgie from hell.

What a tool.

Everyone laughs and follows him to the field while Finn stays back and sticks close to my side. "You ever played flag football before?" he asks quietly, so only I can hear.

"Nah, but I get the gist of it," I answer truthfully. I've never actually held a football, but I don't tell him that. I've watched the game on TV before. I'm sure I can just run around and wing it. I've always been fast. Finn looks at me, unconvinced, but doesn't call me out on my bullshit in front of the other guys.

We split off into two teams of four, and Jared hands out our belts, flags, and clips. I subtly watch Finn put them on and pretend to fumble around with a clip so I don't have to ask for help.

Fake it till you make it, right?

I get my flags situated and can't help but check him out a little while I wait for everyone to get ready. His messy, dark brown hair is nearly chin-length, as if he's in the process of growing it to man-bun level. But also sort of like he just doesn't give a fuck and can't be bothered to do anything with it. It's shiny and soft looking, like a silk sheet I want to run my fingers over. His chiseled face and aristocratic nose make him look like a Greek God. I bet his body looks like it, too, under those loose gray sweats. He has a small scar, about an inch wide, running along the top of his left cheekbone, right under his eye. It definitely adds to the whole broody and mysterious vibe he has going on.

I'm on a team with Finn, Jared, and Ethan as we face off with the others at the imaginary fifty-yard line. We won the coin toss, so Ethan hikes the ball to Jared as Finn goes long. I also run toward the end zone because that's about all I know—catch it and run for a touchdown. Finn bobs and weaves, trying to get past Trace, but no one is guarding me. I'm completely open and feel like a deer in headlights as Jared and I make eye contact across the field.

Shit. He's going to throw it to me.

I run hard and look over my shoulder, seeing the football hurtling toward me, and Eric running at full speed with an evil glint in his eyes. I stick my arms up and jump to catch the ball, but I end up fumbling it because the shape of the ball is just. . . *fucking weird.* It slips from my fingers and bounces awkwardly against the ground. Dammit. I almost had it, too.

Eric slows down and jogs the rest of the way over, cackling like a poor sport. "Nice one, butterfingers! First fumble of the game!" he guffaws.

I can feel the flush slowly creep across my cheeks and tuck my chin to try and hide it. Finn comes storming over, and I'm worried he's mad at me for dropping the ball, but that thought is quickly dashed away when he bends down to snatch the football up and glare at Eric. "Why do you always have to be such a dick?"

"Yeah, not cool, bro," Ethan chimes in.

"Calm your tits. You guys need to quit being such girls all the time," Eric retorts. "Fucking sensitive motherfuckers," he mumbles, but we all hear.

Finn nudges me with the football, forcing me to look right into his eyes as they bounce back and forth between mine. "Hey, don't listen to him. Let me show you the easiest way to grip and throw the ball." Finn is speaking in hushed tones, but Eric the Asshole still hears.

"Dude!" Eric gripes. "We're here to fucking play football, not coach a first-time Pee Wee team!"

"Eric, would you just shut your fucking mouth for a minute, *Jesus Christ.*" Danny shakes his head and huffs out an annoyed breath. He hasn't really said anything yet, and I can tell he's more reserved. So if *he's* annoyed at his friend, I guess I have every right to be as well.

Eric gets a pinched expression on his face, and his already small lips narrow into a thin straight line. He folds his arms across his chest and stands there looking angry.

At me.

I try to ignore the hostile vibes and focus on Finn, but I

feel distracted and on edge. He's explaining the best way to grip the ball, placing a finger over the laces a certain way. He hands it to me, and I try to hold it the way he did, but I fumble it *again*.

Eric barks out a cruel laugh, radiating a superiority that makes me sick. *Smug bastard.*

"Shut up, fuckface." Finn glowers at his *friend*. All this tension is really making me uncomfortable.

"Just ignore him, Oliver," he whispers softly to me, his tone completely contrasting with the way he just spoke to Eric.

"Here, place your ring finger on the second lace at your middle knuckle." He maneuvers my fingers where he wants, his gentle, patient touch making all the little hairs on my arms stand up as goosebumps spread across my skin.

"And then your pinky rests right under the lace here." He finishes showing me the perfect grip. I have to admit, it feels secure.

"Okay, now step forward as you pull your hand back behind your head, laces up." He runs his fingers up my arm and across my shoulder as he explains the motion. His touch burns through my hoodie and ignites my blood.

"Then push it forward, release, and follow-through."

"Yo, T, go long!" he shouts.

Trace runs down the field, and I successfully throw a decent ball, feeling pretty damn proud about it, too. I'm a surfer, not a jock. I steal a glance at Finn, and we're sporting matching goofy grins.

Trace comes jogging over with the football and a big smile, his short dreads bouncing with each step. "Nice one Oliver. You got some good distance there." He turns to Finn. "Now let's teach him how to catch."

Finn and Trace show me how to properly catch the ball

and how to run with it cradled securely in my arms. We practice tossing the ball back and forth, while the others play around behind us, and I catch it every single time. I look over at Finn and smile wide, shaking the football in one palm to show him I got it now. My brief accomplishment is squashed by the vile words of fucking *Eric.*

"I thought only emo kids and goths. . . or fags. . . painted their nails. Which one are you?"

I wince at the hateful slur and rub the back of my neck, feeling extremely uncomfortable again. It's not that I'm ashamed of being gay, it just didn't go that well the last time I came out to my so-called friends, and the last thing I want to do is fight with Finn's. I don't need to slap a label on my forehead that says *I'm gay* in big, bold letters, as if my sexuality is everyone's rightful business.

Finn just growls menacingly. "If you say one more fucking thing, Eric, I swear to God, you're done with flag football. For good." He crosses his arms across his chest and straightens to his full towering height. His posture screams *Try me, I fucking dare you.*

"You'd do that to *me* over some kid you just met *today?*" A flash of hurt crosses Eric's face before he schools his features and returns to being a cunt.

"He's my family now, and I'm really fucking sick of your shit, Eric. You're crossing the line." Finn doesn't back down, and his muscles seem to bulge even bigger as he flexes with barely restrained fury.

It's fucking hot.

Oh no. No, no, no. I cannot go down that path with my new brother.

Eric concedes, obviously not wanting to lose his entire group of friends. "Fine, whatever. I won't say anything else. Let's just play."

We play through a few more possessions, and I finally get my chance to score when I make a clean break down center field, cradling the ball in my right arm while pumping my left furiously—completely ready for this fucking touchdown.

I make it there, all my flags intact, and slam the ball down, yelling, "Touchdown!" I can't control myself as the adrenaline pumps through my veins, and I do my favorite dance move and dive to the ground, smoothly rolling my hips and humping the grass. In a moment of sheer insanity, I flick my gaze to Eric's seething face, stick my tongue out and give him a teasing wink. He looks fucking murderous, and I may have just signed my death warrant.

God, why am I like this?

I hop off the field, wiping my cold, damp hands on my hoodie. Finn runs over to chest bump me, and I have to jump slightly to offset the height difference.

Oof.

Damn, his pecs are seriously hard. I just laugh and rub my poor, abused sternum.

"You're a fucking natural, brother!" Finn exclaims, and his praise does something to me, causing a tingle to run down my spine. I beam from ear to ear, straight cheesing like a fool. I like this happier, less grumpy Finn.

Ethan and Jared both give me a high five and congrats as we line back up, ready for the next play. Jared lets loose another perfect throw, and I take off, running toward where the ball is sailing. Just as I look up, ready to catch it, what feels like a semi-truck barrels into me, knocking me off my feet. I crash to the ground with a resounding thud.

CHAPTER THREE
FINN

"What the fuck is your problem?!" I shove Eric hard as I push past him to get to Oliver. He's just lying on his side, not moving.

Fuck, Dad is going to *kill* me.

I carefully roll him over onto his back, and he gasps for air, his diaphragm once again working. He clutches his ribs tightly and takes a few more heaving breaths, still lying there in a daze. "You're okay," I soothe. "You just got the wind knocked outta you." I help him sit up and dust the debris off his sweatshirt. It's a little damp from the frosty ground but not soaked. He's still wheezing and cradling his left side slightly. I make a mental note to check on that later and pin Eric with a hard glare as I grasp Oliver's hand and gently pull him to his feet.

Eric just holds his hands up as if he did nothing wrong. "You okay, bro? I didn't mean to bump you like that. My bad."

I stand in front of him, feeling oddly protective. It wasn't just a "bump." He full-on body-checked Oliver without tackling him, like this is fucking ice hockey or something. "He's not your bro, and if you ever touch him again, I'll do ten times worse to you, *bro*," I say with all the venom I can muster.

Shit, where did that even come from?

"Whoa, calm down, Finn. It's all in good fun, right, Oliver?" He looks at my stepbrother expectantly, as if Oliver is supposed to defend him. What a fucking joke.

"Uh. . . Yeah, we're cool. It was an accident. No worries, Finn." Oliver smiles hesitantly, trying to defuse the situation like the peace-loving Cali boy he is.

"Whatever. I'm outta here. Let's go, Oliver." I head toward the picnic table to grab my bag.

"You're not gonna finish the game?" Eric shouts after me, but I don't stop.

"No," I simply state, cracking my knuckles and gritting my teeth to suppress the violent urges running through my mind, telling me to go back and kick his fucking face in. I'm not the same happy-go-lucky, sixteen-year-old mama's boy they knew before the accident. I've changed, and there's no going back to who I was. They know this, and they know to let me walk away. I climb into the Jeep, rubbing my hands down my face in exasperation. That lasted all of an hour, and he hasn't even started school yet.

Jesus Christ.

"It's fine, really, Finn." He misinterprets my frustration for anger. I mean, I *am* still pissed at Eric for being such a cunt, but I'm more nervous now. Nervous about all the asses I'm going to have to kick to protect Oliver. Because I've already decided I will. Protect him that is.

No one's gonna fuck with *my* stepbrother.

I pull into Scully's drive-thru, and only one other car is in front of us. We must have arrived right before the lunch rush. The place is styled like a 50's diner, with black-and-white checkered floors, red vinyl booths, and a jukebox filled with old classics. They set up the movie screen and projector in the summer, making it a real drive-in, not just a fast-food drive-thru. I've loved coming here ever since I can remember.

I turn to Oliver. "You ever had this before?" I know it's not a chain, but I have no clue if it's made its way out West.

"Uh, no, never heard of it." Oliver ducks his head slightly to read the menu through my window and his eyes scan the board.

Meanwhile, I open their app to check the nutrition facts for peanut allergies. "Looks like you can eat pretty much anything here, even the frozen yogurt," I say, scrolling through the menu.

"You looked that up for me?" He pauses with a strange expression on his face.

"I mean, yeah. I'm not gonna take you somewhere you can't eat." I try to brush off my concern for him, but I'm pretty sure I failed if the soft look in his eyes is anything to go by.

"Thanks, Finn."

Then he leans further down and peers up to see the top of the menu where all the frozen yogurt choices are. His face is practically hovering over my crotch.

"You said I could get frozen yogurt, too?" he asks, his mouth inches from my dick.

"Mhmm," I manage to choke out.

What the fuck is wrong with me?

I'm not gay. I've never liked dudes. I've never seriously dated a girl either, but why am I having to focus so hard on *not* getting hard right now? I make the challenge even more impossible when I see him biting his pouty bottom lip in indecision. My dick involuntarily twitches in my sweats, and I jerk back, blurting out, "Strawberry! You should get strawberry."

He finally sits back in his seat and chuckles. "Alright, strawberry it is. . . and a double cheeseburger, please."

I add on the same for myself and some mozzarella sticks. After getting our food, I pull around and park so we can eat before heading back home. The mouthwatering scent of greasy burgers and fried cheese fills the cabin as Oliver unfolds the paper bag. He has his burger unwrapped and is moaning into his first bite before I even have the Jeep in park.

"Oh my God, this might be as good as In-N-Out," he mumbles through a mouth full of food.

Gross.

But I'm glad he's enjoying it. I knew he'd be fucking starving after only eating a yogurt for breakfast. We continue devouring our food in complete silence, but it's not uncomfortable. I reach into the backseat and dig through my bag until I find the Gatorades I brought. I hand the blue one to him and keep the yellow.

"Sweet, thanks. How'd you know blue is my favorite?"

I don't know why the innocent question makes me fidget suddenly, but I feel the heat spreading across my cheeks.

Fuck, what is happening?

I *never* blush, and I'm *never* off my game, but Oliver is breaking down my walls without even trying.

"What?" He scrunches his eyes and chuckles lightly, his melodic laugh sending chills down my spine.

I clear my throat awkwardly. "Lucky guess," I mumble.

"Why do you look so flustered then?" he prods, narrowing his eyes even further. "Is there something wrong with it?" He pales and looks hurt, like he actually thinks I would fuck with his drink. *I wouldn't.*

"Of course not. . . I just. . ." I tuck my hair behind my ears and force out a stilted laugh. "This is so fucking embarrassing, and I have no idea why I'm admitting this to you." I meet his curious gaze head-on. "I don't know if you've noticed, but it's the same shade as your eyes. *Electric*."

Oliver's eyes darken and shimmer as he starts to lean forward, but it's like a switch gets flipped, and he composes himself, swiftly sitting back against the seat. He laughs it off. "Damn, bro. Think you could write me a poem? I kinda like it."

I'm glad he's playing it cool; I didn't mean for things to get so intense. But it's like he's lit a spark in me, making me feel things I haven't felt in such a long time. Regardless of the fact that he's a guy and my new stepbrother. I snort out a laugh at his joke. "In your dreams, Cali Boy. I don't do poems."

He rolls his eyes and smiles, showing off his deep dimples that I'm sure have helped him get away with murder his entire life. "Anyway, how much do I owe you for this?"

I wave him off, smirking. "Nothing. Consider it my welcome-to-town meal since we both missed family dinner last night."

"Okay, deal." He chuckles and takes another sloppy bite of his burger. Ketchup and mustard ooze out of the bun and onto his face and hands. For being so nice and polite, he could really use some better table manners.

I finish my burger and crumple the wrapper, stuffing it

back into the paper bag. Oliver takes his last bite and uses half the napkins to wipe his hands and face, but somehow still manages to miss a spot. "You missed some." I gesture to the corner of my own mouth.

He pokes his tongue out and licks at the wrong corner. "Did I get it?"

"No. Here, let me." I swipe my thumb across the corner of his mouth, wiping the ketchup off. I have no idea what comes over me, but I hold my thumb up in front of his mouth. The look in my eyes must be saying, *I dare you,* because Oliver doesn't break eye contact as he leans in, takes my thumb into his warm, wet mouth, and sucks it clean, releasing it with a pop. *Fuck.* I can't help but imagine what else would feel amazing in that wet heat.

I clear my throat and change the subject before I get a full-on erection in front of the new stepbrother I've known for all of two hours. "So, do you even have a winter coat?" I randomly ask, curious if he came prepared.

"I have some fleece-lined hoodies. I'll be fine." I snort at that and shake my head. So fucking naive.

"What?" he asks, scrunching his eyebrows in confusion as he licks at the frozen yogurt, curling his tongue around the spoon and drawing my eyes to his sensual mouth once again. I quickly look away because, seriously, what the *fuck* is wrong with my brain today? It's like I'm thirteen again, and Oliver is the first girl to show me the slightest bit of attention, making my body go haywire.

"I don't think your 'fleece-lined hoodies' are gonna hold up well in negative five-degree weather. We're having an unusual warm front this weekend, but don't let it fool you."

"Shit, negative temperatures?" His tone is incredulous, and I feel bad for how clueless he truly is.

I shake my head and laugh. "You're in for a rude awakening, bro. January is the coldest month of the year. Let's stop at the mall before we head home. You definitely need some winter gear."

"Uh, thanks for the offer, but I can just go with my mom later." He's fidgeting and picking at his nail polish again, and I don't understand why he's acting so shifty.

"The mall's on the way. It's no big deal. Our parents are leaving in like two days anyway. She won't have time."

He looks up at me as a blush settles into his cheeks and whispers, "I don't have that kind of money on me."

Oh.

He's embarrassed because he doesn't have any money to buy winter clothes.

His eyes steel over, and his spine straightens. "Don't look at me like that. I don't want your pity."

Okay, whoa, that kinda came out of left field.

"Dude, no pity here. We're family now. You're my dad's stepson. If he knew you didn't have proper clothes for this weather, he'd insist I buy you whatever you need." What I don't say is that I'm not going to even use Dad's card. I have my own trust and money from Mom's side of the family, and I suddenly want to be the one to buy these things for Oliver.

He bites his lip and still looks a little uncertain. "Well, okay. When you put it like that, I guess it makes sense."

"Alright, to the mall it is then," I say, unable to stop the smirk pulling at my lips.

It's after three by the time we get home. I pull into the garage, and we unload four bags each, heading inside to take them to Oliver's room.

We did pretty well in just over two hours of shopping. Oliver got a black down jacket and a nice dark gray peacoat for school. He also got a handful of sweatshirts, Henleys, flannels, and some kick-ass combat boots that are waterproof and perfect for the snow. I threw in scarves, beanies, and gloves when he wasn't looking because I practically had to force him to buy the second, dressier coat. He was too focused on price when it didn't matter if it was fifty dollars or five-hundred dollars.

When we get to his room, I toss the shopping bags by his closet door. I need to get something off my chest. I wanted us to have a fun afternoon after the clusterfuck that was Sunday flag football, so I didn't bring it up earlier. "If Eric ever hurts you or even touches you again, you tell me, okay? Actually, if he even says hi to you, tell me." It's not really a question, but Oliver doesn't answer.

"Got it?"

"Yes, Finn, I got it. Seriously, it wasn't a big deal." He rolls his eyes.

"Then lift your shirt and let me see."

"What?" he splutters.

"Show me your ribs, Oliver. On the left side." He carried the bags with his right hand and nothing in his left. I'm not backing down from this. I know what broken ribs can lead to from personal experience.

"No," he huffs out, crossing his arms right back in defiance.

Okay, if that's how he wants to play it. I'm not above manhandling him in this situation. He needs to watch out for Eric when school starts. I'm worried he'll escalate things like he always does when he has his sights set on someone.

I uncross my arms and stalk toward him. He immediately stumbles back a step and stutters out, “Wh-what are you doing, Finn?”

“Checking for myself if you won’t show me.”

“I haven’t even looked at it myself! Just hang on a minute!” He holds his hands out in front of him, palms facing me.

I pause at that and change course to his en-suite. “Okay, we’ll look together then. Come on.”

Oliver hesitantly follows me into the bathroom. We both just stand there, facing the mirror, still dressed in our hoodies and sweats. He slowly lifts the bottom of his hoodie, and my eyes latch onto his every movement in the mirror. When his bent elbows make it chest high, he hisses out a pained breath and drops his hoodie. My eyes burn with rage and the need to find Eric, but I meet the shimmering depths of Oliver’s brilliant blue eyes in the mirror and instantly calm down.

“Let me help you,” I whisper as I turn to face him. Something inside of me is demanding that I take care of him. He peers up at me with such helplessness it guts me and simply nods. I lift his hoodie and T-shirt and help him slip his arm out on his good side. I pull the neck over his head and then slide the rest down his other arm so he doesn’t have to lift it.

Jesus. Fuck.

His ribs are already a mottled red and purple, and it’s only been a few hours. I reach out and hesitantly touch his bruised skin. Oliver sucks in a sharp breath at the contact, and I yank my hand back instantly. “Sorry.”

“N-no, it was just cold. It didn’t hurt,” he murmurs, so I place my fingertips back on his tender flesh. I can feel his eyes on me as I concentrate and gently press on his ribs to check for any fractures.

He doesn't complain that anything hurts, so I think he's just bruised. I look up from my semi-crouched position, and our faces are inches apart. There's a beat of silence as we both just stand here and stare at each other. There's definitely something brewing between us, but I'm not prepared to investigate that any further now. I clear my throat and step back. "I don't think anything's broken, but you may want to have your mom take you for an X-ray just in case." I comb a hand through my messy brown locks. "My dad's gonna murder me for letting you get hurt."

"No! Don't tell my mom. I'm fine, seriously. I just bruise easily."

I eye him for a second. I don't know his mom, and I'm not sure why he would be so worried about telling her, but I'm not about to look a gift horse in the mouth so I go along with it. "Okay, well, promise you'll come to me if it starts to look or feel worse?" I ask, even though I know I'll be checking again.

"Deal." He quirks up a grin, and a single dimple pops out. *Fuck*, that is trouble.

I turn away quickly because his dimple and the lean, toned chest on full display right now are doing confusing things to my body. More specifically, to my dick. "Uh, you good to shower?" I ask awkwardly, not sure I can handle it if he says no.

He just chuckles. "Yeah, bro, I'll be fine. Maybe help me put my shirt on after, though?"

"Deal." I mimic his earlier words. "And we should probably ice it and wrap it after your shower. The bruising is pretty bad." I grimace and slip out the bedroom door, leaving him to it.

After I take a quick shower and change into jeans and a dark blue Henley, I walk across the hall and knock on Oliver's door, lightly this time. The door is cracked, but I wait for him to answer.

He appears with just a towel wrapped low around his trim waist. I watch, enraptured, as tiny water droplets run down his toned pecs, traveling over every peak and valley of his lean six-pack. One particular droplet takes a joy ride along the groove of his Adonis belt and disappears beneath his towel. I've never checked out a guy before, but for some reason, Oliver is now the sun, and I've been pulled into his orbit, wanting to revolve around him. And it's completely out of my control. His shine is so bright, and I'm so close, I'm fucking *burning*.

I ignore the knowing gleam in his eyes and get pissed off all over again when he lets me in, and I see his left side covered in the bruises that Eric fuckface Carson put there.

"I'll be right back." Oliver slips into the bathroom and comes back thirty seconds later in skin-tight, black boxer briefs dotted with neon green smiley faces with their eyes crossed out. He pads over to one of the new shopping bags and delicately bends over to rifle through it with one arm. I gulp so loud I almost choke on my own tongue. I'm positive he heard it echoing like a fucking foghorn in this otherwise silent room.

Ass dimples.

He has ass dimples.

Not only does he have dimples on his face, but he has them right above the curve of his ass. I can't help but bite my fist and tilt my head a little to get a better angle. His ass is so firm and tight. The little boxers hug it so snuggly that I have the filthiest urge to walk over there and pull them down so I can bite and kiss his bare ass cheeks.

I want to lick those fucking dimples.

Before I lose all reason and go over there and follow through with my deviant desires, Oliver stands back up holding jeans with the tags still on them and a new black leather belt. "Do you have any scissors?" He motions to the price tags.

I physically shake the lust from my head and walk over to him. "No, I got it." I rip the tags off without tearing the material. While I have the jeans in my grasp, I undo them, squatting down to look up at Oliver through my thick lashes. "Hold on to my shoulder."

He bites his lip and obeys, stepping into them as I hold the pants out. I pull them up his legs, and he does a little hop and shake to help get them over the swell of his ass. I carefully zip and button his jeans, then thread the new leather belt through, choosing which hole I think fits best. "Not too tight?" I whisper on a ragged breath as I stick my hand into the front of his jeans, my fingertips grazing his happy trail, and tug on the belt I just put on him.

"Uh uh, feels good. . . um. . . uh, I mean fits good." He peeks up at me as pink settles on his cheeks, and I decide I like to see him flustered over me.

"Oliver! Are you home, honey?" a feminine voice shouts from downstairs. We both jump apart like we've been caught doing something wrong, which isn't too far from the truth.

"Shit, help me get my shirt on! She can't see me like this, or she won't go on her honeymoon! She deserves to do something for herself. Finn, *please*!"

Hearing my name as a plea on his lips forces me into action, and I grab the old Red Hot Chili Peppers T-shirt on his bed. I slip his arm through the hole on his hurt side and stretch the neck over his head. From there, he maneuvers his other arm through and yanks it down just as we hear a soft knock and see the door push open.

Oliver's mom sees me first. "Oh, hi! Wyatt! It's so good to meet you, sweetie!" She rushes over and encloses me in a surprisingly tight hug for someone so small.

My new stepmother has long, golden blonde hair and aquamarine eyes. Oliver is the spitting image of her, down to her smaller stature. I didn't realize she was so young; she barely looks old enough to have a son my age, whereas my parents were almost thirty when they had me.

"It's nice to meet you too, Mrs. umm. . . Finnegan?" I feel like a complete idiot as soon as the words tumble from my mouth, but what the fuck else am I supposed to call her? I'm sure as hell not calling her Mom.

She laughs, and it's musical and sweet, just like Oliver's laugh. "Oh, call me Viv, honey." She pats my arm lovingly.

"Okay," I agree, "but call me Finn."

"You got it," she beams.

Oliver walks over, giving his mom a side hug that makes my heart ache a little. "Hey, Mom, your hair looks great. Are those highlights?"

Vivian gushes about the salon she went to and how excited she is to visit another country for her honeymoon. She is every bit as genuine and down-to-earth as her son, and there is no way I could possibly hate her. I don't know what the fuck my dad did to win this woman over, but I'm actually really glad he did.

"Dinner's at six. I'd really love it if you could both be there. School starts tomorrow, and Gabe and I leave the next day, so this may be our only chance to have a family dinner for a while." Her energy is so positive and hopeful that I can't say no.

"I'll be there," I grunt. It's the best I can do right now.

"Great!" She claps her hands together and smiles from ear to ear. She has the same damn dimples as her son, too.

"Ollie, you'll be there?"

"Yeah, Mom, I will." He smiles at her the way I used to smile at my mom. Full of love, devotion, and happiness.

She leans in and gives him a peck on the cheek. "See you boys for dinner. I'm so happy to see you both getting along so well!" She exclaims this like we're eight years old and blending a family. Vivian slips out of the door, closing it delicately behind her.

I turn back to Oliver. "You look just like your mom."

He grins crookedly and looks down, rubbing his bare foot back and forth across the plush carpet. "Yeah, everyone says that."

"Where's your dad?" I ask bluntly.

"Dunno. Never met him. Where's your mom?"

"Dead," I say with a bite, even though I'm the one who started this line of questioning.

Oliver rubs the back of his neck. "Shit, Finn, I'm sorry. I had no idea. No one told me anything."

"It's fine. My dad didn't tell me anything either, not until the day before you moved in."

We're both quiet for a minute, trying to digest all that's happened in the last twenty-four hours.

"Let me wrap your ribs. It'll support them and make it easier to move and breathe."

"How do you know all this?" Oliver asks.

"Football," I answer simply. What I don't say is that most of my medical knowledge comes from the fact that I fractured three ribs and had a partially collapsed lung from the accident that killed my mother.

"Do you want to become a doctor, like your dad?" he asks innocently.

My answer is swift and merciless. "Fuck, no. He's the reason I *don't* want to become a doctor."

"Okaaay," he says, drawing the word out. He clearly doesn't know my dad yet. He'll see. Probably at dinner tonight.

He's picking at his nail polish, and I place my hand over both of his to stop his fidgeting. I gingerly lift his shirt, and he holds it up for me while I grab the ACE bandage I stuck in my back pocket earlier. I unwind one end, press it against the ribs on his uninjured side, and wrap the bandage around once until the loose end is secured. I go around his torso a second and third time, completely aware of our proximity. On the fourth trip, I pull the bandage to make sure it's snug, and Oliver lets out a whimper. My eyes dart up to his face. He's biting his lip so hard I'm afraid he's going to draw blood. I reach up and release his poor abused flesh with my thumb.

"Shhh. I know it hurts," I murmur. "It'll feel better when I'm done, trust me." Oliver just nods, and I continue three more times around his torso before securing the end. By the time I'm finished, Oliver has tears pooling in his eyes. He tries to blink them away, but a few escape and roll down his cheeks.

Again, I feel the need to ease his pain and use my thumbs to wipe that now visible proof away. Proof that I couldn't keep him safe for even an hour. Proof that I failed to protect someone who's suddenly important to me. "I'm sorry, Ollie," I whisper, liking the way the nickname rolls off my tongue but hating the pain he's feeling.

"Thanks, Finn. For taking care of me," he whispers back with a sniffle, squeezing his lids shut as more wetness trails down his cheeks and pools in the little groove above his top lip.

"Always," I vow, not giving two fucks if it's too soon to say shit like that.

CHAPTER FOUR

OLIVER

After Finn wrapped my ribs, he went downstairs, snuck me a bag of ice from the kitchen, and then left to finish some homework. My ribs actually do feel a lot better. Now I can take a deep breath or stretch and reach for something without wincing. The ice is helping, too, dulling the ache.

I lean back against my new fluffy pillows and take a second to luxuriate in the softest bed I have ever slept in. And it's mine now. I adjust the ice bag to cover a different spot on my bruised and battered ribcage. I tried to downplay the injury when it happened, but that ass wipe really checked me good. I don't know what the hell I did to instantly piss him off, but Finn seems to think this Eric guy is going to keep giving me shit. I'm not worried, though; I've dealt with worse.

My best friends became my tormentors after I came out to them at the beginning of the school year. When Mom told me she was getting married and we were moving to Chicago, I couldn't wait to get the fuck out of Marlo Bay and away from the homophobic assholes I thought cared about me. I never in a million years expected that the same guys I grew up with would let my sexuality define our friendship, or more accurately, *end* our friendship. They couldn't get past all the times we changed out of our wetsuits together or had sleepovers when we were younger. They made my life a living hell at school, spreading wild rumors about me trying to seduce them or staring at their junk in the locker room. All of which couldn't be further from the truth. I was never attracted to them, never saw them as anything more than my best friends. My brothers. But clearly they did not feel the same way about me, which hurt.

I push the negative thoughts away. That's in the past, and I can't change anyone's bigoted behavior. I have a fresh start in a new state, with a new family and a new school to start tomorrow. I fully plan on making the best out of my last semester of high school, which does not include coming out to anyone. My mom knows, of course, and she knew how I was treated before we left. She was extremely upset and outraged on my behalf, but I made her promise not to go to the school board over it. I didn't want the attention; I just wanted to leave.

I have about two hours to spare before family dinner, and my eyes are starting to feel heavy. I give in to the tiredness and drift into oblivion, where I don't have to worry about being gay or bullies harassing me.

Vaguely aware of the dip in the mattress next to me, I continue to hover in that blissful state between sleep and wakefulness.

"Oliver." The sound of an unfamiliar male voice saying

my name in a hushed whisper has my eyebrows creasing in confusion. I mumble out what I think are words, but my brain is still in a sleepy fog, so I burrow further down into the cloud I'm sleeping on.

A deep chuckle pulls me closer to the land of the living, and I crack one eye open.

Oh. It's Finn. *My new stepbrother.*

"How are your ribs?" he asks, removing the wet towel and melted bag of ice from the bed.

"Better, thanks," I croak out in a sleep-induced rasp.

"That's good. It's almost time for dinner. I would have just texted you, but I realized I don't have your number yet."

"Oh yeah, here. Text yourself." I grab my phone from the nightstand and don't think twice about unlocking it and handing it over. I changed my number back in California so no one could harass me anymore.

Fresh start, remember?

I hear his phone ping with an incoming text.

"There," he says. "Text me your class schedule when you get a chance, and I'll see if we have lunch or anything together."

Oh fuck, I didn't even think about that. I hope we at least have lunch together. I can't go through another semester like the previous one. Being ridiculed, ostracized, *slandered*. Daily. I can't do it again. I don't tell Finn this, though. He doesn't seem homophobic. In fact, the vibes he's been giving off are the complete opposite. I mean, I've never sucked ketchup off the thumb of a straight guy before. I've never sucked *anything* off of *anyone* before, actually.

"Okay, I'll find it in my emails later," I say casually, even though I'm starting to freak out about school a little. Finn gets off the bed, and I stand to do my normal stretch, reaching high above my head and wincing when I'm reminded I can't do that right now. I watch as his eyes dart down to the sliver of skin I know is showing and then quickly away. I'm really starting to wonder what his deal is, but I don't ask because I don't want him to ask me in return. It's one thing not to tell anyone I'm gay; it's on a different level to actively lie and deny my sexuality. I won't do that.

"I gotta take a piss, and then I'll be ready. What's for dinner anyway?" I ask.

"I don't fucking know. Your mom's cooking," he retorts with a smirk.

In that case, I'd bet money on tacos.

Mom's eyes glisten under the bright light of the crystal chandelier as she clasps both hands under her chin, a wide smile splitting her face, dimples and all. Finn and I just came downstairs, and we're walking into what appears to be the formal dining room, and it is fucking fancy. I feel out of place in my skinny jeans and band tee, but whatever, this is supposed to be my home now. Besides, Finn is wearing gray sweats again, and his white shirt has holes. Although I'm guessing he probably spent three hundred dollars for it to look like that.

"Look at them, Gabe. They've just hit it off so well." She sniffles and tries to subtly wipe at her eyes. My mom has always been the sentimental and emotional type and tends to get choked up easily.

My new stepdad takes one of my mom's hands in his and kisses the top adoringly. Finn acts like he dislikes his dad, but Gabe has been nothing but good to my mother. I haven't interacted with him much, but as long as she's happy and he treats her right, he's okay in my book.

"Just like brothers should." He smiles and gazes at her with love.

Finn scoffs at that, but I don't think my mom heard. She's too wrapped up in her new husband at the moment. We both take our seats. Gabe is at the head of the unnecessarily long mahogany table, with Finn on one side and my mom and me on the other.

She buzzes with excitement as she leans over the table and removes all the fancy-ass silver domes covering everything. "I made tacos!"

Yep, called it.

As soon as she lifts the first lid, my mouth waters as the spicy aroma of carne asada tickles my nose.

"I fucking love tacos!" Finn exclaims with a full-blown smile as his gaze homes in on the stack of warm corn tortillas.

My heart stutters a beat, and my stomach flips like I just went down the first big drop on a roller coaster. His smile is amazing, radiant even, but way too rare. I prove my point when said smile twitches and dies not even two seconds later at his dad's insensitive words.

"Language, boy. Apologize to your mother."

Finn flinches as if his father just physically struck him. He grits his teeth, and I can see his jaw clenching from across the table.

"Gabe, honey, relax. We're all just having a good time, about to enjoy some good food and good company." She bumps my shoulder and winks to lighten the mood. Her youthful attitude and positivity can turn any negative situation around.

Gabe grumbles under his breath but lets it slide. "Just watch your mouth at the dinner table, Wyatt."

"Yes, sir," Finn grits out as he stares at nothing on his plate.

It's weird to see him submissive like that. I don't like it. And now I can see why he doesn't like his dad. Gabe may be great to my mom, but he's a prick to his son, and that doesn't really leave me with much hope for my own relationship with him.

Mom once again sprinkles her magic happy dust over everyone and explains each dish she made. Being so close to Mexico growing up, we always had bomb-ass Mexican food around, and Mom learned how to make our favorites.

Everyone piles their plates high, and no one is shy about it. This food is fucking delicious, and we all dig in. For the next twenty minutes, all I hear is the clanking of utensils against plates and the crunch of tortilla chips. I know I don't have to worry about my allergy when Mom is cooking.

I'm the first to finish and lean back in my chair, patting my food baby. "Oh my God, I'm stuffed. Mom, thank you. That was amazing as always."

Finn nods enthusiastically, instantly agreeing between bites of his soft taco.

My mom sips her water and laughs lightly. "Thank you, baby. I hope you saved room for dessert. I made your favorite. Apple pie empanadas."

I groan at that and continue to cradle my stomach—looks like it's going to be twins before the night is over. There's no way I can say no to apple pie empanadas.

I look over to Finn, and his eyes sparkle with mirth as he takes another giant bite of his taco.

Jesus, is that his sixth one?

Guess he's not going to have a problem eating dessert. The dude is a garbage disposal.

"I wanted to talk about a few things with you boys," Gabe says as my mom goes into the kitchen to serve the empanadas and fresh whipped cream.

"Your mother and I will be gone for two weeks." I glance at Finn and see the vein in his forehead pulse and his eye twitch. He holds it together so well and shows no other sign that he wants to fucking *strangle* his douchebag of a dad. I feel like Gabe is purposefully referring to my mom as Finn's mother just to hurt him, and it's a low blow.

"No parties, no girls, no drinking, no drugs. I don't want either of you calling me or Vivian for anything. If you're not on your deathbed, don't call. I don't want to hear it. This is your mother's honeymoon. She deserves the best and deserves to relax, so don't stress her out with any of your teenage bullshit. I also have cameras around the house, so keep that in mind."

Jesus, this prick.

He hides his scorn under the guise of giving my mother the best trip of her life, but he's really just a selfish asshole who doesn't want to be bothered by anyone.

"Same as usual, Dad. It's not the first time you've been out of town."

"Don't take that tone with me, Son. Two weeks is a long time, especially for someone so prone to trouble. I expect you to be on your best behavior and do *not* cause me any headaches for when I return," he sneers. "And if you do decide to do something stupid, make sure you don't bring Oliver down with you. I don't want to hear that you got into another fight at one of Bethany's parties. Doesn't matter who started it."

I don't say anything during the entire conversation. I

feel awkward, like I'm stuck in the middle of someone else's family feud. But I'm not, because this is *my* family now.

My mom comes back into the dining room, balancing a bowl on each arm while carrying two more in her grasp. All her years of waitressing have given her some impressive balance.

Then it's like a switch is flipped in Gabe, and he jumps up to be the doting husband and help with the dessert bowls. I bite my tongue for now. She does deserve this happiness in her life. She's worked so hard—being a young, single mom and taking care of me with only her mother to help. She had me at nineteen, so she's only thirty-seven, and I just want her to be happy.

Finn and I make eye contact across the table, and a new understanding passes between us. Another common enemy.

First, Eric.

Now, Gabe.

Who's next?

My mom places a bowl in front of me, and it smells absolutely divine. I take a huge bite, getting a little of everything—the warm, gooey apple filling, the buttery, flakey crust, and the cold whipped cream, all in one massive bite. I mean, that's just how you gotta do it to truly appreciate the culinary masterpiece that is apple pie empanadas. I can barely keep my mouth shut as I chew, and I'm sure I look like a rabid chipmunk.

Finn's deep chuckle has me peeling my eyes from the cinnamon apple goodness in front of me.

"Dude, I've never seen someone eat so enthusiastically before. Like, you go all in. One hundred and ten percent, no chill."

I can't smile or laugh. My mouth is too fucking full, so I

just narrow my eyes and continue to chew. He throws his head back with a loud laugh. My mom chuckles along with him. She's always tried to get me to eat with better manners, but if I really like something, I can't help myself.

Gabe's cold brown eyes dart between Finn and me, and he curls his lip and wrinkles his nose when he looks at me. As if I fucking disgust him.

I've only known him a few hours, and I'm already sick of his pompous attitude. How can my mom not see it? Even if he is sweet to her.

I can't help but open my mouth, showing him my food when he looks back at me.

His face turns crimson, and he sneers at me, wiping his mouth harshly with his napkin. He clearly won't say shit to me in front of my mom. Gabe physically turns away from me so he doesn't have to watch me eat.

Too bad. If you love my mom, you're stuck with this pretty face. Better get used to it.

"Vivian, sweetheart, you have absolutely outdone yourself. This dinner was delicious." He overdoes the compliments, but Mom just eats it up. She's only ever had to cook for two before.

Finn and I agree because it's fucking scrumptious.

Mom tells us the itinerary for their honeymoon in Aruba—all the historical areas she wants to see, the different beaches, the local cuisine. By the time she's done talking, I know more about Aruba than I ever thought I would.

"Take care of my baby while I'm gone, Finn. He's only seventeen, and he's never stayed this long on his own before."

Finn snorts at that, and I groan. "Moomm, can you

please stop acting like I can't handle myself? It's embarrassing, and I'll be eighteen next week."

"Oh, I just mean that because you're in a new city and don't know anyone or your way around yet. I hate that I'm leaving you so soon after moving here. And for your birthday, too."

"Don't worry about my birthday. We already agreed to celebrate once you get back. It's seriously not a big deal. It's just another day."

"But, it's your *eighteenth*, honey! That's just as special and important as a honeymoon. It is a big deal, and I won't let this slip under the radar, Ollie. We will be celebrating when we get back. As a family."

"Don't worry, Viv. I'll take *very* good care of Ollie for you. I'll even plan something a little *extra special* for his birthday." He's talking to her but staring straight at me, absolutely no expression on his face except for a twinkle in his eye that his dad is probably right about.

Fucking trouble.

"Well, aren't you just a sweetheart?" Mom smiles back at him. I don't think she picked up on it, but could he be any more obvious? There's no way he's not into dudes saying shit like that. I blush and gaze at the empty bowl in front of me. I have no response and can't hold eye contact with him. I can't come out, not yet. I need to get through this last semester without any drama, for my own sanity and peace of mind.

CHAPTER FIVE
OLIVER

Finn pulls into a front row parking spot at Lake View fifteen minutes before the first bell will ring. Being on the football team sure has its perks. This parking lot is fucking massive, and I would not want to be in the back.

I take a moment to admire the main building on campus. Set back a ways from the student lot, Preston Hall is situated front and center in the lush, green grass that makes up LVP's main quad. The massive building is historic and has a slightly gothic feel to it. Tangled vines of mostly dead ivy scale the front of the aged, washed-out gray stone, strangling it with gnarled fingers. It has actual fucking turrets on each end and gabled roofs with spires above each set of windows. When you're in the middle of the quad, I've heard you can even see Lake Michigan in the distance, hence the school name. Basically, it's fucking *awesome* and makes my old public high school look like a shoebox.

I'm torn from my reverie when Finn places his cold fingers under my chin and closes my mouth. "You might want to get the shock and awe out of your system before we get out of the car," he teases. "You look fucking mesmerized." He snorts out a laugh, but I know he's not actually making fun of me.

"Ha, ha. Very funny. You have to admit, this building is pretty fucking awesome," I say, defending my admiration.

"I've been here almost four years, so it just looks like a prison to me."

"Geez, a bit doom and gloom, Finn."

"Sorry, Sunshine." His mouth quirks up on the side. I narrow my eyes at him even though I kind of like the teasing nickname. Let's face it, I like *anything* Finn calls me.

He laughs and grabs his backpack and my messenger bag from the back seat. "Let's go before we're late for your first day of school. Shit, I forgot to take your picture before we left the house." He smirks, and *holy fucking shit,* did Finn just make another *joke*?

"You are on a roll with the jokes this morning, bro. Did you add extra sugar to your Captain Crunch or something?" I tease as we climb out of the Jeep.

A gust of frigid wind smacks me dead in the face, and I pull my peacoat and scarf tighter around me.

Fuck, it's cold here.

Finn walks around and hands me my bag. I grab it, but he doesn't let go. I peer up at him with a question in my eyes, and then it hits me. "I'm fine, Finn. I can carry my own bag." He's concerned about my ribs.

"Fine," he grunts, "but don't carry too many of your books at once, or you'll agitate them. Trust me."

"Okay, thanks," I say shyly at his concern. I take the bag from him and gingerly place it over my head, situating it across my chest.

I smooth down my dark red and navy plaid pants with my gloved hands, extremely grateful that Finn secretly bought me some. I was fitted for the uniform back in California, so the tailoring is on point. The pants are fitted and stop right at the ankle, showing off my shiny dress shoes. The white button-up is pressed to perfection, and my navy blazer fits snug across my shoulders, the school crest on my left chest. I've never worn a uniform before, but I feel fucking *good*. Like I actually belong. Finn helped me rewrap my ribs this morning, so I think I should be okay all day.

Jared steps out of a matte black Challenger that just pulled in next to us and greets Finn with one of his bro hugs. I'm a little surprised when he walks around the Jeep and greets me the same way, only he seems to be more gentle, probably remembering how Eric slammed into me. Or maybe Finn told him how I'm hurting.

"Hey, Oliver. You excited to start Lake View?" he asks in his friendly, down-to-earth manner.

I readjust the messenger bag across my chest. "Um, I am, actually. Fresh start and all that." I smile in that universally awkward way where you press your lips into a thin, flat line.

I look over at Finn, and he's got his head tilted, eyeing me curiously like he wants to ask what I need a fresh start from. But he knows now is not the right time or place, and I mentally prepare for the questions that will no doubt come later.

"That's awesome, dude," Jared says, looking genuinely happy for me. "Let me see your schedule." He holds his hand out and waits while I rummage through my bag. I printed it out last night so I wouldn't have to look at my phone whenever I needed a reminder or someone asked this question.

"Oh sweet, we have American Lit, Art, and Lunch together." I beam at that because Finn isn't in either of those classes with me, but now I have someone to sit with. Jared hands my schedule back, and the three of us make our way up to Preston Hall, Finn and Jared flanking me. I can't help but wonder if they're doing this on purpose, and Finn set the whole thing up. I know we can trust his best friend, but I hate having anyone think I'm weak or powerless.

Once we enter the main hall, I see where all the kids went. No one was hanging around outside because it's too fucking cold. It seems this is the place to congregate in the morning before class. The main area is completely open beneath the dark-wooden beams and vaulted ceiling. The students call it the Mall. You can look up at the railings of the other two floors, as well as the flags of what appears to be at least fifty different countries, all lining the perimeter.

I follow Finn and Jared to a group of guys and girls. I recognize a few of them and nod to Ethan, Danny, and Trace. I don't see Eric anywhere, *thank fuck.* Finn introduces me to the other guys standing around and the girls hanging on them. Everyone seems pretty friendly, which puts me at ease.

"I'm gonna go show Oliver his locker," Finn mumbles after a couple minutes of small talk. I can tell he's had enough and wants to leave. I follow him down a few winding hallways, and I'm already turned around. *Shit.*

"Your locker's right here." Finn raps his knuckles on number two-fifteen. "And mine is right here." He smirks as he opens number two-fourteen, right next to me.

"And what are the chances that our lockers would be side by side when you've already been here for more than half the year?" I raise a questioning brow.

He just shrugs. "What can I say? Mrs. Jameson loves me."

"The guidance counselor?"

"Yep, I emailed her last night. I was concerned about my brother having to switch schools in the middle of the year and wanted to make the transition as smooth as possible." He smiles wide, which is fucking charming as hell.

I can't help but grin right back at him. All the thoughtful things he's doing for me make me feel special. Cared for. He tries to act all grumpy and broody, but under all of that is a really sweet, caring, and loyal guy.

For instance, this morning, Finn stuffed most of my textbooks into his backpack since I needed to bring them all with me today. No one even noticed that his bag was full and mine was mostly empty.

See? Fucking thoughtful.

He places my books into the locker for me. I grab the AP Statistics one for first period, my school-issued tablet, and a spiral notebook, stuffing them back into my messenger bag.

The warning bell rings, and I follow Finn to our class. I'm glad it worked out that we have so many classes together, including the first one of the day. It definitely helps ease my excited and anxious nerves.

When we walk through the classroom door, I'm surprised to see Jayden sitting there. This is a senior class, and he's only a sophomore. He smiles wide, the fluorescent lights reflecting off his silver braces, and waves us over. He has regular black-framed glasses on today and looks a little older now, but not much.

"Hey, Oliver! You can sit in front of me. No one sits here," he says as he points to the desk in front of him.

Finn walks down the other row and fist bumps Jayden before sliding into the desk next to him. "Sup, Jay?"

"Hey, Finn." He grins, way too happy for first-period math.

I sit in front of Jayden and turn in my seat to look at

them. The bell hasn't rung yet. "Hey, I didn't know you were some kind of boy genius or something. What are you doing in this class?" I ask, genuinely curious.

He just shrugs like it's no big deal. "I've always been really good with numbers. I want to go into astrophysics in college, so I'm trying to get as many AP credits as possible for the standard courses."

"*Damn*. Aren't you like fifteen?" How the hell does he already have a fucking life plan? I don't even know what I'm doing after graduation. I couldn't think past getting out of California and starting over, but now that I'm here, I guess I need to figure shit out and quick.

Jayden's smile stretches, his dark brown eyes sparkling. "Yep."

I laugh and shake my head at him, turning around in my seat as the final bell rings.

The class is really boring and tedious for first thing in the morning, but at least we have the child genius, Jayden. I can feel Finn's eyes on me as I chew on the end of my pen, trying to make sense of a complicated bivariate distribution that Mrs. Simmons is writing on the whiteboard. I tilt my head and peek at him from the corner of my eye. He's leaning back in his seat, legs spread, dark blue eyes smoldering. They're so intense that I quickly look away, confused as to why he's staring at me.

Not long after, the bell rings, and we all scurry from our seats. We say goodbye to Jayden and head off to US History, which I'm excited to see that we share with Trace and Ethan. Mr. Rattler is a cool older man and makes the class fun, so it passes quickly.

I'm not looking forward to splitting up from Finn; he's kind of become my security blanket this morning.

Finn turns to me after we both shut our lockers. "Okay, do you remember how to get to Spanish?"

"Yeah, it's just the small building at the back of campus, by the pond. Sable Hall?"

"Yeah. Just follow the main path that cuts through the quad there and back afterward. I'll meet you at our lockers before lunch. I'm not sure who has Spanish with you."

"I'll be fine, Finn, seriously. Thanks for all your help around school this morning. It means a lot." I scuff my dress shoe against the dark wood floor and flip the few loose strands of my hair off my forehead.

True to the Finn I've come to know the past couple of days, he just nods and grunts, "Let's go."

I smile to myself, knowing someone has my back no matter what.

Finn and I split up in the middle of the quad when he heads off to Auto Shop, and I go to Spanish. I didn't know he was interested in car mechanics, but I guess I shouldn't be too surprised looking at his and Gabe's garage.

I hesitantly step into Spanish and peer around at the sea of faces, searching for anyone familiar. Or shit, even slightly friendly looking.

"Yo, Oliver! Come sit with us!" Someone hollers obnoxiously loud.

Fuuuck. This is like the worst-case scenario.

I smile stiffly and reluctantly shuffle up the row to the back of the class, where Eric and a really pretty redheaded girl are sitting.

Two redheads—this can't be good.

"Hi, I'm Hazel." The girl smiles wide and sticks her

dainty hand out to shake. It looks like a claw with blood-red talons on the end. *Jesus.* Those look fucking sharp. She has a typical slutty schoolgirl costume on. Excuse me, I mean *uniform.* I'm getting a weird vibe from her, but I smile politely and shake her hand anyway.

"Oliver," I say simply. Maybe I'm being dramatic, but I swear she has the same evil glint in her eyes as Eric.

"Oh, I know who you are. You're Wyatt Finnegan's new little brother." She smirks, and it's condescending and nasty. I internally roll my eyes at her weak jab. Yes, I'm younger than Finn. . . by a month. And yes, I'm smaller than Finn. *Big fucking deal.*

"Yeah. . .?" I say, unsure of what her point is.

"Well, you seem like a really sweet kid, Oliver, so it wouldn't feel right if I didn't give you a warning."

"A warning?" I parrot as my eyebrows furrow together in confusion.

What the hell is she talking about?

"Yes, honey." Her fake sweetness makes me sick. She places her claw-tipped hand on my arm, and I'm thankful for the long sleeves and blazer between my skin and her venomous grip. I'd probably be allergic to her touch.

"Wyatt is. . ." she trails off and waves her other hand in the air as if searching for the right wicked words.

She settles on "Unstable."

"What are you talking about?" I'm sure I look confused as hell and glance around, hoping someone besides the crazy bitch in front of me will answer my question.

"Well, as you know, Finn and his mom were in a terrible car accident last school year. Hit by a drunk driver. On the night of the state championship, actually." She sighs deeply and dramatically as if it truly upsets her to talk about it.

"Hazel. . ." Eric warns, finally speaking up for his so-called friend. "You don't need to go there."

"No, Eric. I think I do." She gives him a murderous glare, and he shuts right up. "Oliver needs to know who he's sharing a home with. So, as I was saying, after his mom died, he cut me off. No more hooking up, no more gifts, no more dinners. We were about to make it official, too. I just know it. But then, the accident happened, and Finn changed. He's not the same person anymore. He's depressed, cold, distant, *violent*. Do I need to continue with the negative adjectives? Just look up 'psychopath' in the thesaurus." She huffs and flips her long red hair over her shoulder.

Fuck.

No, I didn't know that. I knew his mother wasn't alive, but I didn't know the *how* or even the *when*. My heart aches for Finn even more now. I school my features and don't let Hazel see my shock or sadness. It's exactly the kind of response she's looking for. I know these types of people, and they're toxic. I thought I left all that behind me, but clearly, you can never truly escape negativity and hatred. It's everywhere. Her perspective is so self-absorbed and skewed that I'm pretty sure *she's* the psychopath.

"Hazel. I think you're wrong here. Finn went through a tragedy. Of course he's not going to be the same person. And I'm sorry, but he's been nothing but amazing and welcoming to my mom and me."

She sighs audibly and crosses her arms over her chest, pushing her boobs further up. "Don't say I didn't warn you," she snips and turns back around in her seat as Señor Garcia starts class.

I forget about Hazel and Eric and immerse myself in the lesson. Living in Southern California my entire life has made me nearly fluent, including an excellent accent, if I must say so myself. I can tell Señor Garcia is impressed when I stand up and introduce myself to the class in near-perfect Spanish.

I look next to me, and Eric is just glaring.

Great.

First, he's jealous of my touchdown, and now I'm too good at Spanish. What a fucking *hater.*

I turn back to the front and ignore the douchebag next to me for the rest of class.

I'm not even sure if I should tell Finn what went down. What Hazel said is fucked up, and she's obviously not over him. I don't even want to acknowledge how I feel knowing that Finn was with her. It was clearly in the past, but I can't help the jealousy burning through me. I decide I don't want that negativity, and I'd rather Finn come to me when he's ready to share, not have it forced out of him because of what one bitchy little girl said.

When the bell rings, I am so ready to get out of this hostile environment that I jump up a little too fast and wince at the pain in my ribs. I adjust my bag so it's only on my right shoulder, relieving any pressure on my left side. I head down the aisle and see Eric watching me.

He does not need to know that he hurt me.

I force a smile. "You got lunch next?" I ask casually.

"Yeah." He nods once. He has a poker face on, but I'm not sure why.

"Cool, man. See ya there, then." I practically jog out of the room to get away from him.

Once outside the class, I start power walking toward the exit when I feel my phone vibrate in my bag. I only have two contacts, so it's either my mom or Finn. I look down to dig through my bag for it when someone bumps into my left side, *hard.*

I suck in a sharp breath and bend forward slightly so I can't see who it is, but no one stops to check on me.

Sonofabitch, that hurt.

I hobble to the men's bathroom, keeping an arm wrapped protectively around my side. I try to breathe past the feeling of knives stabbing my bones and simultaneously weave my way through a crowd of people. The pain is so acute, a cold sweat breaks out across my brow.

Almost there.

I push through the bathroom door and let out a sigh of relief.

Thank fuck.

No one's in here, and this bathroom is one with a couch, too. I'm lucky the bathrooms are so fucking fancy in this place as I stumble over to the leather couch in the corner and drop my bag. I carefully lie down and drape my good arm over my eyes as I clutch my left arm tightly to my chest on my injured side. I try to catch my breath for a second before the nausea makes me run for the toilet.

CHAPTER SIX

FINN

I check the time on my phone. It's only one minute later than the last time I looked, but it's been over ten since the bell rang. Oliver still hasn't shown up to our lockers, and he's not answering his texts either.

Goddammit. I knew I shouldn't have left him to walk back alone, but I don't think he would have appreciated an escort.

Fuck!

I slam my locker door shut and rush to the back exit of the main building and straight across the quad toward Sable Hall.

My breath comes out in little frosty puffs as I get closer to the small building at the back of campus. Worst-case scenarios are running through my mind right now, and I can't stop them.

Eric? His allergy? His ribs?

Then I see a fiery red mane storming through the sea of kids around me.

Fucking Hazel Bell.

"Hey, Wyatt," she purrs as she cuts me off directly in

front of the building and runs her shiny red claws across my chest. She's like an evil little kitten, always scratching and hissing at people. I can't believe I ever used to fuck her, let alone almost date her. I shiver, and it's not from the near-freezing temps outside.

She couldn't understand that I wanted a break after the accident and have some time to myself. I was not in a good place, and I needed someone, anyone, to sympathize with me, but she just showed her true colors. She proved that she truly is the entitled, self-centered brat everyone thinks she is.

"I don't have time right now, Hazel," I growl as I remove her hand from my chest and let go. She lets it hover in the air for a second before using it to whip her hair off her shoulder.

"Hmm, and why is that, Wyatt?" She holds a finger to her chin as if deep in thought. "Are you looking for your *brother,* perhaps?" she sneers.

I take a challenging step forward, even though I would never put my hands on her. "Where is he?" I demand.

She cackles like the witch that she is. "I just saw him run into the bathroom at the back of the building. He didn't look so great. What did you guys eat last night?" She laughs more, so I side-step this crazy bitch and run up the stairs, taking off toward the bathroom.

I find Oliver on the couch in the back of the bathroom in a separate vanity room with carpet, mirrors, and a really comfortable leather couch. I'm not sure if he's sleeping, but he's clutching his ribs tightly.

"Hey, Sunshine. You okay?" He startles at my deep voice

as it echoes off the spacious walls. I see the wince on his face when he moves too fast.

"Someone bumped into my ribs in the hallway after Spanish," he murmurs, still holding his side, but sitting up now. "And I thought I was going to be sick from it."

I grit my teeth. "Did you see who it was? Was it Eric? Hazel?" I question.

"What? No. I mean, I don't think so. How did you know I had Spanish with both of them, anyway?"

"I didn't," I reply shortly, "but I do now. And I don't fucking like it."

He scrunches his eyebrows together in confusion. "Can we just go to lunch? I think eating and taking some ibuprofen will help."

I help Oliver stand the rest of the way up, and he grimaces. "Are you sure you're up for the cafeteria?" I question, a little concerned with how uncomfortable he seems to be.

"Yeah. I'm not leaving sick on the first fucking day, Finn," he snaps, and I let him get away with the attitude because I know he's hurting.

"Alright, let's go, then." I grab his bag and hold it low, discreetly. He opens his mouth like he's about to protest, but I just stare him down. It's non-negotiable. He's not carrying that bag right now.

Oliver stands tall, even though I know his ribs feel like he was hit by a freight train because he basically was. I admire that he doesn't want to show weakness around others, especially assholes who would relish in it and use it against him. . . or against me.

Assholes like Eric, Hazel, *my dad.*

The cafeteria is still really loud and busy, even though lunch is almost halfway over. We stopped first by our lockers to stuff our bags in; there's no point in standing in line carrying that shit. You only need to scan your student ID, and you can select anything you want to eat. Our parents pay enough annual tuition to run a small country, so they provide the best of the best for the students.

"Hi, Mr. Chase. I have your special food restriction lunch for you," the nice old lady with a white bun and hair net says, holding out a styrofoam container wrapped in plastic.

Oliver flushes and stutters a thanks, grabbing the container and placing it on his red plastic tray. I hastily grab two slices of pepperoni pizza, a side salad with ranch, and two waters. I didn't even think about his lunch; I bet Vivian set that up.

We walk over to my normal table next to the floor-to-ceiling windows. You can see the entire quad and the thirty-foot-tall obelisk towering over everything smack in the middle. The dark waters of Lake Michigan glitter in the distance.

I sit next to Ethan, and Oliver sits next to me, with Jared on his other side. Everyone is already mostly done eating and just snacking on some chips and candy.

Oliver slowly peels off the plastic wrap and lifts the lid as if he expects something to jump out and bite him. He crinkles his nose in disgust when he fully opens it and slumps back in his seat.

"What the fuck is that?!" Eric guffaws, tipping his head back and drawing unnecessary attention to our table. "Prison food?" His booming laughter is obnoxious and disrespectful, and I kick him in the shin under the table since he's sitting across from me.

"Shut up, fuckface," I snarl. I'm really starting to wonder why I was ever friends with him. He's a bully and an asshole who gets off on the suffering of others.

"Ow! Jesus, Finn." Eric narrows his eyes at me, reaching under the table to rub his shin. I hope it bruises. It's the least he deserves for all the marks he put on Oliver.

I look over to Oliver's lunch and grit my teeth because it *does* look like fucking prison food.

What the hell is the school thinking? Is this really the best they can come up with?

A bologna and cheese sandwich on plain white bread, a bag of barbecue chips, and an apple. That's it. We're ordering groceries tonight and packing our lunch from now on. This is utter bullshit.

Oliver grabs the chips and apple, then shuts the lid, pushing his tray away in distaste. I know how much he actually loves food, so it pisses me off when he's not able to enjoy it.

Jared, the nice guy that he is, subtly pushes over half of the artisanal sandwich his family's personal chef prepares for him and his little sisters' lunches.

Poor Oliver just clears his throat and smiles sadly. "Thanks. It looks and smells really great. But the reason I have this *prison lunch* is that I'm allergic to peanuts and have to be careful about what I eat."

"Damn. Sorry, man. I didn't know," Jared apologizes.

"No reason to apologize. I'll just eat this apple and catch up later with dinner," he chuckles, but I see the frustration in his eyes. He's probably never been able to eat what he wants, when he wants.

Surprisingly, Eric doesn't talk shit about Oliver's food

allergy, and everyone goes back to eating and talking about sports or which girl they're trying to bang at the moment.

While everyone's distracted, I reach into my inner blazer pocket and pull out the two small ibuprofen pills I stashed there earlier. I tap Oliver's thigh under the table and hold out my palm. He takes them and shoots me a small, grateful smile. He swiftly pops them into his mouth and swallows them without water.

I stuff the last bite of greasy pizza into my mouth and guzzle my water as the lunch bell rings. I feel better knowing Jared is in Oliver's next two classes. He won't let anyone fuck with him. I texted him last night, telling him what was up with Oliver's ribs. He was pissed about it, too.

I pull my beanie down lower and stuff my hands in my coat pockets, anxiously waiting outside the gym doors for our last period of the day. I love playing sports, but I fucking hate gym class. Dodgeball, tug-of-war, volleyball, all that bullshit. It's not fun, and it just pisses me off.

Jared walks up with Oliver, and they're both laughing and talking animatedly, little puffs of cold breath dissipating into the air around them.

"I still think French Impressionism is the most beautifully detailed style ever. I mean, come on, Monet? Renoir? They were completely innovative for their time! Combining light, small brush strokes, and all those minuscule details to portray the most beautiful dream sequences and fantasies they could imagine. It's completely amazing," Oliver raves.

Okay, whoa. He's mentioned painting, and I saw the canvases in his room, but damn, the kid knows his art. I have no idea what he's talking about, but it's cool that Jared does.

"Hey," I say when they both stop in front of me. "I take it art went well?"

"Yes! The art studio is incredible. Practically any medium I could ever want to try, right at my fingertips!" Oliver gushes, bouncing on his toes as he breathes heat into his fingers. His nose is turning pink from the cold.

His happiness makes me want to smile, and Jared just chuckles. "I'll catch you guys later. Gotta get to class."

"See ya, dude!" Oliver shouts at Jared's retreating back, and he lifts a hand in return. I'm thankful I have such a loyal best friend. He walked Ollie across campus in the opposite direction of his own class. We didn't tell Ollie, of course.

We push through the heavy double doors of the gymnasium, and it feels a bit like leading him into a dungeon as we head down the steep steps to the locker room.

As soon as we open the door, Oliver wrinkles his nose at the ever-offensive stench of dirty socks and musty uniforms. "Too rank for you, Sunshine?" I tease.

"Uh yeah. My sport doesn't involve sweaty balls and athlete's foot. Just saltwater and a board," he teases right back. I bark out a laugh, and a grin tugs at his lips.

"I like the sound of your laugh," he whispers before we walk into the main area where all the guys are changing.

"I don't. . . not much makes me laugh or even smile anymore. But you do," I confess. His smile grows, and I can see every one of his pearly whites.

Oliver takes my hand in his and gives it a reassuring squeeze. "I'm glad, Finn. You deserve to smile and laugh every damn day."

His touch is so soft and tender. It's not something I'm

used to anymore, and I have to swallow past the lump stuck in my throat.

"We better get dressed. Coach hates it when we come out late."

I stride past everyone and head to the back, Oliver on my heels, and see Danny at the lockers, getting changed. Danny's a cool dude, so I let him in on the information about Oliver's injury since the three of us have gym together. It's darker in the back corner—away from the showers and mirrors—and doesn't have the same amount of fluorescent lighting as the main area by the sinks.

"Sup, Danny?" I hold my fist out, and he bumps mine back.

"Yo." A man of few words, and I appreciate that. Danny Vallejo's your guy if you want to hang out and chill with someone who never brings drama or long conversations.

He nods at Oliver, who gives him a small wave in return.

I lean down to whisper in Oliver's ear. "Change fast, but no one should notice."

He hesitates but nods and scurries to the corner behind Danny and me. I hand him the uniform I already picked up from Coach. He gingerly yet efficiently unbuttons his dress shirt and slips the heather gray Lake View Prep tee over his head.

Phew.

He's covered.

I swear it's like these guys are fucking vultures that can sniff out injured prey from a mile away. And I'm going to make damn sure Oliver isn't that little wounded mouse.

I relax for a second and change into my gym uniform, the cotton shorts a little too short for my liking. We have hoodies and sweatpants in the same colors for when we go outside, but we usually don't in the winter. It's just too fucking cold.

I turn around to check on Oliver, and *damn*. The tight blue shorts look fucking amazing on him. It's like I can feel each heartbeat, slow and steady, pumping throughout my chest and then south to my groin. I want to close the distance between us, push him against the tiled wall face-first, and yank those little shorts down. . . I bite my lip, cutting the fantasy off right there. *Where the fuck are these thoughts even coming from?*

I clear my throat and glance over at Danny. He stares at me curiously, a sparkle I can't define shimmering in his chocolate eyes.

Shit.

I forgot he was here for a second.

I drop my gaze and swiftly stuff all of my shit into my locker. "You guys ready?" I ask before turning around to see Oliver on the bench, gritting his teeth and struggling to lean down and tie his own shoe.

I walk over and crouch down in front of him. "You can ask for help, you know?"

His eyes flicker up to mine and immediately back to his shoes, his glare burning a hole through them. "I can tie my own fucking shoes. I'm not an invalid."

I lower my voice to make sure only he can hear, not even Danny sitting behind us. "Hey, I know you're hurting and frustrated, but don't take that fucking shit out on me, bro. I'm on your side, remember? I'll always be on your side, okay?"

I gently move his hands out of the way and pick his foot up, placing it on my bent thigh. "Now, shut up and let me tie your fucking shoe." A flush creeps up his neck, and he makes an annoyed grumble but lets me continue.

"How'd you get your shoes on by yourself this morning?" I ask, trying to lighten the mood but also kind of curious.

He pins me with a hard glare, but there's no real heat behind it. "They're slip-on dress shoes. No laces, asshole," he mutters, but I see a dimple peeking out, and it causes my own lip to quirk up in return.

"Also, I hadn't just been body-checked in the hallway, so I could bend down more easily this morning."

"Okay, dude. But it's not a big deal to ask me for help." I peer up at him as I finish the last knot. "We're brothers now, and I'd never see you as weak just for being hurt."

He bites his lip and gives me a sharp nod in acknowledgment, still picking at his nail polish and not making eye contact. I sigh and stand up. I can't fault him for not wanting to show any vulnerability, even to me. I would be the exact same way.

I look back at Danny scrolling through his phone, at least pretending to give us the illusion of privacy. The remaining guys have already piled out of the locker room and into the gym. I take a deep breath and pray that this class goes smoothly.

Lucky for us, we're spending the next two weeks "honing our hand-eye coordination" by playing racquetball. We break up into small groups of four, and I grab Oliver and Danny. I scan the open gym for our fourth when I make eye contact with Hazel Bell sitting on the bleachers with the other cheerleaders. She waves dramatically and smiles wide, like we're the best of friends.

Hell no. This girl is fucking toxic, and I've already had enough of her today. She is *not* joining our team.

Hazel saunters over to the three of us, swinging her hips with unnecessary flair because, trust me, none of us are looking.

"Hey, Wyatt. Boys. Coach said he wants some co-ed teams, so I figured I'd join you guys since Oliver and I are already fast friends." I crease my brows in confusion, and her eyes twinkle with malicious satisfaction.

She's always trying to stir up drama. She thrives on it and needs it daily, like the disgusting kombucha tea she always drinks.

I glance at Danny and Oliver; they do not look thrilled with the idea either. I'm about to open my mouth to protest when Coach Donavan blows the whistle.

"Alright! Four to a room, and this isn't gossip hour, folks! I want to see some real practice going on!"

A chorus of unenthusiastic voices rings out in acknowledgment, echoing off the wood panel walls of the giant open basketball court.

Everyone scatters toward the back of the gym where a set of double doors leads to the private rooms. We have multiple dance studios, a weight room, racquetball courts, and two swimming pools. You name it, and the LVP Athletic Department has it. Most of the buildings on campus are historic, but the gym was rebuilt in the early 2000s and renovated two years ago. They even added a five-lane bowling alley to the unused half of the basement.

The four of us head for the last racquetball court at the end of the row. The room has three white walls, with the fourth being one giant glass window. The floor is a high-quality, high-gloss maple that reflects the buzzing fluorescent lights above. We all grab a racket and a ball from the equipment bin in the corner.

"Let's just practice and warm up for now," I say, and no one disagrees. It's been a long day, and I don't think any of us want to work too hard.

"One sec, guys. I need to tie my hair up." Hazel puts on an unsolicited show for the three of us when she bends at the waist, dramatically flipping her flaming red hair upside down and making her tiny gym shorts ride up her ass even more. I glance at Danny and roll my eyes because I don't know if she's trying to win me back, seduce Oliver, or just show her body off. But she's barking up the wrong tree because no one in this room gives a shit.

After her hair is piled on top of her head in a messy bun, she picks up her racket and smiles fakely at Oliver. "Oliver! Wanna practice with me?" He flicks a glance my way and hesitates, which really makes me wonder what they talked about in Spanish.

"Um, sure," he says politely. I'm not sure the word "no" is even in the kid's vocabulary.

Danny and I stay to one side of the room while Hazel and Oliver start hitting the ball off the wall on the other side. I'm not too worried about his ribs. Racquetball isn't very strenuous, and it's not like we have to try hard. But I am concerned about the whispering and giggling that's coming from that area. My stomach hardens as I watch Hazel place her fingers on Oliver's forearm and lightly trail them up to his bicep, where she grabs on and leans into him, laughing like he's just said the funniest thing in the world. With her hand still on him, she looks over to me with an evil grin meant to provoke.

And now I have my answer. She's trying to use Oliver, *my stepbrother*, to make me jealous. She has no idea that the jealousy burning through me isn't over her. It's over *him.* I want her to take her venomous talons off him.

Oliver does not seem into the touch at all. In fact, he looks supremely uncomfortable with the flirty caress, building on my theory that he actually likes guys. Oliver pastes a fake smile on his face and gently slips out of Hazel's grip, serving the ball against the wall and starting a decent volley with himself.

Danny and I alternately hit the rubber ball against the wall, and time passes quickly. Next thing I know, Coach is knocking on the glass, telling us to call it a day.

"See you in Spanish tomorrow, Oliver!" Hazel chirps, then scowls at Danny and me. "Later, *boys.*"

I just sigh and head toward the locker room, relieved this day is finally over.

CHAPTER SEVEN
OLIVER

That was the longest fucking school day of my life, and I really hope it gets better. I'm excited about the opportunities I'll have by attending Lake View, but I'm even more unsure of my place in the social hierarchy after today. I know Finn is at the top, so I can only hope I slide in there, unnoticed and unbothered. I definitely don't want to make any enemies, although I feel like it might be a little too late for that. At least Finn and I can grab our stuff and leave without showers. Having gym last period definitely makes up for having math first.

Once we get home, we rush off to our respective rooms to shower, change, and knock out our homework early. It's my last night hanging out with Mom before she leaves for her trip, so I want to have the entire evening free.

I'm sitting at the plain white writing desk in my room, chewing on the end of my pen as I tackle my last Stats problem. I hear a gentle *tap, tap, tap* on my door frame before Mom pushes the door open.

"Hi, honey. How was your first day?" Her smile is so big and bright that I can't bear to squash her hopes even a little. She perches on the end of my bed, and I swivel around in my desk chair to face her.

I give her a matching grin that I know shows my dimples. "It was really great, Mom. Lake View is awesome. My locker is next to Finn's, and we have half of our classes together. I have classes with some of Finn's football buddies, too."

She clasps her hands tightly together, making her knuckles go white. "Oh, that's so nice to hear, Ollie." Her eyes start to water, and I stiffen. I hate when my mom cries, even if they're happy tears.

"After everything that happened in California," she sniffles, "I'm just so happy to see you meeting new friends and getting along so well with your stepbrother." I get up from my desk chair to sit with her on the edge of the bed, wrapping my arms around her smaller frame.

"It's okay, Mom. It's not gonna be like that here, I promise." I kiss the top of her head and close my eyes, breathing in her motherly scent of sunshine and rosewater.

"I'm so thankful for Finn. Taking you under his wing like that," she whispers.

"Me too, Mom," I say, just as softly.

A weird prickling sensation ghosts across the back of my neck, and I turn my head to glance at the open door. Finn is standing in his doorway, brows furrowed and dark eyes way too intense.

Shit. How much of that did he just hear?

Judging by the scowl on his face, maybe everything. I look back at Mom, who follows the path my eyes just took.

When she sees Finn leaning against his doorframe, she straightens up and pastes a happy smile on her face, quickly wiping her cheeks.

"Finn! How was school, sweetie? Are you guys hungry for a snack?"

Right on cue, my stomach rumbles so loud I put my hand over it as if that act alone can keep the embarrassing noises from escaping.

Finn pads across the hall and enters my room. "School was good, and I am absolutely starving. I know Oliver is, too. The cafeteria didn't exactly come up with the best lunch for him."

Mom turns to look at me with concern. "Oh?"

I can feel the heat rising on my face, and I rub the back of my neck, uncomfortable with what's happening. "Um, yeah. I didn't like it."

Finn snorts, "It was more than not liking it. They gave him a dry bologna sandwich, a bag of chips, and an apple." I flick my eyes to Finn and widen them deliberately, trying to signal him to shut the fuck up.

"It's fine, Mom. Seriously. I can just pack my lunch like I've always done."

"But honey, Gabe pays a lot for you boys to have the best education, and that lunch is definitely not up to par nutrition-wise. I'm going to email the school."

"Mom," I groan, tipping my head back and staring at the ceiling in exasperation. "Please do not do that. Unless you're going to tell them to cancel it. I really don't want to make a fuss." I implore her with my gaze, begging her to let it go. She knows I want to fly under the radar this last semester.

She sighs heavily, and I know she's given in. "Okay, Ollie. I'll just email them to cancel it. But I'm placing a grocery order for delivery tonight, and I'll help you with meal prep for the week." She winks, always ready to turn a negative situation into a positive.

Mom stands to her full five-foot-five-inch height and heads for the door. “In the meantime, I’ll get out the left-over chips, salsa, and guacamole for a snack. Come down when you finish up.”

After Mom leaves and her soft steps pad down the stairs, Finn shuts the door and turns around to face me. I’m still sitting on the bed when he asks, “What happened in California?”

My laugh is counterfeit. Bogus. Forged in awkwardness and insecurity. “Heard that, did ya?”

“I did.” He doesn’t move from in front of the door, but he’s waiting for an answer he’s not going to get.

I walk over to my desk and busy myself with organizing my notebooks, pens, and textbooks to delay answering his question.

“Nothing important happened.”

“You’re a terrible liar, Oliver. You can’t even look at me when you say that.”

I glance up at him and then quickly back down to zip up my school bag. *Shit,* he’s not even wrong. I *can’t* look into those dark sapphire pools and lie.

“Yeah, well. Maybe I just don’t want to talk about it, okay?”

“Okay.”

Hmmm. That was a little *too* easy.

“For now,” he adds.

I scoff but don’t argue about it. And I still can’t look at him. “I’m going to go eat something.” I walk over to the door, expecting him to leave first, but he just opens it and steps back a fraction of an inch, still nearly blocking the door.

Fine. You know what, two can play this game.

My heart gallops like a herd of wild horses as I squeeze my way past him through the door frame.

Our chests brush. My groin is achingly close to his. But I still don't look up.

Once I'm free from the towering, magnetic presence that is Wyatt Finnegan, I hightail it down to the kitchen to stuff my face.

I'm fucking *starving* after my prison lunch strike.

I'm stretched out on the buttery leather of the oversized theater room couch, headphones blasting my favorite band, hands behind my head, and foot bouncing to the beat. I don't hear Finn's approach.

"Whatcha listening to?" he asks as he leans over the back of the couch, plucks one of my AirPods out, and pops it into his own ear.

His lip twitches like it's battling against gravity to quirk up into any semblance of a smile.

"Rebelution. Nice."

My eyes light up. "You like them?" I didn't know meat and potato-loving Midwestern boys knew about Cali reggae.

"Yeah, bro. Vibes."

My jaw drops open because, yeah, it is total fucking vibes. He throws a wolfish grin my way, and I clamp my lips shut.

Why is he always catching me with my mouth wide open?

Okay, that sounds really bad, and I'm glad I didn't just say that out loud. "I saw them once in San Diego," I say instead. "It was super chill, and there was so much positive energy. Even with Micah bitching the whole time because some drunk girl spilled her beer on him after the first song, making him smell like stale alcohol the entire time," I chuckle.

"Who's Micah?" Finn asks as he walks around and sits next to me, picking up my legs and placing them over his lap so I can continue to lie down.

I pale at his words when I realize what I've said, hardly even noticing that my legs are now resting on his thighs. It's the first time since everything went down that I've even thought about my ex-best friend in anything other than a negative light. It pushes the knife in my back even deeper, bringing up the hurt and shame all over again.

"Um, no one. Just an old friend," I reply, looking down and chipping away at more of my neon green polish. It's about time I redo them. Maybe orange this time.

"Liar," Finn rumbles, and I find the courage to brave his gaze. His eyes swirl with stars and far away galaxies no one will ever find. An endless night sky to stare into and reflect upon. Dark to my light. And it feels appropriate.

I squirm under his intense scrutiny because I *am* lying. Once again. Not because I don't trust Finn. I just don't want him to know about my pathetic past and how all of my friends turned on me. It's embarrassing and dredges up old wounds I do not want to face.

"Does this have to do with the 'nothing important' that happened in California before you left or the fresh start you're looking for?"

I focus back on my nails. My pinky is almost free of any green, just a few more chips. Finn reaches over and places his big hand on both of mine, squeezing them to stop the nervous habit.

"Ollie." The sound of my nickname on his lips makes all

the little hairs on my arm stand up and a tingle run down my spine. I shiver.

"Please, Finn. Can we not do this right now? It's my mom's last night to hang out, and I don't want to upset her." It's a lame copout, but also kind of true.

Before Finn can even respond, she shouts from the kitchen, "The Chinese food is here, boys! Come dig in!"

I immediately swing my legs off Finn and jump up, power walking to the food, but Finn's deep rumble halts me.

"This isn't over, Oliver."

I peer over my shoulder at him and take in the tense set to his jaw, the hard eyes, and for some reason, his threat goes straight to my dick. The fucker twitches in my basketball shorts, trying to come to life. I whip my head back around and rush from the room.

"Where's Gabe?" I ask Mom before I shovel another bite of sweet and sour chicken into my mouth. The rich aromas of garlic, soy, and caramelized sugar swirl around us, enhancing the delicious flavors even more.

Mmm. Sweet honey glaze.

"Oh, he had a few last-minute consultations to squeeze in before we left." I nod my head, still chewing. I know Dr. Gabriel Finnegan is one of the best cardiovascular surgeons in the country, but I don't know much else about him.

I glance at Finn, who has his head down, focusing hard on devouring his beef and broccoli. I'm not surprised that he doesn't give a single fuck about where his dad is or if he'll even see him before our parents leave. And I don't blame him after last night. I can't even imagine how shitty Gabe treats Finn when we're not around.

"What time is your flight in the morning? Will we see you off before school?" I ask Mom.

"Our flight is at eight, but we're leaving the house around five, so best to say goodbye tonight," Mom responds.

"M'kay," I mumble around a mouthful, and we all continue eating our dinner in silence. We're at the smaller, more casual dining set in the corner of the kitchen instead of the formal dining room like last night. This is much more my style. I can actually reach across the table and grab another scoop of food without asking someone to pass it down.

Finn surprises me when he sets his fork down and starts a conversation with my mom. "We could all watch a movie in the theater room if you're up for it, Vivian?"

Mom places her palm over her heart as her voice goes soft. "I would love to, Finn. Thank you."

I look over to Finn fondly and smile when he asks, "Are you all packed then?"

"Yes! I'm so excited for the trip. My suitcase was zipped up and ready before we even left California," she exclaims.

We both chuckle as we all stand up to help clear the table.

"I bet Ollie wants to binge-watch *Fast and Furious* after taking a look at our garage the other day," Finn teases. He's not wrong, though. I fucking love those movies.

"Oh yeah?" Mom asks, as if I'm not in the same room as them. "It does scream Dominic Toretto."

I dart my probing gaze over to Mom and scrunch my eyebrows in confusion.

How the hell does she know who that is?

Mom rolls her eyes. “Don’t look at me like that, Oliver. I’m only thirty-seven. I liked Vin Diesel long before you came into the world, and I was wiping your little butt instead of crushing on boys.”

Finn barks out a raspy laugh, but I just huff, pretending to be annoyed when I’m anything but. That was pretty fucking funny.

After we put away the leftovers and load the dishwasher, I place my arm around Mom’s shoulders and steer her toward the theater room.

I turn around and wink at Finn behind us. “Come on, Finn. My mom wants to show us the teenage heartthrob she used to have taped to her bedroom walls in the ’80s.”

Mom gasps in mock outrage, “Oliver! It was the early 2000s! How dare you!”

She can’t control her laughter as a loud snort escapes her, making me burst out with a big, obnoxious laugh that echoes down the hallway.

The deep, sexy rumble of Finn’s reserved laugh makes all of the fine, blond hairs on the back of my neck stand up. I’m glad we’re about to watch a movie with my mother in the room. I think I need the buffer.

“I meant what I said last night, Wyatt.” A deep, raspy voice pulls me from sleep. I must have drifted off while sketching in bed after the movie. My door is slightly ajar, allowing the voices to seep in.

“I never doubted that you did, Dad.”

“Okay, well, let me make it even clearer now that Oliver isn’t here. Unless you’ve had a heart attack and need my particular brand of expertise, don’t call me.”

"When do I ever call you?"

"That's not the point. Make sure you don't while my wife and I are on our honeymoon."

"You don't think Vivian will want to check in on her son? Catch up?" Finn scoffs, already knowing the type of parent my mom is.

"Don't you dare presume to tell me what my wife is going to do. I am well aware of the kind-hearted woman I married," Gabe hisses back like the fucking viper he is. Always ready to strike his son down emotionally.

I stealthily climb off my bed and tiptoe to the door. I gently lie down, flat on the ground, to stay hidden and peek out of the crack unnoticed. I want to see this bully for myself.

"I've already told Vivian not to worry about Oliver, that you'll look out for him. Watch over him at school and at home. And I'm holding you to that, Wyatt. Oliver is new to a place like this and people like us. The boy is a bit odd. Different, if you know what I mean."

"No, I don't. What the fuck are you trying to say, Dad?" Finn growls menacingly.

"I'm not insinuating anything, Wyatt. I am just stating the obvious. No one can miss the bright green nail polish. He's very... *eclectic.*"

I can't see Finn's face because his dad is even bigger and blocking my view, but I don't miss the low guttural sound vibrating from his throat, and it causes my abs to tighten.

He really does have my back.

"Anyway, Wyatt. This is not a debate. Vivian can check in with her son whenever she wants. Although, I have encouraged her to communicate via text as we will all be on different schedules. But this is a time for my new wife and me to form a deeper connection. We do not need to be concerned with trivial drama."

Finn just snorts like this is nothing new to him. "So I shouldn't expect a souvenir then?"

Gabe takes a menacing step forward, but Finn doesn't back down. "Listen here, smartass. Don't cause any trouble, and don't pull Oliver into it if you do. If you upset my wife, there will be hell to pay when I return, boy."

"Have a lovely trip, *Dad*," Finn sneers and slams the door in his father's face, rattling the framed photos that line the long hallway. Gabe huffs out an irritated breath and turns to head to his wing of the house, mumbling to himself.

Not even ten seconds later, Finn's door bursts open before I even have the chance to push myself up off the ground. He slowly eases my own door open as if he knew I was on the ground spying this whole time.

I'm poised to heave myself up when I sense an overwhelming presence above me. I peer up at him through my lashes and give him a hesitant smile. His gaze is intense as he stares down at me, dark brows pulled together.

"Umm... I... I dropped my... um... pen," I stutter out.

There's no denying that I was just eavesdropping as Finn glances over to my desk on the opposite side of the room. Yeah, that was a pretty shitty excuse.

He just sighs and says, "Get up." I push to a crouch, careful of my healing ribs, and Finn holds his hand out. We lock forearms, and he lifts me the rest of the way to my feet.

"I know you were listening, Ollie, and I'm glad. You need to fully understand the level of asshole my father is."

"Why does he treat you that way?" I ask, unable to hold back the question.

"He hates me."

"What? Why would you say that?"

"Because he does, Oliver. And all you need to know is that he's a heartless bastard who only cares about himself. I hate to tell you that since your mother just married him, but it's the truth."

I don't know what to say. My heart aches for Finn, and I wonder if this has anything to do with the car accident that killed his mom. I won't ask, though. That's for Finn to tell me whenever he's ready. I hate Hazel even more at this moment for putting the pressure of that knowledge on my conscience.

"It's late, Oliver. Get back in bed. I'll go grab another bag of ice for you. Even if you're feeling better, you need to keep icing it every night until the bruising turns yellow and green."

I don't argue. "Thanks, Finn."

CHAPTER EIGHT
FINN

I heard Ollie sneak downstairs at five in the morning to secretly say goodbye to his mom, *again*. It's something I would have done, so I don't judge him because Vivian is an amazing mother. She turned in around ten-thirty last night, right after the first movie ended, and we both gave her hugs and well wishes for a fun, safe trip. It's been really nice the past two nights, eating dinner and hanging out with her. She infuses a caring warmth into this cold, dead place and brings light and happiness, just like her son, and I can only hope that my father and I don't tarnish their spirit.

Oliver meanders into the kitchen after I finish my last bite of Lucky Charms. Once again, he looks fucking tempting in his perfectly tailored white button-up with the tie hanging loose around his neck.

"Good morning," he chirps, full of energy, without having had any coffee. It's a conundrum I'll never understand. I grab my travel mug and fill it to the top with steaming black coffee. I'm going to need another cup today;

I'm exhausted after last night. Dealing with my dad always is.

"Morning," I manage to reply, even though speaking before eight should be fucking illegal.

Oliver chuckles as he sets his sights on the fridge. "Someone's not a morning person."

"Understatement," I mumble, clearly only able to grunt out single-word responses before I've consumed my first cup of coffee. I'm okay on the weekends when I can sleep in, but before school, I'm practically a hibernating bear who's been prematurely awakened from his cave.

"Okay, got it. No talking until your first cup of caffeine kicks in."

Oliver boosts himself up to sit on the kitchen counter by the sink and eats a quick, healthy breakfast of Greek yogurt with granola and raspberries. Completely opposite of my own favorite breakfast choice.

I grab our brown paper bag lunches from the fridge and tuck them into my backpack so they don't get squished. I paid attention to everything Vivian ordered and even had her tell me some tips and tricks to help navigate the whole peanut allergy thing—when Oliver left the room, of course. I want him to eat as well with me as he does with his mom and not have to worry. I continue leaning against the kitchen island, sipping my bitter coffee while Oliver finishes eating.

"Need help?" I nod toward him, indicating his halfway buttoned dress shirt and loose tie.

Oliver swallows his last bite and darts a quick glance my way. "Uh. . . yeah, if you could."

Here we go with the unnecessary embarrassment again.

"Come here." I hold out my hand and let him decide what that means. He hops off the counter and walks over to me. Instead of his hand, he places the ACE bandage he had in his pocket, just like I thought he would.

Since I'm a good four inches taller than him, I sit on the stool and pull Oliver to me by his wrist and into the empty space between my thighs. I don't even ask him. I just start slowly unbuttoning the rest of his shirt.

Button by agonizing button.

I flick my eyes up to meet his. I know this is an extremely intimate position, an extremely intimate act, but I continue on. I don't know if I do these things to push his comfort zone or my own. Probably both.

I slide my hands beneath the collar of his shirt, and he trembles slightly from my touch. His eyes are still down-cast, watching my every move with rapt attention. I skim my hands down his arms, tracing over the muscles of his smaller yet toned biceps, taking the shirt with me. Before it can drop to the floor and get wrinkled, I catch it and gently place it on the barstool next to me.

I take a second—okay, maybe more than a second—to admire the beautiful male specimen before me. With his perfectly coiffed blond hair, delicate features, lean body, and loose tie hanging haphazardly around his neck, he looks like a fucking fantasy. His fitted, plaid pants ride low on his hips, showing off the black underwear band and sexy as fuck grooves of his V. His tan is striking against the paler tone of my hands as I let them linger on his warm skin a little too long.

Fuck me. He looks good.

He *feels* good.

The more I start to think about my sexuality, the less these feelings scare me.

So what if I like guys?

I'm not even sure if that's the case, though. I've never been turned on by another dude before.

Until Oliver.

Shaking the confusing thoughts from my mind and the creeper stare from my face, I wrap Oliver's ribs tightly, ensuring the most support for the long school day ahead. He doesn't whimper as I pull the bandage taut, which is a good sign that he's healing nicely.

"All done," I say as I hold the shirt out, allowing him to slip back into it and button it himself.

"Thanks," he says bashfully but continues to stand between my spread thighs, like he wants to say something else.

"You good?" I rumble.

He visibly blushes and speaks in a too-quiet voice. "I don't know how to tie a tie."

"Really?" I ask in disbelief as I sit up straighter and reach for the tie still hanging limply around his neck.

He breaks eye contact and shrugs. "I've never had a dad to show me or even a need to wear one." He glances back at me and answers the question on the tip of my tongue. "My mom did it yesterday morning after a YouTube tutorial."

My lip quirks up because it's funny how he already knows what I was thinking after only a few days together.

"It'll be easiest if I show you how to do it by putting it on myself." I slip the dark red tie around my own neck and proceed to explain each loop, cross, and pull. I take the loosely tied tie and slip it back over Oliver's head, tucking it under his collar and tightening the knot.

"Pretty easy, right?"

"Yeah, it doesn't seem too hard," he agrees. "Thanks for showing me."

"Anytime."

We gather our things and walk toward the garage, ready to get this school day over with and be one step closer to the weekend.

"So, are you guys having a party while your parents are gone?" Jayden asks innocently from across the lunch table. It sounds so fucking weird to hear 'your parents' said out loud to both Oliver and me.

"You're only fifteen. What do you know about partying?" Trace teases and playfully gives his brother a noogie.

"Trace, stop," Jayden whines as he tries to push his much larger brother away from him.

"Go back to the nerdy sophomore table, twerp. You're in my seat," Eric demands, looming behind Jayden's chair. I don't interfere because I know Trace won't let it go too far. He always has his little brother's back.

"Jay's sitting with us today. Back off," Trace says casually as he takes another bite of his cheese pizza, otherwise ignoring the asshat behind him.

Eric grumbles but doesn't put up a fight and just slinks to the end of the table, plopping down next to Danny and across from Ethan.

I look back to Jayden and answer his earlier question. "Nah, little bro. No parties at the Finnegan residence." I glance at Trace. "You know how my dad is."

He just nods sagely and takes a loud slurp of his chocolate milk.

"Bethany is back from Cancun on Friday, anyway," Jared informs us from his spot next to me. "She's celebrating her grand return with a massive house party since her parents are staying another week." He rolls his eyes because we all know Bethany is fucking *extra*, but we love her anyway.

"Those things get fucking wild, Oliver. You should definitely come," Ethan grins wickedly, showing off his slightly too big and too white veneers. He sort of looks like a vampire with his ivory skin, inky black hair, and dark brown eyes. But the girls seem to dig it and hang all over him. Some guys, too, although that is not widely known. Only Jared, Bethany, and I know that Ethan is bi. The four of us have always been closest.

Oliver just looks at me. "Umm. . .?"

"Do you want to go?" I ask.

"I haven't been to many parties, but it could be fun, right?" His big eyes implore me.

I turn to Ethan, answering for Oliver, "We'll be there. I'll text Bethany and let her know."

"Sweet!" He leans over and high-fives Oliver like they're fast friends. "You smoke, bro? Being from Cali and all?"

Oliver blinks big, owlish eyes, and it's funny that he seems nervous to answer in front of me. I raise a single brow in question, as if to say *go on*.

"A few times. It's been a while, though. But I could definitely use some relaxation."

"Well, I got some really good bud right now, so I'll roll up a couple of blunts for me and you at the party." Ethan winks at Oliver. "It'll get you nice and relaxed." His slow, deep laugh is full of innuendo.

What. The. Fuck.

I clench my fists under the table, digging little crescents into the soft flesh of my palms.

A light blush settles on Oliver's cheeks, and I'm pissed I wasn't the one to put it there. I pin Ethan with a deadly glare that screams *cut it the fuck out*. I know he's a naturally flirty person whether he's actually into someone or not, but this shit needs to stop right the fuck now.

His sultry laugh turns stiff and wooden. He knows not to fuck with me. He's seen the aftermath of the guys who have dared.

I got into quite a few fights at Bethany's parties right after the accident last year. For no other reason than someone thinking they can talk shit to me because they're drunk and want to poke an angry bear. People learned real quick when Jesse Reynolds left the party needing three stitches in his bottom lip. I never start anything, but I admit to ending it every time. And I always slept it off in Beth's guest room, never once accepting a ride from anyone but myself.

Ethan clears his throat and pops a pretzel into his mouth. "It'll be fun."

That's more like it. I relax slightly in my chair and look down at the dark red indents in my palms. I sense someone watching me and quickly close my hands. I glance out of the corner of my eye and see Oliver watching me with scrunched brows.

"Can I go, Trace?" Jayden asks with wide, hopeful eyes. His optimistic question switches up the mood of the table.

"No. Juniors and seniors only."

Jay's face falls, and he tucks his chin, picking at the crust on his ham and cheese sandwich.

Poor kid.

But T is right. A sophomore doesn't need to be around the drinking, drugs, and sex that Bethany's parties usually entail. And they only seem to be getting worse as we get older.

Trace, being the great big brother he is, compromises. "But we can play Xbox all day Saturday. Just you and me."

He slings an arm around Jay's shoulder and gives him a little squeeze.

"Alright, cool." Jayden tries to play it off, but I can see the smile tugging at his lips.

I finish up my bag of pretzels and turn to Oliver. "You heard from your mom at all?"

"Yeah, she texted a couple of hours ago. They're all checked in and just relaxing before they go out to the main pool and bar. Did you hear from your dad?"

"No," I scoff. "And I don't expect to. Don't you remember the pleasant conversation I had with him about it?"

"Yeah. Sorry, Finn."

"Don't be. I'm not."

The warning bell rings, and we grab our trash and dump it before heading to class.

The rest of the day flies by, even gym, and I'm ready to get home, order some pizza, and have a beer. I cannot wait to enjoy the next two weeks without the constant threat of my father's shitty attitude looming over me.

"Did your dad leave you money for food or. . . um. . . say how much we could spend on his credit card? I'm not sure the grocery order my mom made last night will last us two weeks," Oliver says shyly from across the kitchen island where we have our homework spread out.

God, he's so fucking polite it makes my teeth ache.

The chill sounds of Ollie's favorite reggae play softly through the built-in Bluetooth speakers around the kitchen.

"We're ordering pizza tonight. And don't worry about money. I got us, bro."

He frowns adorably. "What does that mean? He doesn't care if we order in?"

"I have my own money," I huff out, not wanting to get into specifics but also not wanting him to feel one ounce of false debt toward my asshole father.

Sure, he's made a lot of money from being a top surgeon, but he doesn't have family money—old money—like Mom did. Nope. Dad is new money, and I can't help but feel like he resents me because my trust fund is bigger than his entire life savings. And I now have access to it. I'm staying here until I graduate out of respect, what little I have left for him, and because of the graduation clause in the trust. Although, now that Oliver is here, you can bet I am definitely staying.

"I can't spend your money on food, Finn!" Oliver actually looks horrified, which makes my lip twitch.

"I have plenty. One pizza doesn't mean shit."

Oliver scrambles off of his barstool. "Well, let me grab ten bucks so we can split it, then."

"Ollie. Stop." My command is deep and sharp, cracking out like a whip.

"What?" He pauses at the edge of the kitchen, looking over his shoulder with twisted brows.

"I don't want your ten bucks. Keep it. I'm going to show you what a real pizza looks like. Follow me," I say, standing up and heading for the stairs so I can get more comfortable in my room. Oliver blushes but doesn't fight me on it, following along as I pull out my phone.

"Angelo's Pizzeria has *the* best Chicago deep dish. They even have a gluten-free, nut-free option. I checked." I smirk over at him, and he flashes his dimples right back.

That's right, bro. I'm always gonna check on that for you.

"You mean that weird blasphemy of a pizza where the sauce is on top?"

I gasp and clutch my chest. "Oliver. . . I don't even know your middle name. . . Chase. What *you're* saying is blasphemy!"

"It's Walter," he mumbles, but I see that dimple peeking out.

I burst out laughing because I was not expecting that.

"Shut up. It was my grandpa's name." Another dimple pops out, so I know he's not mad.

"What's *your* middle name then?" he asks.

"Carter. It was also my grandpa's name," I repeat his own words back to him.

His smile drops, and we stare at each other for a minute, standing in the hallway between our two bedrooms. There's an intensity in the air, like live electricity crackling between us. It's dangerous and ungrounded, and I'm worried I'll get shocked if I reach out to touch him.

Oliver is the first to break when he clears his throat. "That's a pretty cool middle name, much better than Walter."

"Nah. I like yours. . . Ollie Wally," I tease, an uneven smile slanting my mouth.

Oliver groans and rubs his hands down his face. "Oh my God, I haven't heard that since elementary school."

I chuckle and walk into my room. "Come chill in my room, Ollie Wally."

He rushes in after me. Big, owlish eyes implore me. "Wait. Please don't actually start calling me that."

"Don't worry, I like Sunshine much better." I wink, and he blushes. "I'll save Ollie Wally for special occasions."

"Please don't."

"You like it."

"Not this one. Call me anything but Ollie fucking Wally." He shudders with revulsion and climbs onto my bed next to me. I just shake my head and concede.

"Alright, if it bothers you that much, I won't say it. Even though it's fucking adorable," I say with a sly grin.

He just huffs and slouches further down against my upholstered headboard, crossing his arms and essentially pouting.

"It's pretty adorable when you pout like that, too." I turn my head to stare at him. He has the faintest line of freckles along his cheekbones.

I wonder if he'll lose them and that tan after his first winter in Chicago?

He stares straight ahead at the TV on the wall, narrows his eyes, and scrunches his nose and mouth into a scowl.

"That's not helping your case either, bro." Honestly, he looks cute no matter what kind of face he makes.

He flops his arms down on the bed dramatically and huffs out a big breath. "I am *not* adorable. I'll show you fucking adorable."

Oliver sits up and kneels on the bed facing me. He tucks his neck in, somehow creating the appearance of a triple chin even though he probably weighs a buck sixty soaking wet. He crosses his eyes and sticks out his tongue, and a startled laugh erupts from deep inside me because. . . .

"What in the ever-loving *fuck* is that face, dude?" I manage to say while cracking up. I've never seen anything like it and decide not to disappoint him with the fact that it was actually pretty fucking adorable as well.

"Told you. *Not* adorable." He smirks, looking supremely satisfied with himself.

I just shake my head and reach for his wrist. "Come

here, you little shit," I tease, yanking gently on his arm until he tumbles down next to me.

"Let's order our pizza. I'm fucking starving." I grab my phone and open the app again to complete our order.

It feels oddly domestic, and I kind of like it. I feel. . . relaxed, happy even. I take another sip of my beer and turn the movie down when a loud car chase happens. We're almost done with *Tokyo Drift*, the third movie in our *Fast and Furious* binge, but Oliver is starting to crash. His head keeps sliding down the back of the couch until he jerks awake. After the third time, I get impatient and gently pull him down to lean against me. I lift my arm and tuck him under my shoulder. He snuggles into my side, his cheek and mouth accidentally nuzzling my nipple through my thin white shirt. My reaction is involuntary—my nipple *and* my dick start to harden.

Fuck. Shit. Fuck.

These feelings are so confusing, but I can't deny what my body is telling me. I haven't wanted anyone in over a year. I was sinking into a pit of despair and self-loathing, drowning in the misery that was my life. And then I was just numb. I locked everything down so tight that I had nothing left to feel. Certainly nothing left to give to anyone else.

Until my new stepbrother waltzed into my life, spreading his sunshine and light fucking *everywhere*.

Now that it's just the two of us—no parents, no lectures, no *bullshit*—my feelings are starting to intensify. I want him. I don't care about labels. I don't care if he's gay, if

I'm gay, or bi, or whatever. I just know that I want Oliver Walter Chase.

I lean away from him and place my beer bottle on the end table. "Ollie," I whisper, finding the courage to act on my growing feelings with a few beers coursing through me and Oliver's innocent eyes not focused on me.

I gently stroke his cheek with my fingertips and run my thumb along the seam of his plump pink lips.

"Mmm," he moans and slips his leg over mine, intertwining them and pressing his hips against my thigh.

I bite my lip because *fuck*, he's hard. I can feel my stepbrother's hard dick rubbing on my thigh, and it's making my own cock throb with pure desire.

He starts to thrust against my leg harder, grinding his shaft against my leg. I know I need to stop this because he's not even awake, but damn, it's fucking hot. I wonder if he could come in his sleep right now?

I put my hand on his hip and whisper in his ear, "Oliver, wake up. You're dreaming." Just then, a huge explosion happens on TV, and he jolts awake. He looks around, confused for a minute, then realizes where he is—cuddled against me with his leg threaded between mine and his hard cock pressed against my thigh.

Even in the darkness of the theater room, I can see his face turn beet red as he looks up at me hesitantly. "Uhhh. . ."

"Hey, shh. Don't be embarrassed. It's just me. Come here."

It's now or fucking never, I guess.

A flicker of confusion briefly passes his eyes, then understanding and heat fill them. He sits up and hovers next to me on his knees, unsure what to do next. He's in those fucking silver basketball shorts again, and I can *really* see the evidence of his arousal straining the front of his shorts. I've only been with one girl before, but I imagine kissing a guy can't be too different.

I grab his hips and maneuver him so he's straddling me. He makes a cute little squeak and holds onto my shoulders. My mouth quirks up to one side as I stare at this angel-faced boy.

"Finn. . ." he questions. "What are you—" I cut him off when I slam my lips onto his. He's frozen for a second, but then he starts to kiss me back. I lick at the seam of his mouth, and he opens for me. I caress his tongue with mine and bite his pouty bottom lip before plunging my tongue back into his mouth like I'm fucking him with it. I need to show him who's in control right now.

This time, he says my name on a whimper when I pull away from his mouth. "Finn. . ." he whines.

I press my forehead to his. "Have you ever kissed a guy before, Ollie?"

"No," he breathes out against my lips.

"Have you ever kissed *anyone* before?"

"No," he repeats as he pecks little kisses around my mouth and up my jawline, where he bites my ear lobe, causing goosebumps to pebble down my neck. I shiver at his sensual touch.

Fuck though.

He's a virgin.

I mean, I guess I am too when it comes to guy stuff. Not that we're doing anything else; it was just a kiss.

Can I really be his first. . . everything?

Shit, now I'm getting flustered. I can't do this. How can he even know what he wants if he's never been with anyone else before?

What was I thinking?

I pick Ollie up by the waist and set him next to me. We need to cool down before we take this too far. I run my hands through my hair, making the shaggy strands even more tangled. It's almost long enough for a ponytail; maybe I should do that. "Um, it's late. We should get to bed."

"Finn, wait." I can hear the hurt in his voice. "Did I do something wrong?"

I force a quick smile, "No, Ollie. I just. . . it's really late, and we have school early."

Lame. Lame, lame, lame.

It's a shitty excuse, and he knows it.

I grab my half-empty beer bottle and practically run from the room. I don't look back. I can't handle the pain and rejection I know is shining in his eyes.

CHAPTER NINE
OLIVER

R*ejected.*

Unwanted.

Loser.

The negative thoughts take over my mind, swirling around with every other name or slur I was ever called back in California.

Fag.

Freak.

Pathetic.

Finn triggered me with his cool indifference and dismissal of the hottest fucking kiss of my life. Okay, the *only* kiss of my life. But it brought up every insecurity I've tried to lock away since leaving Marlo Bay and felt like a punch to the fucking gut. My mind was whirling last night, and it took me hours to fall asleep after Finn ran from the room like it was on fire.

I don't even know if I was bad at it or if Finn freaked out because he was kissing a dude. Now I feel awkward and uncertain, and I don't know how I'm going to act around him when I'm inevitably forced to leave my room and go to school in about an hour. It fucking sucks.

Trying to pull myself out of this pessimistic funk, I grab my favorite neon orange polish, Citrus Sunrise, and re-do my nails. There's something about bright colors and painting that soothes my soul. I can only hope that these next few days fly by so I can lock myself in my room all weekend. Art is like therapy for me, and I really need it after last night.

I'm just blowing on my nails when Finn knocks lightly at my bedroom door. "Want any scrambled eggs?"

"No, thanks," I answer hollowly.

"I made like half a dozen. Don't make me eat them all." He opens the door even though I didn't tell him to come in.

He sees my hand poised in the air, nails still glossy and wet, as I continue to blow them dry.

His eyes narrow imperceptibly, and if I hadn't already started to pick up his tells, I would have missed the jump in his jaw as he clenched it tightly.

What the hell is his problem?

I can express myself however the fuck I want. It's *art*. It has nothing to do with being gay.

"I'm busy. . . and not hungry," I say coldly. I hate this complete flip in our dynamic. I wish we could go back to how it was before the kiss. No matter how mind-blowing it was. Well, to me, at least.

"Just come eat. I made toast with the nut-free bread your mom got. And there's orange marmalade." His lip ticks up on one side.

I roll my eyes but can't stop the goofy grin from spreading across my face. "Okay, you got me. Can't say no to orange marmalade."

I get up from my desk and head for the door. Finn grasps my bicep just before I pass him.

"Do you need help wrapping your ribs this morning?" his deep voice rumbles.

Why is he acting like we didn't just have our tongues in each other's mouths last night?

"Nah, I already did it. I got it now." I brush him off and slip out the door and down the stairs.

I slink into one of the overstuffed barstools tucked into the mammoth kitchen island. It's fast becoming my favorite spot to eat, snack, and do homework.

Finn already has two plates piled high with scrambled eggs, bacon, and toast. There's even a cold glass of orange juice on top of a napkin.

My heart does a little flip, and my belly swoops low. He's acting like nothing happened, and it's so confusing.

I wait for Finn to start eating before shoveling food into my mouth because I still have *some* manners.

Finn's scrambled eggs are perfectly fluffy, and the turkey bacon is crisp and not greasy. The toast is still crunchy and glistens with butter, just how I like it. I grab another piece and slather it with marmalade.

Damn.

He can cook a good breakfast, and I tell him as much.

"Thanks," he mumbles around a mouthful of bacon.

Things are still off, and I know we'll have to talk about it eventually. But for now, I let the food bridge the gap.

The somber gray clouds and overcast skies match my mood, and it looks like it might snow soon. My loafers feel heavy as I take step after reluctant step toward Sable Hall like I'm trapped in quicksand. Finn and I haven't said much to each other since breakfast. I hope the rest of today goes by fast because I'm just not feeling it.

At least AP Statistics and US History flew by. There's never much time to talk in Stats anyway—we dive right in and work up until the bell rings, every damn day. Ethan and Trace are in US History with us, so they easily distracted Finn and me from our awkwardness. Now I just have to get through Spanish before I can eat the delicious ham and provolone sandwich Finn has in his bag.

Every time he ignores me or acts like the kiss didn't happen, an echoing pulse of pain flutters in my center. Around my heart. And the painful vibrations nearly make my eyes water.

My thoughts are in the clouds as I trudge down the path, hands in pockets and neck tucked low into my scarf. The bitterly cold wind whips my hair all around me, making the chill settle deep in my bones. I don't even make it halfway to the building before a small arm loops through mine, and a flash of red appears in my peripheral vision.

"Hey, Hazel."

"Hello, Oliver," she chirps, like she wasn't a frigid bitch just two days ago. "Did you get through all of your workbook pages okay?"

"I did. Spanish just comes easily to me because of where I grew up." I adjust my messenger bag and practically beg the path in front of me to warp time and space and create a black hole so I can get the fuck away from Hazel.

"Hmm," she hums, and I have no idea what nefarious plans could possibly be running through her head with that reply.

She notices my nail polish as I continue to awkwardly

fidget with my strap. "Oh, I'm loving this new color, Oliver! We should totally get manis and pedis together sometime," she gushes, and her artificial smile doesn't even meet her eyes.

Um. Hell to the fucking no.

"Thanks. I actually just like painting them myself. It relaxes me, like art."

"Hmm. How humble of you. I can't be bothered. That's what nail salons are for, right? Why do it myself when I can pay someone else?" She cackles like the stuck-up ice princess she is.

My chuckle is stilted and forced as we finally make it up the front steps of Sable Hall. "Makes sense," I concede, even though it doesn't really.

"Of course it does, silly! Time is a commodity I can't waste, and you shouldn't either. Daddy always says to pay someone else to do your dirty work," she snickers.

Yeah. Okay. Whatever.

How the hell did Finn put up with her shit? Even if he *was* getting his dick sucked.

Fortunately, Hazel left me alone in Spanish, as did Eric—the rest of the day flies by in a blur of American classics, paint, and more fucking racquetball.

Neither of us says anything the entire ride home, and I hate it.

How could we go from the instant connection we had. . . to this frigid aloofness?

I finish my homework within an hour of getting home and relax on my bed, sketching ideas for my first art project. It's not due for over a month, but the theme is simple and quite fitting. It's a single word that can mean so many different things to everyone.

Home.

We can use any medium. We just have to be able to explain in front of the class every choice we make and the reason behind it. I'm using my oil paints, but I have to sketch it out first, and I'm not even sure what *home* means to me anymore.

There's a sturdy knock on my door, followed by Finn's muffled voice. "I'm just reheating some pizza from last night. Want some for dinner?"

I don't get up, and I don't answer the door. Something else has caught my eye.

"Nah. I'm not hungry right now. Working on a project!" I shout back so he can hear me through the door. I hate that it's like this, but he's the one who walked away from me.

Low grumbles filter through the thick, wooden door, but then I hear him go downstairs, heavy feet thumping on each step.

I focus back on what grabbed my attention before Finn knocked. A golden glow filters through the cracks of my blinds, and I walk over to pull them up.

Deep indigos, purples, and pinks splash across the horizon in abstract shapes that my fingers are twitching to replicate. My room must face west because this sunset is fucking breathtaking as it disappears behind the forest of pines at the edge of the property. I race back to my desk and grab my case of oil pastels so I can capture more than just a black and white sketch.

My reflection in the glass is ruining everything, so I open the window, uncaring of the below-freezing temperatures blowing in. I need to see everything. Capture everything.

I stick my head out and glance from side to side. The roof is pretty flat right here. I bet I could climb out and sit while I sketch the setting sun. Deciding not to think too hard about it and miss the beautiful palette of colors, I grab the throw blanket from the end of the bed and wrap it around my shoulders. I tuck my sketch pad and pastels under my arm and stick my AirPods into my hoodie pocket. I carefully lift my leg and step through the window to my new, quiet, safe place. I sit cross-legged in the corner, where two exterior walls meet, creating a small alcove that somewhat blocks the howling wind from throwing me and my art supplies off the roof.

I pop my headphones in and let the soulful beats of Labrinth fill my ears. I don't want to miss even one second of this beautiful sunset as I frantically swoosh, smudge, and blend the vibrant colors onto the page, essentially duplicating the view in front of me.

It doesn't take long for the sun to fully descend and the last of the day's light taper off behind the sea of trees.

But I don't stop sketching.

Instead, I grab every shade of gray and my single white and black pastels and flip to a new page, ready to draw the awakening night sky. I add rich purples and deep blues, wiping my fingers on my pants in between every smudge.

I'm lost in the art. In the passion. I don't realize I've been out here for over an hour and that my fingertips are starting to go numb.

"Oliver?!" I hear my name shouted before my bedroom door clicks open. He must have a key. . . or a screwdriver.

"*Jesus Christ!* It's fucking freezing in here! Where the fuck are you?" Finn yells.

Maybe it's petulant, but I don't answer him as I smudge the last crater into the luminescent moon on my paper.

Movement out of the corner of my eye catches my attention, and I turn to look at Finn as he pops his head out the open window.

"Ollie! What the fuck, dude? How long have you been out here? It's like twenty fucking degrees! I can see my breath in your room!"

"What time is it?" I ask as I stand up and wobble slightly, bracing my hand against the rough, brick exterior. My legs must have fallen asleep because I feel like I'm walking on pins and needles.

"Goddammit! Be careful, Oliver!" Finn shouts as he reaches for my hand and carefully pulls me in through the window, shutting and locking it swiftly.

"It's almost nine. When did you go out there? Your fingertips feel like icicles, and your lips are turning purple, for fuck's sake," he scowls.

Oops. Guess I was out there longer than I thought.

"Um. . ." I hesitate to tell him because he looks really pissed right now. He grabs my sketchbook and flips backward through page after page of twinkling night skies and huge, silver moons until the warm, vibrant hues of my new favorite sunset fill the sketch pad.

"Since the fucking sunset? Really Oliver? This isn't fucking California, dude. You could literally get hypothermia or pneumonia from being out there in the cold wind that long."

"Okay, Mom. Geez, get off my case, would you?" I realize too late that it's the most insensitive thing I could have possibly said, and it makes me feel like as much of an asshole as Gabe himself.

Finn looks off to the side and flares his nostrils like a bull getting ready to charge. His jaw is clenched so tight, and I know he's furious.

I step forward and hold my hand out tentatively. "Finn, I'm sorry, I shouldn't have said that. I got swept up in the gorgeous view and lost track of time. I won't go out there every day," I add quietly.

"You won't go out there again, period," Finn demands, as if he has any say.

I spin around and pin him with my best glare, poking my finger into the middle of his solid chest. "You don't get a say in anything I do, Finn. You made it pretty damn clear last night that you don't want me. That I'm not *worthy* of you. Was I that terrible of a kisser?" I clamp my mouth shut and look away to the now dark, closed window.

Why did I just word vomit that?

The blinds are still up, and I can see the tall, imposing frame of Finn hovering behind me in the reflection of the glass. But I don't dare look back at him in real life. I'll stick with the window version as the pang of rejection steals my last remaining strength.

Soft yet calloused fingertips brush my cheek, turning my head back to face him.

"Don't ever say you aren't worthy. I don't think that, and you should *never* think that either, Oliver." His gaze is unwavering, and it pierces my soul.

"Look, I care about you, Ollie. I *worry* about you. But. . . we just can't take it *there*."

I wrap my arms around myself, pulling the nearly frozen blanket tighter around me. "So it was bad?" I whisper.

Sighing deeply, Finn unwraps me from the useless throw, pulls the fluffy, down comforter off my bed, and wraps it around me. He leads me to the bed and helps me lie down in my human burrito.

"You're not a bad kisser, Ollie, not at all. It's just. . .

you're a virgin and my stepbrother. And I don't even know if I'm bi or just curious... Or maybe it's just... *you*." He ends the last word in a whisper, and while the shy, boyish look sparkling in his eyes hits me right in the chest, his next words punch me right in the gut.

"But we can't do this. *I* can't do this."

"Nothing's changed, though," he's quick to add. "Just no more kissing."

I try to hide the disappointment in my expression, but I'm pretty sure I failed. I've always had a shit poker face.

"I'm going to heat up some chicken noodle soup for you. You need to warm up and didn't eat any dinner. Just forget last night ever happened, okay? We'll finish the school week and have a good time at Bethany's party. You'll see." He pats me on the shoulder, and I don't know if he's trying to convince me or himself.

Because there's one other problem with that. I can't forget it. I can't get the taste of Finn's lips off my tongue.

CHAPTER TEN
FINN

The next two days at school go by uneventfully, and Oliver and I have settled into a routine of sorts. Even if it's strained and nothing like it was the first few days after we met.

I fucking hate it.

I know he's upset and not over it, but I stand by what I said last night—no matter how much I want to do the opposite. It's just too messy, too tangled. It's never a good idea for two stepbrothers to hook up. *Ever*. My dad already hates me, but if he knew we kissed or if he saw some of the heated stares between the two of us, he would probably fucking kill me. And I am definitely not ready to die.

Besides, in a way, I'm protecting him from the toxic storm that's hovered over me for the past fourteen months. He doesn't deserve to deal with any of my negative bullshit. I'm hoping Bethany's party will bring us out of this weird funk we're stuck in. Her parties are always a good time, and I'm curious for Oliver to meet the one and only girl in our friend group. She's been one hundred percent friend-zoned since the third grade, much to her dismay. I'm pretty sure she's had a crush on all of us over the years, including Eric.

I drum my fingers on the steering wheel as I stare up at the large, brick mansion on the hill, complete with white Colonial columns, a full-width porch on both the first and second floors, and a third level on top of that. The spotlights showcasing the grand estate are a frosty blue tonight, illuminating it like a beacon in the dark. I never even asked Bethany what the theme is tonight. Because she always has one.

Cars line the road below the hill as eager kids start the hike up to the party. I put the Jeep in park and turn to face Oliver. I need to set some ground rules first. "Don't accept a drink from anyone. Mix your own, or I'll mix them. Don't wander off where I can't see you, and definitely don't follow anyone to another room, especially a bedroom."

Oliver stares down at his hands in his lap as he picks at the neon orange nail polish that's already starting to chip because he fucks with it every time he's feeling anxious. He's wearing a plain white T-shirt under a black and orange flannel that's hanging open. The new puffy black coat he got last weekend remains unzipped, and his dark, ripped skinny jeans are skin tight. His bright orange chucks match his nail polish, and his nose ring sparkles gold tonight.

He definitely stands out here, next to all of these preppy-ass rich kids. And I do not include myself in that. I have on simple dark jeans, a fitted black Henley, my favorite combat boots that don't need to be tied, and a black peacoat. I don't know what style it is, and I don't give a fuck. You might call it emo if you count the beanie on my head and the swoop of dark hair nearly covering my left eye. But still, Oliver's *give no fucks* California style might paint an even bigger bullseye on his back, and I'm the only one here to guard that target.

"Okay, Finn. No problem," he says in a soft voice, giving me a shy, uncertain smile as he peers at me through the golden blond hair that's flopped over his forehead and partially into his eyes. He didn't style it into his normal meticulous swoop, and I like this messy, careless vibe.

"Let's go," I grumble and open the door to get out, trying to ignore these weird fucking feelings his innocent smiles are *still* giving me. I never should have kissed him because now everything is even harder to deny.

I pause and wait for Oliver to get out before locking my Jeep and proceeding to climb this steep-ass driveway. Oliver stumbles in his haste to keep up with my longer strides, so I grab his elbow and steady him as we scale Mount fucking Everest.

I texted Bethany before we left, so she's waiting on the front porch when we finally reach the summit. She's rocking in a white, wooden chair like an eighty-year-old woman or like she just finished brunch at Cracker Barrel.

"Oh my God, Finn! You're here!" She squeals and jumps up, causing the rocking chair to bang backward into the brick with an audible crack.

"Oops," she giggles as she covers her mouth with her hand and looks over her shoulder. She whips her head back around and jumps into my arms, giving me a big squeeze. I hug her tightly because Beth has always been like a sister to me.

"Missed you," she whispers into my ear and then hops down to face my new stepbrother.

"Hi, I'm Bethany. It's so good to finally meet you! I've heard so much about you!" she exclaims like I've brought a girl—or boyfriend—home to meet the parents, and she's trying to embarrass me. She holds her hand out for Oliver to shake, her little button nose wrinkling as she flashes a full, genuine smile at him.

"Oliver. Nice to meet you, too." He blushes and gives her hand a quick little shake but doesn't seem interested in the full rack she has on display. In fact, he doesn't even glance down once. Even *I* glanced. They're just so. . . *bam*, in your face.

Maybe he isn't bi. Maybe he's just gay.

I should have asked him when we had our heart-to-heart last night.

I mean, is it rude to just ask him?

Fuck, probably.

Bethany giggles and grabs my hand. "Come on, you two. I'll make you some of my famous party punch!" I roll my eyes because I've been the victim of Bethany's party punch far too many times in my short eighteen years on this planet.

I grab Oliver's hand as Bethany pulls on mine and leads us through the enormous open-plan living room into her state-of-the-art, sterile white kitchen. It looks so fucking pristine, even with all the assorted liquor bottles and mixers on the counters.

"Finn, you can put your coats in my dad's office and grab them whenever you want throughout the night."

I nod in thanks and peer around at the fairy lights strung up from the ceiling, the giant ice sculpture of a. . . *sloth*? And the assortment of blue and silver balloons, streamers, plates, cups, napkins. . . *Fucking everything*.

"Winter Wonderland?" I guess.

"You got it, Finny!" She boops me on the nose as I swat her hand away like we've done since we were eight years old, and I used to chase her around the playground, daring her to boop me one more time.

"What's with the sloth, though?" Oliver asks in confusion.

Bethany nearly spits out the sip of alcohol she just took as she chokes and sputters around a laugh. I pat her on the back, trying to help her catch her breath.

"Sorry, sorry," she says, dabbing at her eyes and glittery pink lips with a little snowflake napkin. "I just can't stop laughing whenever someone asks me about it. The guy at the shop only had one sculpture that was ready and available for purchase, so I jumped on the opportunity. Usually, you have to commission these things weeks ahead of time."

She saunters over to the ice sculpture, her short, black cocktail dress swaying dangerously close to exposing the bottom of her ass cheeks. Her chocolate brown hair hangs in a slick sheet down to the middle of her back, and her skin glows golden after her extended winter break in Cancun.

She twirls on the spot when she reaches the odd ice animal and gives it a little pet, aquamarine eyes sparkling with mirth. "So, yeah. Finn, Oliver, meet my new party mascot, Seymour the Sloth." She cackles like a crazy person —an endearing one, but crazy nonetheless.

"Maybe have some water after that drink, yeah?" I nod my head to her half-empty cup of *whatever*.

She just rolls her eyes. "I'm not *that* drunk, Finny. But anyway, let me be a good hostess and make your drinks!"

"Not drinking," I say as I pat my front pocket, making my keys jingle.

She pouts a little but continues to pour all kinds of shit into a blue plastic cup and holds it out for Oliver to take, an expectant look on her face.

Oliver seems unsure as he bites his lip and glances over

at me for reassurance, and it causes an odd warmth to spark in my chest.

He really does trust me.

I nod once, letting him know it's okay to take a drink from Bethany. She's an exception to the rule.

The only exception.

"It's my signature drink!" Bethany exclaims in her bubbly voice. "It's vodka, orange, pineapple, Sprite, and a splash of Everclear. Try it." She pushes the plastic cup further into Oliver's face as he reluctantly takes it from her grip.

"It doesn't even smell like alcohol," he says as he sticks the cup up to his nose and sniffs hesitantly.

"That's the point, silly!" Bethany giggles. "It doesn't taste like it either, but it'll get you wasted before you even finish that cup."

Oliver takes a small, tentative sip, then follows up with three huge gulps as if it's cold water and he just ran a full fucking marathon. I reach over and gently pry it from his grasp. "Slow down, bro. It's not a race."

Oliver looks up at me with glassy eyes and flushed cheeks.

Fuck, he's already tipsy.

"Sorry, Finn. Bethany's right. It tastes reeeally good." He bites his lip again as he peers up at me. My eyes zero in on his mouth as his teeth tug at the soft flesh of his lower lip. If he doesn't stop doing that, I'm going to do something stupid. Something I'll regret in the morning. Now that I know what he tastes like, the temptation is even stronger. But I promised Vivian I'd look out for him, not be the one he needs protection from.

I shake my head, clearing these dumbass thoughts from my mind and focusing back on my *stepbrother*. He's still looking up at me, completely unguarded and trusting, just waiting for the word on what's next.

I hand Oliver his drink back and grab a water bottle out of the cooler for myself. I won't ride in a car that I'm not driving; I just can't. Even if I could, I'm not getting drunk around this many assholes with Oliver here. I'm not getting high either. I won't risk it. I won't risk *him*.

We amble to the living room, where the music is much louder, and I can feel the bass thumping through the hardwood floors.

I lean over to shout into Bethany's ear that we're going to make our rounds and look for the guys. She tells me to watch out for the nasty viper slithering around—a.k.a. Hazel Bell. I thank her for the heads-up because I am definitely going to try and avoid *that* snake. Bethany and Hazel have always had a frenemies type of relationship, full of competition and fake niceties. But ever since Hazel was so selfish and cruel after the accident, Bethany has fucking *hated* her.

We drop off our winter coats in Bethany's father's office and look for Jared. I find him upstairs in the game room, eyes glued to the massive eighty-inch television screen mounted to the wall and a PS5 controller in his hand.

Trace, Danny, and Eric are here as well, and it looks like they're deep in some kind of Fortnite competition, with what appears to be twenty shots lined up in four rows on the coffee table.

"Finn! Oliver!" Jared hollers and waves extravagantly when he sees us hovering in the doorway. "Come join the party, my dudes!"

Well, he seems about three sheets to the wind, as does everyone else in this room. The microfiber sectional is enormous, so Ollie and I walk in without passing in front of the TV and sit at the far end.

"So, we're in between lobbies right now if one of you wants to join the competition. It's simple. If you don't place first, second or third, you take a shot." Trace grins with glassy brown eyes.

"I think I'm good with Bethany's punch. This shit is strong," Ollie says as he holds his plastic cup in silent cheers.

"And I'm not drinking," I add.

"Oh, come on! Don't be a pussy! Take a shot, Oliver," Eric sneers as he leans in aggressively and grabs a shot glass, causing some to spill over the side and onto Bethany's glass coffee table. He thrusts it out in front of him and lifts one brow in challenge.

Before Ollie can decide, Hazel comes strutting into the room in a silver sequined minidress and delicately perches on the arm of the couch next to Eric. She grabs the shot glass from his outstretched hand and downs it in one go.

"Damn, Oliver! You gonna let a chick show you up?" Eric goads. Then he starts chanting obnoxiously.

"Shot, Shot, Shot!"

Somehow he gets the rest of my friends to join in, even the normally silent Danny. Hazel grins maniacally because she knows what she's doing. She's trying to push my buttons by fucking with my stepbrother.

Ollie's cheeks pinken as everyone continues to chant. He quickly scoops up a shot from the table and tips it back, only slightly wincing.

"Happy?" he asks with a sideways smirk that pops a single dimple out.

"Yes!" Trace exclaims. "Wanna play now?"

"Nah, I'm shit at Fortnite on a good day, but add in a

few drinks, and it won't be pretty." Oliver chuckles self-deprecatingly, and even though these are some of my best friends—minus Hazel—I need to get the fuck out of this room.

"Let's head out back to the patio. I need a fucking breather, and there's a fire pit," I whisper into Oliver's ear.

We stand up, and I tell the guys I'll catch them later.

I glide my hand down the polished oak of the ornate banister as we head down the double staircase, not unlike my own. We stop and grab our coats before I ghost my hand over Oliver's lower back and steer him toward the back patio.

I open one of the French doors and urge him through first. The cold night air smells like fireplace smoke and snow—we're supposed to get a foot overnight.

We make our way toward the fire pit. It's one of those fancy ones installed directly into the stone deck, and there are space heaters everywhere, too. Bethany has fairy lights strewn up in magical loops along invisible fishing lines that connect the house to the pine trees lining her property. It truly does look like a winter wonderland out here—the heated, saltwater pool creating steam that hovers over the surface of the clear water like a whimsical fog.

Oliver and I sit on two dark, wicker chairs clustered together with a small end table. Two couples are lounging on the large couch across the fire from us, but I don't recognize them. They might be juniors.

"Sup, dude?" The guy with white-blond hair says casually. The fire illuminates the light color, making his head practically glow. I try not to stare and nod back in greeting. "Sup?"

"Bro, you played a killer final season. Cindy, this is the guy who took us to state *two* years in a row! And won!" he raves to the pink-haired girl next to him. "Sorry 'bout your mom, though. Sucks, dude. You know where you're goin' to college yet?"

I tense up, my back going ramrod straight. Even though I know it's a completely normal question to ask a senior during their last semester of high school, I don't want to discuss it with a nosy stranger at a party. And did he have to bring up my mom, too? I'm not in the mood for this drunk kid's bullshit right now, even if it is benign.

Sensing my discomfort, Oliver pipes up to divert the attention off of me. "Can we just drink and not talk about school right now? Did you guys try Bethany's party punch? It's freaking amaaazing!"

The two girls on the couch giggle and agree, asking Oliver to play a drinking game with them. He once again defers to me, and I tell them we'll join them in a few minutes.

Once they've all walked away, I turn to face Oliver. "Why did you do that for me?"

"Do what?"

I narrow my eyes at him. "You know what."

He doesn't back down from my stare and just sighs and rolls his eyes. "I felt you tense up and knew you didn't want to talk about it with that guy."

I squint my eyes even more at him. "Did my dad tell you something? I'm really goddamn sick of him." I don't raise my voice. I don't want to scare him, but I know he can feel my anger.

"What? No." He holds his hands up in mock surrender. "Seriously, I have no idea what you're talking about, Finn."

"Okay, whatever," I grumble, turning back to stare blankly into the fire and lose myself for a moment.

"Hey." A soft, warm hand caresses mine and pulls me

from my spiraling thoughts, and I just stare down at it, unseeing. A second hand touches my cheek and steers my gaze to meet bright blue eyes shining with. . . *Fuck,* I don't even know what, but it feels too intimate.

"I don't know what's going on in your head right now, but you can talk to me. I'm not asking you to spill your deepest, darkest secrets, but we're brothers now, and I want you to know there's someone here for you. When you're ready."

His gaze is so pure and so genuine that I feel a lump of emotion clogging my throat. I clear it and awkwardly look away, mumbling a simple, "Thanks, bro," even though the feelings I'm having for him are anything but brotherly.

After a few games of beer pong with the junior girls and another cup of Bethany's party punch, Oliver and I once again leave the warmth of the house to venture outside for some peace and quiet. He's nursing his third cup, and I think I'm going to have to cut him off after it. Just as I'm about to say as much, Ethan and Bethany burst out the back doors and make a beeline for us.

"Your friendly, neighborhood ganja man is in the house!" Ethan shouts and plops down on the wicker couch across from us, Beth right beside him. She grabs the throw blanket draped over the arm and covers her bare legs. The fire pit and heaters help a lot, but it's still below freezing.

"Ready to light up, Oliver?" Ethan asks.

I glance at the boy in question as he chugs the rest of his third drink and slams it down on the end table, swiping his jacket sleeve across his mouth.

"Ready!" he exclaims with a slightly too loud shout.

Bethany giggles and agrees, so Ethan pulls the overstuffed blunt from behind his ear and stokes the cherry to life with a few quick puffs. He passes it to Bethany, who inhales deeply, holding it in like a pro. She holds the blunt up to me in offering, but I give a quick shake of my head. Someone needs to stay responsible and aware tonight.

Oliver leans forward and takes it, pinching the blunt between his thumb and pointer finger as he takes a long pull. He holds it for two seconds before it all escapes as a massive, hacking cough.

Ethan and Bethany cackle wildly, but it's not funny. That shit hurts if you cough it out. I take the blunt out of his grasp and pass it back to Ethan before handing Oliver my water bottle and rubbing his back as he chugs mouthful after mouthful until he's drained the entire thing.

Ethan is still laughing like a madman. "Dude! You are going to be sooo fucked up after coughing that hard. Damn!"

Oliver leans forward, elbows resting on his knees as he lowers his head, trying to catch his breath after that rough coughing attack. I continue to softly rub his back, and when the rotation comes around to him again, he just shakes his head and croaks out a raspy, "Pass."

Taking a deep, shaky breath, Oliver slumps back in his seat and stares off into the forest with a vacant, dazed expression on his face.

Shit. He's completely fucked out of his head right now.

"You okay, Cali Boy?" I ask as I nudge his shoulder to gain his attention.

His half-lidded, bloodshot eyes meet mine, and I barely see a flicker of recognition there.

"M'fine," he slurs as his glazed-over eyes continue to hold my stare.

Jesus Christ.

The first snowflake lands on the tip of my nose, and I drop my head back to peer up at the dark expanse of night sky filled with twinkling stars and dancing snowflakes making their way down to the ground.

"The party's been great, Bethany, but I think I need to get this wasted-ass kid home, and it's starting to snow, too."

"Aw, but you can stay over if you want. All the guys are. We're having a slumber party, just like old times."

"I think we're going to pass tonight so we don't get snowed in here all weekend. But thanks, Beth."

"At least make sure you grab some food from the buffet before you leave. Oliver is for sure going to have the munchies." She giggles, tugging the blanket tighter around her lower half.

"Food?" Oliver asks, bloodshot eyes opening only slightly wider with the mention of snacks. All three of us chuckle at that.

"Yeah, we'll get some food, Cali Boy," I agree.

"Ooo! Make sure you try the little meat and cheese pinwheels. They're to die for!" Bethany gushes.

I lie and say I will because she doesn't know about Oliver's peanut allergy, and now is definitely not the time to get into that type of conversation when he can barely stand on his own. In fact, he starts to ever-so-slowly lean to the right as we stand here trying to say goodbye to my friends.

I snake my arm out with lightning-fast reflexes and drape it over his shoulder, pulling him into my side so he doesn't tip over.

Ethan is still smoking his blunt, even though it's tiny now, and he can barely hold it between his long fingers.

"So, I guess we probably won't be playing football on Sunday?"

"Nah, there's a winter storm rolling in later tonight. There's no way we won't be covered in snow by Sunday. I'll just see you guys at school on Monday." And then we turn to leave through the house, and I'm wondering how the fuck I'm going to make it down the steep driveway with Oliver in this condition.

CHAPTER ELEVEN
OLIVER

A bright light pierces my closed lids, glowing orange, and making me wake far sooner than my body wants to. I toss an arm over my eyes to block the sun pouring in through the cracks in the blinds. I really need some fucking blackout curtains in here.

As my brain starts to come back online, I'm slightly disoriented for a few seconds before the memories from last night flood in.

Bethany's party punch.

The blunt.

Slipping and falling on my ass in the slush and taking Finn down with me.

I peek under the covers and groan because. . . yep, that last one must have really happened. My pants are off, and I forgot I chose to wear the tiny black briefs with the little purple eggplants all over them.

Fucking great.

I rub my hands roughly down my face, trying to scrub the sleep *and* the embarrassment from my mind. I sit up against the wooden headboard, still feeling slightly dizzy.

A piece of paper in my periphery catches my gaze, and I see that Finn left me a note, two pills, and a bottle of water on the side table. The note is written in simple, neat handwriting—very impressive for a guy.

Take these.

Drink this.

Come downstairs to eat.

Short and to the point, I wouldn't expect anything else from him. I do as the note says and scurry over to the window to see why it's so exceptionally bright out this morning.

I pull the cord for the blinds and unveil a shimmering white landscape that is so beyond *foreign* to me that I feel like I'm on a different planet. The sky is cloudless and blue, and the sun reflects off the perfectly undisturbed field of snow, making me squint.

It's fucking *majestic*, and I'm itching to grab my oil paints. I've never tried to paint snow before, and now I'm dying to see if I can. Judging by the height of the perimeter fence, there must be a foot of snow out there, *at least*.

My excitement over the snow gives me a little adrenaline boost, and I power through a quick shower. I dress in dark gray joggers and a black zip-up hoodie over a plain white tee. I quickly comb my hair back, leaving it to dry and do its own thing and pull on my favorite new pair of wool socks.

I grip the banister tightly as I walk gingerly down the stairs and stroll into the kitchen as casually as I can, like I didn't just get wasted off my ass the night before.

The smell of Finn's fancy coffee filters through my senses, and I think I'm starting to like the strong aroma. He's perched at the island, like always, sipping his black coffee from an *Avengers* mug and scrolling through his phone.

"It fucking *snowed* last night!" I shout at Finn embarrassingly loud and completely out of the blue. Not even a *good morning* first. I mentally facepalm myself as Finn just raises a single dark brow in question.

"You're looking well this morning, Sunshine," he teases. I can't help but smile back because, yeah, despite the slight hangover, I do feel great today. Excited.

"I want to play in the snow," I blurt, ignoring his observation completely.

Finn's deep, throaty chuckle warms my bones. I have the creepiest urge to climb into his lap and nuzzle his neck like a content little kitten.

"That we can do, Cali Boy. Glad to see you aren't completely hungover. You were pretty wrecked last night. Nice undies, by the way," he smirks.

"Oh my God," I moan, covering my probably crimson face with both hands. "That's so humiliating."

The next thing I know, I feel Finn's larger, slightly rough hands grasp my wrists and pull them away. His dark gaze enraptures me, and I can't tear my eyes away.

"I like them." He shrugs and drops my wrists. "And sorry, but I had no choice. Your ass was wet, and so was mine. Thanks for that, by the way. My tailbone hurts like a bitch."

Oh, right.

I busted my ass and, subsequently, Finn's ass at the bottom of Bethany's driveway. "Shit. Sorry, Finn," I say, casting my gaze aside.

"Don't worry about it. I'll just ice my ass when you ice your ribs." My eyes dart back to him, and I catch the boyish smirk before it disappears. "But seriously though, how are your ribs doing? It's been almost a week. If they're not feeling substantially better, we should think about getting you an X-ray."

"No. I'm fine. Seriously. They feel like eighty percent better." I may have fudged that a bit, but I don't need help anymore, so he won't know that.

"Okay, good. There's a plate of eggs and hash browns in the microwave and a glass of orange juice in the fridge. You need to eat something. Soak up some of that leftover party punch."

"Ha, ha, ha. Very funny. I think I held my own pretty well, actually. I didn't even get sick." I cross my arms and hold my head up high because it's true. I didn't get sick or blackout. Sure, maybe I passed out, but I remember everything just fine.

I grab the plate and orange juice and sit at the island, digging into Finn's fucking *amazing* eggs. Perfectly fluffy, as always.

Once finished, I take my dishes to the deep farmhouse sink, where I clean every dish, pot, pan, and utensil piled up.

"I could have done that," Finn mumbles.

"No way. You cook, I clean. It's like a universal life rule or something. You know?" I toss over my shoulder.

"Okay, if you say so," he chuckles.

When I finish up, I set the sponge down and hang the floral towel over the oven handle. "So, can we play outside now?" I know my dimples are showing, and I probably look like a hyper five-year-old, or worse, an over-excited puppy. But whatever. I've never seen, let alone *touched*, snow. I need to get out there, like right now.

"Yeah, go add some more layers, and I'll meet you in the mudroom."

I run off to do as I'm told and add a thermal over my T-shirt, put my hoodie on over that, and switch my joggers for some jeans with no holes in them. I slip my knitted black beanie over my still damp hair and wrap a matching scarf around my neck. I dig through the back of my closet until I pull out my brand-new waterproof boots. I can't fucking *wait* to slip these bad boys on. The shiny black leather and chunky straps look sleek, and I can choose to leave the laces loose for a more casual style if I want. But I'm fucking playing today, so I tie them tight and knot the laces twice.

I practically bounce downstairs. I wish I could slide down the banister like I always dreamed of doing as a kid, but I might need to wait until my ribs heal one hundred percent for that. And also when Finn isn't around because I know he would be *pissed*.

I stroll into the mudroom where Finn is already bundled up and grab my thick, puffy coat. Finn hands over my gloves and sunglasses, and we are good to go.

We exit through the back patio doors and step into the most surreal ice world I have ever seen. The pine trees lining the property are no longer dark and serrated but fluffy and white. The huge expanse of softly rolling hills beyond the deck is blanketed with a sheet of white that sparkles like thousands of tiny diamonds. The smooth, unblemished powder is just begging to be disturbed by sled tracks or a snow angel. I want to do *everything*. Everything I missed out on as a kid living in Southern California. I don't care if I look ridiculous—it's happening.

We carefully climb down the snowed-over, wooden steps of the massive back deck and venture out into the calf-deep snow. As soon as my boot sinks with my first step, I lean down and scoop a handful of snow from the ground to shove into my mouth.

Finn just shakes his head at me. "You're fucking weird, dude. Haven't you had a snow cone before?"

"Yeah, but that ain't got shit on trying the real thing straight from the sky!"

"Fucking weird," Finn mumbles to himself. "Watch the pool. There's a safety cover, but don't walk on it. I don't trust it with all the extra weight of the snow."

I nod and veer away from the giant, slightly raised rectangle where I know the pool is. Once we pass the stone decking and frozen landscaping, we're standing in the middle of Finn's giant backyard. I spin around and peer up at the house—*the mansion*—and my breath catches at the sight before me.

Every peak and valley of the roof is solid white, and giant icicles hang from the gutters. Frosted snowflakes outline the edges of every window, just like the old lace doilies my grandmother used to set everything down on. It's picturesque, and I can't wait to experience this during the next Christmas season. It must be absolutely *magical*.

Once I have my fill of the breathtaking view, I mentally scroll through my snow day checklist to decide what's first.

Sledding. It has to be sledding.

As if he can read my mind, Finn says he'll be right back and heads to the quaint little storage shed on the right side of the property, tucked up against the edge of the forest. He comes back five minutes later with two plastic sleds under his arms.

"Thought this would be the most fun to start out with. Before you get too cold. Because you *will* get cold," he smirks.

"Never!" I shout with a pump of my fist and way too much enthusiasm for someone who's supposed to be slightly hungover. "Too much adrenaline pumping through me to be cold!"

"We'll see about that, *Cali* Boy," Finn declares with a grin, emphasizing the Cali, and hands over the blue sled, keeping the red for himself.

"I still don't understand your constant energy without any caffeine," Finns says. "It makes no sense," he adds, mumbling.

I just chuckle and attempt to climb up the closest small hill. "You know what they say," I shout over my shoulder. "Positive thoughts breed good moods and boost energy! I don't need any coffee!"

"Who the fuck says that?" Finn questions as he catches up.

"Me!" I yell and cackle like a crazy person.

"You still high, dude?"

"Shut up." I roll my eyes and shove his arm playfully. Although when we're leg locked in a foot of snow, I guess a shove isn't all that playful.

Finn loses his balance and grabs onto my forearm, taking me down with him in some kind of karmic justice.

"That's the second time in less than twenty-four hours, bro!" Finn hollers and scoops up a handful of snow, packing it into a ball. "It's fucking on, now!" He stands up and looms over me, still sprawled out on my ass in the wet snow.

Guess we're skipping sledding and moving directly into snowball fight territory. I hold my hands up in surrender and try to show off my big baby blues. "Mercy," I plead.

"Never!" he mimics and throws the first punch when he

slams the snowball down on my beanie—a cloud of white powder raining down around me.

"Oh, okay. I see how it is!" I jump up and try to maneuver away into a more defensive position, but the snow is deep, and I feel like I'm in one of those sumo wrestler suits as I waddle through it.

Finn hits me in the back with another snowball, and his deep, throaty chuckle warms some of the cold that's starting to seep into my bones.

I finally make it to the shed and duck out of sight to form some of my own ammunition. Not even one minute later, Finn barrels around the corner of the shed, nailing me with snowball after snowball like he's one of those pitching machines at the batting cages Mom used to take me to.

When the barrage ends, I jump up with my armful and a loud battle cry as I peg him right back until I'm out of breath and out of snowballs.

We're both still laughing breathlessly when he holds a hand out. "Truce?"

"Truce," I agree and shake on it.

We brush the snow off each other's shoulders and hats.

"So, sledding then?" I ask, walking toward a small hill.

"Let's do it."

"Dude! Imagine flying down Bethany's driveway on one of these! That would be sick!" I exclaim as we trudge through the deep snow. I've lost count of how many times we've gone down, but it still hasn't lost its appeal.

"That's like a death wish, bro. It's not like they have brakes."

"True," I concede.

"Besides, you would not want to be snowed in there overnight with all the guys and Eric. You'd probably wake up with a dick drawn on your forehead, and then I'd have to kill someone."

I can't deny how my insides twist up at that statement. Finn's overprotectiveness just. . . fucking turns me on, to be honest. I know my nose and cheeks are already pink from the cold, so I don't think he notices the blush creeping up my cheeks.

I change the subject. "Think I could surf down one of these little hills?"

"Surf?"

"Yeah, like on the sled. Sled surfing? It's probably a thing, and I bet I can do it."

"No."

"No, you don't think I can do it? Or no, it's not a thing?" I tuck the sled under my arm and head for the biggest hill available in Finn's backyard.

Finn's boots crunch through the snow as he follows behind me. He yanks the sled out from under my arm.

"I meant no, you're not doing anything that fucking stupid. If you wanna surf, we can go snowboarding with proper gear. Wilmot Mountain is only like an hour away, in Wisconsin."

I already know I would kill it at snowboarding, but I want to try something right now.

"Come on, Finn. Just let me try. It'll be fine."

"No."

"Fine. Just let me take one more trip down, and then I'm done," I lie.

He frowns, and I see his eyebrows dip together beneath his sunglasses. He's weighing whether he should believe me.

Oh, well. Better to ask for forgiveness and all that.

Finn hesitantly hands over the sled, and I smile as genuinely as possible.

He waits at the bottom of the small-ish hill with his arms crossed. Shit. He's gonna be pissed at me.

Taking a deep breath, I remind myself that I am my own fucking person, and I don't need anyone's permission right now. I drop the sled on the ground and proceed to place one boot on it, testing the stability.

"Don't you fucking dare, Oliver!" Finn explodes, but I don't look up at him.

I cautiously place my other boot on the sled and hold my arms out, balancing like I'm on a board. I think I can do this. Seems stable enough.

Here goes nothing.

I push off with one foot and quickly place it back, feet spread and angled sideways. I laugh as I start to pick up speed and the crisp, cold air smacks me in the face. I'm near the bottom when I realize I don't have a way to stop. I settle on jumping ship and leap off the sled before I crash.

Oof.

I'm caught by two steel bands and a brick wall. Finn essentially catches me and hugs me tightly to his chest. After another second, he pushes me back by the shoulders and holds me out at arm's length.

His glare is molten hot. His nostrils flaring. "Goddammit, Ollie! Don't fucking do shit like that again, okay?"

He drops his gaze to our feet, looks back up again, and his expression has changed. There's vulnerability and a flash of hurt now. "You lied to me."

Shit. I did. And that was really fucked up.

"Finn, I'm sorry. I just need to be able to make my own decisions sometimes."

His jaw clenches, but he nods. I know he understands. He probably wouldn't have listened to anyone if he wanted to do something slightly reckless.

I don't want to bring the mood down, so I ask, "Snow angels?" And that pulls a small smile from his mouth.

"Dude, it'll snow again. You don't have to experience it all in one day."

"Yeah, I know. This is the last thing. We can save the snowman for later."

Finn sweeps his arm out in front of him and lifts a single brow as if to say, "Go on, then."

"You're not going to do it with me?"

"No way. It's too fucking cold to lie down." He shakes his head.

I trudge over to a new, undisturbed spot and fall backward. Soft white powder puffs out around me as I sink into the pile of snow. I lie there for a second, staring at the bright sky. I move my arms and legs like I've seen on TV and then carefully climb out of my snow impression.

"Nice," Finn comments from over my shoulder. And it is. A perfect little snow angel.

But now that we've been out here for a couple of hours, my body starts to shiver.

My breath comes out in little white clouds while I hop in place and rub my arms roughly. I'm trying to bring the warmth back to my blood and get it circulating again. I mean, my teeth are chattering, for fucks sake. I've determined it's not natural for humans to live in such environments. No matter how fun they look.

Finn places his big paws on either side of me and squeezes my gloved hands on top of my biceps, locking me in and halting my frantic movements. He raises a single eyebrow at me.

"What? Don't even look at me like that. You were right, and I think I'm done now. It's so fucking cold my balls have climbed back inside my body, and they're huddling there together, seeking warmth and shelter. I'm pretty sure my nutsack looks like a shriveled up turtle shell right now."

A surprised laugh erupts from Finn, and he widens his eyes and covers his mouth like he surprised himself. Well, he fucking surprised me too because I have never heard him let loose and laugh so freely and so loudly before.

His body shakes as he tries to hold back, but he finally gives in and lets the braying laughter escape.

I beam back at him. I fucking love happy Finn.

"Better get inside before they fall off then," he chuckles between gasping breaths.

CHAPTER TWELVE
OLIVER

After a long, steamy shower to thaw my bones, Finn and I lounge in the theater room, watching old reruns of *Pimp My Ride* while we snack.

Playing in the snow must be like swimming or surfing. It really works up an appetite because I am inhaling the charcuterie board Finn expertly whipped up for us.

The fire is now roaring, warming the room and casting a golden glow across Finn's sharp features. His long hair is wet, and little droplets fall from the ends and land on his T-shirt. He stuffs another cracker into his mouth and watches the show with rapt attention.

I really only like to see the before and after of the pimped-out ride, but Finn seems to be riveted to the TV during the actual fabrication scenes.

"I know you take Auto Shop, and your garage is insane, but you really like this car stuff, don't you?"

"Yeah. I've always loved cars. More than football, even," he reveals.

"So, do you want to own a mechanic shop? Or have more of a *Pimp My Ride* scenario? You could go to school for business." We haven't talked about our futures yet, and I'm curious about his plans.

"Yeah, business might be good." He rubs the back of his neck. "I'll probably take at least a year off before college—don't tell my dad. And I was actually thinking more like a car museum."

"Museum?" I ask, my brows rising in surprise.

"Like for rare, antique, or super expensive cars. Cars from history, cars from movies. That sort of thing."

I just stare at him with my mouth hanging open. "Holy shit, Finn, that sounds fucking amazing! Oooo! Oooo!" I snap my hand out and grab his muscled forearm. "You *have* to get a car from *Fast and Furious*!"

He smirks. "Planned on it."

I'm still reeling from this fucking awesome revelation when Finn asks me about my own plans after school.

"Um, I guess I haven't thought too much about it, even though I know I should have it planned out by now." I grab a slice of prosciutto and shove it into my mouth—chewing slowly and buying time.

"I was just so focused on getting out—I mean packing up and moving—that I didn't apply anywhere. Guess I'm skipping a year or two as well. Maybe I'll try and get my art in a gallery. See if I can make it." I shrug, not feeling too confident about my lack of a solid plan.

"You'll figure it out. I've seen your art. I believe in you."

His simple words warm my already toasty cheeks, and I smile shyly back at him. "Thanks, Finn. That means a lot."

Finn grunts and changes the subject. "I'm hungry for some real food. Let's make spaghetti."

"You can cook spaghetti?" I follow him to the kitchen, where he walks into the pantry and comes out with an armful of items before grabbing a couple things from the freezer. He sets out his simple ingredients of dried noodles, a jar of sauce, ground beef, and garlic bread.

"Spaghetti," he repeats, with a small tilt to his lips.

"Okay, I'm down with this." I try to discreetly look at the fine print on the garlic bread as if I'm looking at the cooking directions.

Before I can find what I'm looking for, Finn answers my unspoken question. "All of this stuff checks out. You don't need to worry when I'm cooking. You can just enjoy it like you do when your mom cooks."

God. My heart.

We work in tandem from there—moving seamlessly around each other in the kitchen like we've been doing this for years. The meal is quick, simple, and delicious.

After dinner, Finn and I find ourselves back in our favorite room, on one of our favorite couches, with an old horror movie on. *Scream*, I think. Finn poured us a couple of glasses of Gabe's best scotch, which he swears his dad won't notice is missing.

We're sitting close—my entire right side is pressed against his left. I'm acutely aware of every inch that our bodies connect. Every nerve ending in my system is like a live wire sparking at his touch, and I can't focus on the movie for shit.

My heart starts to beat faster, but I'm not the first to make a move.

Finn folds his knee and turns on the couch to face me fully. "I've tried to be chill about it. But I want you so fucking bad, I can't hold back anymore. Tell me you want me too, Ollie?" The burning tether between our heated gaze is red hot and smoldering, and his words are a desperate plea I can't deny.

"Yes." My answer is breathy and light. Floating off my

lips and dispersing into the air like a silent wish made on a dandelion puff.

"Can we redo our first kiss?" he asks shyly, and it's so unlike him that I'm stunned silent for a beat too long, and his hopeful smile starts to fall.

I snap out of it. "Yes. Please." Another breathless whisper from me.

Finn leans forward and presses his lips to mine, testing the connection.

Soft. Gentle. Chaste.

I can't help but moan at the feel of his velvety, plush lips against my own again. He takes advantage of the opening and plunges his tongue into my mouth. The once sweet peck turns into a demanding, exploring kiss.

A real kiss.

It's deep and urgent, like he wants to devour my fucking soul, and I'm helpless to stop him. His tongue tastes me, lightly stroking my own.

Finn gently runs his hands up my neck and holds my jaw with his palms, stroking my cheeks with his rough thumbs. The touch is so tender and so intimate that an embarrassing whimper escapes my lips. Finn just sucks it down along with my tongue.

He bites my bottom lip and growls. "I've wanted to chew and suck on this pouty lip ever since I barged into your room that very first morning," he admits. My stomach flutters at his confession, and those flutters travel straight to my dick, causing it to throb with a pleasurable ache.

Finn wraps his arms around me and leans back, taking me with him until he's lying flat on his back, me on top.

I involuntarily press my hips into Finn's, shamelessly grinding myself against his thigh. Without breaking the kiss, he pushes his thigh more firmly between my legs, and

I can feel his own hardness against my stomach. I groan at the contact, needing more but not so sure I'm ready for that. I break away from the kiss, panting embarrassingly loud.

"Finn," I breathe out.

"You taste so good, Cali Boy."

My abs tighten at his words.

"Is just kissing okay for now?" I ask, feeling unsure. "I'm not sure I'm ready for more yet." I'm being honest and open, and I hope he sees that.

"*Just kissing* is fine with me. Come here."

He guides my face back to his mouth and ravages it while the movie continues to play in the background, unwatched.

I'm not sure how many glasses of scotch later, but I wake with my face plastered to a hot, hard, and *bare* chest. We're tucked under the throw blanket, still on the couch in the theater room. The TV is dark, and the last embers from tonight's fire glow softly. The room is stifling—especially with our hot, sticky bodies pressed together.

Why are we both shirtless?

At least our pants are still on. I sit up, and Finn stirs.

"What time is it?" he grumbles.

I squint at the clock on the wall. "Three-thirty. Let's go to bed."

We amble down the hall to our rooms, and Finn tugs my hand toward his room before I can even think about turning into my own. I don't argue or try to stop it. It feels right. I just want to cuddle—for now.

Finn grabs two small water bottles from the retro mini-fridge on the corner of his oversized nightstand. "Drink up before bed."

So bossy. But I do as I'm told. The cold, refreshing water soothes the leftover burn from too many glasses of scotch.

We don't speak. We both just drop our pants and climb under the cool silk sheets in just our boxers. I shimmy to the center of the bed, where Finn lifts his arm, and I settle into the crook, resting my cheek on his chest.

He silently kisses my forehead, but I feel it with every atom of my being.

"Night, Cali Boy."

"Night," I mumble before I drift back into a dreamless slumber.

CHAPTER THIRTEEN
FINN

Yesterday was pretty fucking amazing—spending the day having fun in the snow and doing things I haven't done since I was a kid. I feel a little lighter for it. I know we still have the big, gay elephant in the room, but things are better now. Back to the way they were. The way they should be.

We'll have the talk today; I can't keep putting it off. Especially if we're really going to do this.

I sip my steaming black coffee and stare out the large, arch-top kitchen window. The back deck and yard are still completely snowed over.

I hear the soft footfalls of Oliver's wool socks on the marble floor before I see him stroll into the kitchen. He just got out of the shower, and I love when his hair looks darker —his eyes stand out even more, and the contrast is striking.

"Good morning," he says, giving me a shy quirk of his lip.

"Morning. Sleep well?" I know he did. He slept longer than me.

"Yeah," he chuckles. "Guess the scotch knocked me out."

Oliver grabs a Greek yogurt and a banana and sits at the island next to me. "Damn, it didn't melt at all," he observes. "Think we'll get a snow day?"

"Probably not. They'll have the roads cleared before tomorrow."

I let Oliver eat his breakfast while I finish my second mug of coffee before I bring up what happened last night. "So. . ." I start.

His gaze moves from the window to zero those neon blue eyes on me. I swallow hard because it's always so intense and so *probing*—like he can see more than I've allowed him to. Fuck, it rattles me. I just blurt out my question because what the fuck does it matter at this point anyway?

"Are you gay, then?"

He glances down, then up, and a blush settles on his cheeks. "Yes," he says simply, hesitantly. Almost like he's afraid I'll reject him, even though I had my tongue down his throat last night, and my hard cock was straining against my boxers, trying to poke its way through to make first contact.

I lean forward on the barstool and press my lips softly against his. He kisses me back, adding tongue, and tastes like raspberries and temptation. Oliver pulls back and peers directly into my soul. "Are you?"

"Am I gay?" I repeat needlessly. He just nods and waits for my answer, gazing at me with a sudden, sharp focus.

I clear my throat. "Um, I've never thought I was. I. . . I've only been with one girl, but I definitely liked it."

His face falls, and I look straight ahead again, peering out of the window at the winter wonderland before us. I feel the heat build in my cheeks, and I hate it. "But I know I like you, Oliver. And I've never felt like this before."

I need him to see the seriousness in my eyes, so I brave his intense gaze once again.

"Not even close. It's probably unhealthy, really. This unreasonable and slightly obsessive need to protect you, to kiss you, to—" He cuts off my confession by slamming his mouth on mine. He reaches out and tangles his hands into my unruly dark strands, tugging them until I bend my head exactly how he wants it.

He doesn't get to run the show, though. I lick into his mouth, stroking his tongue with my own, teasing and caressing until he's moaning and whimpering into my open mouth. I break away after a minute so we can catch our breath.

"Do I need to put a label on it? Or can we just see where this goes? Obviously, low-key."

Oliver smiles understandingly. "Of course you don't need a label, Finn. I would never pressure you or rush you to figure yourself out. It's not always an easy answer."

And I definitely believe that because I don't know if I'm bi or demi or maybe I just like Oliver.

I mean, is that even a thing?

"I'll figure it out. But for now, we have to keep this a secret anyway. Our parents would freak, and my dad would probably think I fucking seduced you or something. He always thinks the worst of me."

"I agree," Ollie says. "They shouldn't know. Not while we're in high school, at least."

"Oh, thinking long-term, are you?" I tease and bump my shoulder into his so he knows I'm just fucking with him.

"Maybe." He grins, and I can't fight my own smile because I feel like this could be something that lasts too.

After herding that elephant from the room, we split up to conquer homework for a couple of hours because I know the academy will definitely be open tomorrow. At some point, who knows when, my brain is done, so I shove my books and tablet back into my backpack and slip my headphones around my neck, jogging upstairs in search of Oliver. He's probably painting in his room. He better be in his room and not on the fucking roof again, or I may not hesitate to bend him over my knee and teach him a lesson.

Jesus. A few kisses with a boy I really like, and I'm apparently a kinky bastard. Guess that proves I never actually liked Hazel because all we did was missionary.

I find Ollie exactly where I expect him to be. In his room, with smudges of colorful paint all over his hands and white T-shirt. He's wearing those thin gray sweats, and they cling to his firm, round ass. His door is open, so he sees me walk in and takes his AirPods out.

"What are you working on?" I ask.

"Well, I know I have plenty of time, but I was just getting some ideas out of my head for our end-of-year art exhibition—it's half of our grade."

I peer around at the canvases he has set up and stroll to his desk to check out his sketchpads. I see more sunsets, but I also see something interesting. Something that catches my eye. I pick it up for a closer look and ask, "What's this?"

His eyes dart over to me and widen for a second before he snatches the pad from my hands. "Um, that one's personal."

If I'm not mistaken, those were *my* eyes. . . and they looked. . . *sad*. Is that how he sees me? How other people see me? I let it slide because I'm not going to force him to show me anything he isn't comfortable with.

"So, what's your favorite medium?"

"Oil paints."

"That's very. . ." I pause to find the right word but end up posing it as a question. "Sophisticated?"

Oliver just laughs. "My grandmother was an artist. We have like a dozen of her oil paintings, and I've admired them my whole life. I can only hope I'm half the artist she was."

"Where are they now?"

"In storage."

I frown at that. "Why aren't they here?"

"Um, I don't think my mom wanted to impose on the current decor of the house."

"That's bullshit. This is your house now, too. Give me the info for the storage unit. I'll handle it."

He huffs out an incredulous laugh, but I'm dead serious. I can have them here in two days, and I'm doing it. I hold my hand out and tap my fingers against my open palm. He sighs and unlocks his phone, plopping it in my hand.

"It's under Pacific Self Storage."

I scroll through his contacts and send the info to myself. I'll make the necessary arrangements later this afternoon. It'll be a nice surprise for Vivian as well.

I've already been thinking about the empty room on the other side of the hall bathroom. He needs an art studio. I don't know how long he plans to stay here or how long *we* decide to stay here, but the art has taken over his bedroom. He deserves his own space, and I can provide that, so I will. I just need the snow to melt and some time to slip out to the art supply store. I'm going to build the studio of his dreams for his birthday.

CHAPTER FOURTEEN

FINN

It was warm enough on Sunday that the tall snowbanks melted. The student lot is slushy and salty by the curbs, and I hate this perpetual state of messiness that lasts all season long. We trudge through the lot wearing our waterproof combat boots, attempting to avoid the mud. Bethany is standing by the front doors of Preston Hall with Eric, and she waves exaggeratedly at us. We both give her a small one in return.

"Hey, Finn?" Oliver whispers.

"Yeah?"

"Don't tell anyone it's my birthday on Wednesday, please. I kind of just want to hang out with you, at home." He stuffs his hands in his coat pockets and looks down at the muddy snow as we continue to march toward the main building.

My chest tightens at his honest words.

"I want that too," I whisper back. He looks up at me and smiles, dimples popping.

What is this boy doing to me?

I feel like the Tin Man who finally gets a heart.

"Hey, guys! How was the rest of your weekend?" Bethany chirps with her usual peppy spirit.

Oliver answers for both of us, "It was fun. This is the first time I've seen snow."

"Oh my gosh! That's so exciting!" She links her arm with Oliver's, and they walk ahead of Eric and me into Preston Hall, chatting away.

"Sup, Eric?" I ask to acknowledge him, even though I don't give a shit what's up with him.

"Nothing, man. I see you got your brother home safely from the party. That's good. I heard he was a wasted mess by the end of the night. Fucking lightweight." He laughs cruelly and sounds like a jealous psycho, always focused on Oliver.

Why is he bringing this up first thing in the morning?

"Fuck off, Eric. It's too early to listen to your bullshit."

Jared swoops in once again, the rest of the guys behind him. "What's this asshole saying now?" he asks, slinging his arm around said asshole's shoulders.

"Nothing," I state, not needing to repeat it. "He's just talking shit, as usual."

"Oh, look, it's my favorite group of man-children."

Seriously?

I pinch the bridge of my nose and take a deep breath. Did I wake up on the wrong side of the bed or something? Because I seem to be having really shitty luck this morning.

"Hey, Hazel," Ethan sneers. "Look, guys. It's our least favorite hellspawn."

Hazel bares her teeth and flips her long red hair over her shoulder. "Hmm. . . well, you didn't seem to think so Friday night when you had your tongue down my throat."

I flick a surprised gaze to Ethan, and all the guys go silent, anticipating the worst from me. Probably an epic freakout of some sort, possibly violence. But they're wrong. He can fuck her if he wants; any of them can. I don't give two shits anymore. I'm just a little shocked. I thought he hated her like the rest of us. I guess alcohol can really lower your normal standards.

"Finn—" Ethan starts, but I cut him off.

"I don't care, dude. Seriously." Then I let my eyes link with Hazel's, her malice shining bright. "Fuck whoever you want, Hazel. I. Don't. Care. Okay? We were never together and never will be. Move the fuck on." I head inside, trying to catch up to Oliver and Bethany. Ethan says something about beer goggles and it never happening again, but I don't wait around to listen to anyone else. Maybe that was a little cold to do in front of all the guys, but she needs to get it through her thick fucking skull that we will never be together. And I hope it finally sinks in.

"I'm so glad you have lunch with us, Oliver!" Bethany exclaims from her place on Ollie's other side. They apparently have Spanish together as well, and I'm relieved he now has somewhat of a buffer from Eric and Hazel in there.

"Yeah, me too," he mumbles around a bite of the chicken salad sandwich I made this morning. It amuses me to watch him try to tame his ravenous eating habits and not shove half the sandwich in his mouth in one bite. It's the biggest form of compliment you can receive from the kid. If he shoves it in his mouth, he loves it.

"Now you get to try all the goodies I bring. Rosaline made her famous oatmeal peanut butter cookies yesterday." Bethany pulls a large Tupperware from her oversized bag and places it in the middle of the lunch table. Everyone freezes instead of digging in like usual.

"What? What'd I miss?" She looks so confused, her sleek ponytail swishing as she peers side to side at everyone.

Of course Eric would be the one to burst out laughing at the awkward silence. "Poor, sensitive Oliver here can't eat peanuts! Wouldn't want his pretty boy face to swell up and pop!"

Eric joking about something as serious as Oliver's allergy boils my blood.

"Eric, you better shut the fuck up right now before you wake up with God," I threaten, clenching my fists under the table until I feel the bite of my nails in the soft flesh of my palms. Grounding me.

Eric huffs out in disbelief as he peers around at everyone. "Jared? Ethan? What the fuck? Are you seriously going to let him threaten me like that?" He holds his hands out, palms up, as if he's innocent and not an awful cunt.

Danny speaks up, and everyone listens because it doesn't happen all too often. "Eric, you need to lay off Oliver. You've been on his ass since the second you met him. It's too much, and I'm about to be anywhere but where you are for the foreseeable future until you're over this weird-as-fuck fixation." He stands up and grabs his backpack and lunch tray, strolling to the trash cans and exiting the cafeteria, going wherever Danny Vallejo slinks off to. The man is truly an enigma.

Eric scoffs and rolls his eyes. "Dude never talks, and when he does, it's dramatic as fuck." He turns his steely gaze to Oliver. "My only fixation is on how much of a loser you are and how you're always just *there*, in the way."

I shoot to my feet, my metal chair screeching against

the tiled floor. It might just be the adrenaline, but I swear my vision tunnels. The entire cafeteria goes dead silent. In my periphery, I see Oliver and Jared jump to their feet. Ollie places his hand on my forearm and squeezes, silently telling me not to do it. I know this fuckface isn't worth it. Isn't worth my entire fucking inheritance—not that Oliver even knows that part. He just doesn't want me to get expelled.

I have to graduate from Lake View, or Dad gets control of my trust until I'm twenty-five. I'll be damned if that happens because I let Eric get under my skin so bad.

"Aw, look. Finn is pussy-whipped by the kid who paints his fingernails!" I growl under my breath and try to remember what that first therapist taught me about my anger and counting to ten slowly.

Luckily, Trace and Jared, the two biggest guys at the table, each grab one of Eric's elbows and walk him out of the cafeteria while he cackles like a rabid hyena. Ethan gives us a sad smile and follows the circus out.

That leaves me with Oliver standing by my side and a shell-shocked Bethany and Jayden sitting at the table with their eyes wide and jaws dropped.

I wish I could cocoon Oliver in the warmth and safety of my arms right now. And whisper into his ear not to listen to a single hateful word Eric just spewed. But I can't. Everyone's watching.

Bethany snaps out of it first. "Oliver, Finn. Oh my God, are you guys okay? Has Eric been like this the whole time? He's like. . ."

"Completely lost his marbles," Jayden fills in.

The lunch bell rings, and I'm fucking relieved. It's one step closer to the end of the day when I can touch Ollie the way I want to, and there aren't a thousand judgmental eyes watching our drama unfold.

I'm not surprised to find Hazel salty as fuck and pouting in gym class, and not in the cute way that Ollie does. At this point when it comes to her and Eric, she's the lesser of the two evils, which really shows how far Eric has gone off the rails. Between Danny's normal silence and Hazel's quiet moping, racquetball is extremely peaceful and passes quickly. None of us even acknowledge Hazel, but I have zero sympathy for the selfish, manipulative girl who has no compassion for others.

I change into street clothes for once—a black sweater and dark jeans with my combat boots. We usually just throw our gym sweats on over the tiny shorts and get the fuck out of there, but the snow has melted enough that I decide to run to the art supply store downtown after school.

Oliver eyes me speculatively on the way home. "Where are you going?" I'm surprised he didn't ask me in the locker room.

"Well, there's this awesome surfer boy from California that I'm starting to grow pretty fond of, and his birthday is on Wednesday, so. . ."

He chuckles and tries to convince me not to buy anything, just like I knew he would. "Finn, I don't need anything, seriously. Let's just order Angelo's again and have some beers. That's all I need."

"We can do that too if that's what you want, but I have some plans of my own." I pull into our garage and put the Jeep in park but leave the door open. I lean in and press my lips to his for a quick kiss. I know I surprised him, but he recovers fast and rewards me with a giant smile, complete with my favorite dimples.

"Now, go into the house, make a snack, do your homework, and take a nap. Hell, take a bubble bath if that's your thing. But, just relax, and I'll be home in a couple hours." He blushes, and I know he secretly likes it when I boss him around. He always listens.

Oliver scurries out of my Jeep, and I wait until he's inside before I head downtown, avoiding the highway as always.

I find a spot on a side street and parallel park my Jeep with expertise. I peer up at the colorful neon sign of the Art Emporium, located in the bottom corner suite of a major building downtown. I already know Oliver would love this place, and I haven't even stepped foot inside. I'll definitely be bringing him back.

Sometimes it blows my mind just how much my mindset has changed since meeting Oliver a little over a week ago. Now, I'm thinking about whether he would like something or not. I even find myself planning for things in the future. Things that will make me stay when all I've wanted for the last fourteen months is to get the fuck out and never look back.

I'm greeted by a short wisp of a girl. She has mousy brown hair and retro pink-framed glasses. Her apron has a rainbow of paint smeared on it, as do her shoes.

I probably sound like a pompous prick, demanding the best of everything, but I'm in a hurry to get back to Ollie. "I'll take every shade available in your best oil paints and acrylics. The most expensive set of brushes. Sketch pads. Easels. Those little colorful sticks he always has smudged everywhere—"

"Pastels?" Mary Anne supplies helpfully.

"Yes. Those. Your best. And anything else a serious artist could possibly want for their own studio."

I see the wheels turning and the dollar signs flashing across her eyes.

"Spare no expense. And I'd like next-day delivery for the big things."

She practically beams at me and says, "Yes, sir!" Even though I'm pretty sure we're the same age. Then she turns on her heel with a skip in her step to find the best of everything.

If Oliver doesn't want anyone else to know about his birthday, I get that. But it doesn't mean I'm not going to go all out for him. It's his eighteenth, and there's no one else here to celebrate his awesomeness except me.

CHAPTER FIFTEEN
OLIVER

"Happy birthday, Cali Boy." Finn's lips tickle me as he whispers into my ear, the soft caress of his words pulling me from sleep.

I grin, not opening my eyes. "Thanks. What time is it?" I mumble groggily.

"It's midnight. I wanted to be the first to wish you a happy birthday. Go back to sleep now." He brushes my hair back, and my stomach flips when I feel his lips ghost over my forehead. I'm already drifting off again, a goofy grin still on my face, when I hear my door click shut behind him. This is going to be a good birthday.

The bright morning sun filters through the cracks in my blinds, waking me before my alarm goes off. I stretch my arms above my head, arching my back until it pops. I'm wide awake as usual and ready for a great birthday with just Finn and me. I'm going to try to convince my mom I don't want a party when she gets back, but I won't hold my breath that she'll listen.

After a quick shower, I change into my uniform and check the texts from Mom that came through shortly after midnight. I chuckle, knowing she'd be bummed if she found out she wasn't the first to wish me a happy eighteenth birthday.

I wander downstairs, the scent of bacon filtering into my nose before I hear the hissing and popping from the skillet. Finn is standing at the stove, wearing his academy uniform and. . . a fucking *apron*.

"Is this my birthday surprise? Because I am fucking here for the apron, brother."

Finn spins around with a half-grin. "Oh, this is just the start. Better get prepared." The sparkle in his eyes tells me he's probably not joking.

"Go sit at the island. It may not be in bed, but I'll still serve you a damn good breakfast."

I one hundred percent agree with that and take my seat. Finn pulls a towering stack of waffles and a giant platter of scrambled eggs out of the warming drawer of the wall oven. I still haven't gotten used to how fancy my new home is. Mom and I didn't even have a dishwasher until I was twelve, let alone a fucking warming drawer. But I'm definitely not complaining about it when Finn places a warmed plate in front of me with three waffles stacked high and a single-lit birthday candle on top.

"I'm not singing to you, but go ahead and make a wish," he grumbles. As if he didn't wake up at least an hour early to make me a special feast.

I don't tell him I think my wish has already come true. Instead, I close my eyes and silently hope for all this to last. I blow out my candle and remove it, replacing it with two slices of butter and drowning the stack in delicious maple syrup. I pile my other plate high with eggs and bacon and dig in. I moan when the first bite of waffles hits my tongue

—crispy on the outside and warm and fluffy on the inside. *Perfect.*

Before I can swallow my first bite, my phone rings with an incoming FaceTime call, and I accept.

"Happy Birthday, baby boy!" Mom squeals as soon as her face pops into view.

I finish chewing my bite and swallow. "Thanks, Mom. How's your trip going?" She's been sending me a massive amount of photos and text updates, but it's nice to hear from her in person.

She gushes for a few minutes while I eat my food, unwilling to let it go cold or soggy. "I see you're eating a nice birthday breakfast. Did you cook all that?" She eyes me curiously because she knows I'm not really into cooking, just eating.

"Nope." I pop the "p" and tell her how Finn has been cooking a lot and that it's been amazing. He's sitting next to me, silently eating and letting me talk to my mother.

"Aw, Finn! Can you hear me?"

I angle the phone so she can see him sitting next to me.

"Hey, Vivian."

"Thank you for feeding and taking care of my baby. I knew I could count on you."

I chuckle because Finn goes a little pink in the cheeks. "It's nothing. I have to eat, too."

"Well, it still means a lot to me that you're being such a great big brother to my son." We glance at each other over the phone and cringe slightly. It's going to be a really awkward conversation if it ever gets to that point when we have to tell them we're together. *Romantically.*

We hear a door shut through the speaker and see Finn's dad walk into the room behind my mom. She turns around and motions him over. “Honey, I have the boys on FaceTime.”

Gabe strolls over and sits in the chair next to Mom, putting his arm around her and smiling. He looks. . . different. Lighter? Happier? I’m not sure exactly, but it’s clear the vacation and my mom are good for him and his temperament.

“Happy Birthday, Oliver,” Gabe says with a warm smile that’s surprisingly genuine. “Wyatt,” he nods to his son in greeting.

“Dad,” Finn reluctantly replies. I can tell he’s eyeing his dad the same way I am. Something is different about him. More positive. Hopefully it’s my mom rubbing off on him.

“So, before we left, your mother and I set up a bank account for you since you were seventeen. Your mom’s name is still on it, but you can go to the bank to remove it when we return. I just deposited five thousand dollars to start you off and as a birthday present.”

Say whaaat?

I’m honestly a little speechless. That’s really. . . thoughtful. And way too much, but I don’t want to disrespect him by denying his gift.

“Wow. I think I might be speechless. That’s incredible. Thank you so much, Gabe.”

“It’s good to start your adult life with a bank account and some savings. I’m just helping you get a jump on that. And you won’t need this for tuition or meal plans. This money is strictly yours.”

I risk another glance at Finn, and we lock eyes for a split second. Neither of us has told our parents we didn’t apply to any colleges and that we’re probably taking at least one gap year. But today, on my birthday, is *definitely* not the time to bring it up. Instead, I just smile and thank Gabe again.

"Okay, well, we have a dolphin cruise booked at eleven, so we need to get going. But I want an update at the end of the day on how your birthday was!"

"Sure thing Mom. Have fun."

We say our goodbyes and take our plates to the sink, working together to get the mess cleaned up before heading to the academy.

School flies by without any issues, which is a relief. Lately, it feels like there's some kind of drama at least every other day. I was trying to escape that shit when I moved, not dive head first right back into it.

Finn pulls into the garage and shuts the Jeep off, turning in his seat to face me. "Okay, so you'll see the first part of your surprise as soon as we walk in."

That has me perking up in my seat. "Really?"

He flashes me a wicked grin, boyish and devilish. "Let's go."

When we step out of the Jeep, Finn walks around and grabs my hand, tugging me toward the door like an impatient kid, making my stomach flutter. He's just as excited to show me his surprise as I am to receive it. A rush of warmth floods my veins, and I fall a little harder for this lost boy with so much depth.

We bound up the steps and walk through the mudroom, entering the hallway outside of the kitchen.

I suck in a sharp breath of air at what's in front of me.

I can't believe it...

A black cat sitting precariously on the edge of a wooden

table, guarding a bowl of fruit. The atmosphere is dark, but the cat's eyes and the fruit are bright, creating a beautiful contrast I've always admired.

"Finn. . ." I whisper, unable to properly form words.

"Shhh. Just wait."

Finn tugs on my hand again, and I'm helpless to stop him, following behind like a children's pull toy until we come to our next stop.

A horse stands tall and proud in a field of wildflowers, its dark mane blowing gently in the breeze. The purple sunset behind a forest shines through the trees, highlighting the beast's regal stature.

We keep moving, and I just keep seeing them. *All* of them. My grandmother's paintings, tastefully dispersed throughout the house. I can't believe Finn got them here in a few days. I'm shocked at his thoughtfulness.

Tears prick my eyes when we get to the last painting. A mother holding her baby. More accurately, my mother holding me. The look of pure love on her face is undeniable—the emotion is captured perfectly. Every brush stroke is preserved and timeless, and I can't help but tell Finn the story behind this one.

"I was nine before I noticed the baby had six fingers instead of five."

"What?" He huffs out a startled laugh.

"My grandmother. She accidentally painted six fingers on one of the baby's hands. No one noticed until I did, but she fixed it. You can't even tell."

I turn away from the painting that means so much to me. "Finn. . . What? How?" I know he got the number for the storage unit from my phone, but I figured he was just going to pass it to his dad to handle.

"You and Vivian deserve to make this your home. You

shouldn't even have a storage unit, and you damn sure shouldn't have these paintings packed away."

Hearing the reverence in his voice for my grandma's paintings makes me fall for him all the more.

I throw my arms around his neck and squeeze tight. "You have no idea how much this means to me. To my mom. She's going to flip out," I chuckle around a wet snif-fle. "Thank you."

He wraps his arms around my torso and squeezes me back. "This is just the appetizer. You ready for the main course?"

"Main course? Like ordering a pizza?"

"No," he laughs. "Come on." I let him continue to pull me where he wants because I like it. *So what*?

I find myself upstairs, in front of a closed door a few down from my bedroom. "What's this?" I ask.

"Your main surprise. Go in." Finn sweeps the air with his hand, palm up, in a very *Wheel of Fortune* gesture.

I turn the brushed nickel door knob and slowly push it in. I couldn't stop the gasp that escapes my lips even if I wanted to. My eyes flit around frantically, not stopping on one thing for more than two seconds. There are easels, drying racks, and invisible shelves filled with every color under the rainbow. I have a drawing table and a desk. A fucking refrigerator. A super retro red velvet couch is tucked into the corner, with an abstract rug and a huge flat screen TV mounted on the wall. It's all very artsy and colorful and *me*. How the hell did he pull this off?

It's a studio. A full fucking art studio.

I spin on my heel and stare at Finn with my mouth agape. His deep chuckle washes over me, sending a shiver down my spine. I can't find my words, so I close the distance between us and smash my mouth to his. I grab hold of his dark locks and angle our heads so that I can taste him better.

I finally unlatch my lips from his after a few minutes and stare straight into his dark blue depths. "Thank you. Thank you so fucking much. No one has ever given me so much." My voice catches on the last word. The amount of time, money, and energy he would have had to put into this in a matter of days is astounding. His generosity and kindness are unmatched. I just wish he could see himself the way I do. Under the hard, angry exterior is a sweet, kind boy that I just want to wrap my arms around and protect.

"I'm glad you like it, Cali Boy." He presses another tender kiss to my mouth and spins me around, pulling my back to his front. He engulfs me in his muscular arms and rests the side of his head against mine.

"I left the walls blank on purpose. The room is here, the supplies are here, and now it's yours to do whatever you please. Paint a mural, if you want."

My mind spins with a million possibilities, and I'm itching to get my hands on all the new paint. But I'd rather have my hands on something else right now, so I follow Finn out of my new studio, latching the door behind me.

"I already ordered the pizza—should be here around six. We could grab some beer and snacks and watch a movie while we wait?"

"Sounds perfect," I agree.

Finn slings an arm around my shoulders, his considerable bulk weighing me down as we head to the kitchen in search of food.

CHAPTER SIXTEEN
FINN

"I have one more present for you," I say, taking a risk. Oliver shoves his last bite of cake into his mouth and looks up at me with chipmunk cheeks and chocolate frosting smeared across his chin. I huff out an airy laugh and shake my head.

How can he look so cute when he eats like a complete savage?

Doesn't matter though. I'm still going to suck him off if he'll let me. I've been thinking about it a lot lately, and I really want to do it. I know how good it feels, and I want to give that same pleasure to Oliver.

"More presents?" he asks with a chocolate smile. His eyes glimmer with excitement. Oliver has no idea. I'm about to blow his fucking mind—and his dick.

"If you want. . . And if you're ready, I want to give you a birthday blowjob."

Oliver chokes as he tries to swallow the massive bite of cake in his mouth. He coughs, and I hand him his bottle of water.

"Jesus, Finn! You can't just say shit like that to a guy!" He pats the front of his chest and clears his throat.

His cerulean eyes meet mine, and his cheeks flush a slight pink. We've only made out and grinded against each other so far. No one came. Well, not unless you count me in the shower, jerking off to the memory of his soft lips exploring mine. It only took a few tugs before I spilled all over the shower wall like I'd never touched myself before.

"Are you sure?" he asks.

"Yes. Leave the cake. Let's go to my room. Now." I may be sucking his dick, but I'm still the one in charge here.

Oliver doesn't have to be told twice. He jumps up from his place at the kitchen island and races for the stairs. If he wants to be chased like a little bunny running from the big bad wolf, I can definitely oblige.

My bare feet slap against the shiny marble floor as I chase Ollie down the hall, through the formal living room, and up one side of the grand staircase in the foyer. His laugh is buoyant and infectious, and I find myself laughing and out of breath by the time I herd him into my bedroom, slamming the door shut behind me.

He turns around at the end of the bed and faces me—cheeks flushed, smile big and blinding. I stalk toward him, and my grin morphs into a predatory smirk. He swallows audibly but doesn't move a muscle.

I stand inches away, peering down at his nervous face. He's so beautiful like this, and I settle those nerves with a searing kiss, showing him how badly I want him.

It takes strength, but I peel my lips off his and push him backward. He falls to the bed, bounces, and settles on his elbows, gazing up at me. He bites his lip, waiting for my next move.

I place a knee on the end of my king-sized bed and prowl toward Oliver, crawling up his body until I reach his lips again. I plunder his mouth with my tongue, both of us groaning and rutting against each other. I slip my hand under his favorite black hoodie, trailing it up his stomach and enjoying every bump along the way. His lean muscles are sexy as fuck, and I need to see them. I push his hoodie up, and he takes the hint, leaning forward to pull it over the back of his head. He lies back down, breathing heavily while I greedily take him in. He still has faint yellow and green bruising on his ribs, but it doesn't take away from his fucking amazing body.

"Cali Boy, *God*, what are you doing to me? You're so fucking sexy." He doesn't have time to reply before he's whimpering out my name as I lick and kiss all over his torso. I find his tiny pink nipple and wonder if he'd like it if I sucked on them the way girls like it. Before I can second guess myself and my newfound love of a man's body, I go for it.

First, just a small lick and his abs contract. Then, I take the small bud into my mouth and suck, drawing out a long moan from Ollie. Finally, I bite down gently and his hips thrust up, desperately looking for more stimulation. Okay, so he likes it. I make a mental note. I lavish the same attention on the other side before I pull back and make eye contact with Oliver—silently asking for permission to take this further. Further than either of us has ever gone with a boy. He bites the corner of his lip and lifts his hips, giving me consent to continue.

I lean back on my heels and yank Oliver's silver basketball shorts and boxers down in one fell swoop. It's twenty degrees out, but he still wears them around the house all the time, teasing me with the outline of his dick. The anticipation of seeing it has been killing me, and *fuck*, it does not disappoint.

His cock bobs out, and it's fucking beautiful—long, not

too girthy, and curves slightly to the left. It's perfectly proportionate, and my mouth waters just looking at it.

Two weeks ago, if you had told me I'd be salivating over a dick, I probably would have punched you in the face.

I lean down and swipe my tongue from root to tip, swirling it around the head.

"Oh, fuuuck," Ollie groans out, fisting the bedsheets in both hands like it's more than he can take. But I haven't even started yet.

I lick up the beads of precum already oozing from his slit.

Tangy and salty, but not terrible.

Again, if you would have told me I'd be contemplating the flavor of jizz two weeks ago, I'd have punched you in the fucking face.

I suck his swollen, pink crown into my mouth and swirl my tongue along the underside. He thrusts his hips up and places his hands in my hair. He doesn't apply any pressure and doesn't try to force me to take more. I do, though. Take more. I push my mouth down as far as it will go, nearly taking him into the back of my throat. I just hold myself there, his pubes pressed to my nose and chin. I can feel his dick growing bigger in my mouth, so I pull back and pop off.

He's breathing heavily, chest rising and falling rapidly. He grips his hair tight, fisting the strands like he's wound so tight he's about to snap. "Finn. Don't stop. . . please." He punctuates his words with a thrust, making his hard cock bob.

I decide I like him like this—eager and pliant. *Needy*.

I put him out of his misery and slurp his angry tip back into my mouth. I lick and suck with vigor, bobbing my head up and down while I stroke the rest of his length in tandem.

He moves his hips with me, chasing his own release. It doesn't take long before Ollie yells a strangled shout while his cum shoots into my mouth, landing on my tongue. I swallow it all. Then I plop down on the bed next to him, waiting for him to recover.

He just lies there for a moment, enjoying his post-orgasm endorphin rush. After another minute, he rolls onto his side, unconcerned by his nudity, and tucks his hands under his head. "Finn. *Holy shit,* that was incredible. I can't believe I've been missing out on *that* my entire life," he whines, and I just chuckle. I knew it would blow his mind.

Ollie reaches out to slip his hand under my shirt, but I stop him before he can get too far.

"You don't have to do anything. That was for you," I explain.

"But I want to. I really, really want to." His voice is pleading and whiny; who am I to deny the man on his own birthday.

"Good. Because I really, really want you to," I say. "And I'm clean. I was tested after Hazel, and I've never been with anyone else. Just throwing that out there so there's no question."

"I'm clean, too," he replies, and I snort.

"Duh. Virgin," I tease, smiling at how ridiculously adorable he can be without even realizing it.

He gets a twinkle in his eye and slides his hand into my sweats, slipping beneath the underwear band and going straight for my cock, pulling it out. Guess he's getting me back for the virgin comment because there is *nothing* virginal about the way he's grasping me right now.

I groan at the feel of his soft, warm hand squeezing my cock. He caresses me from root to tip, twisting his hand over my sensitive head on each upstroke. I moan at the incredible sensation. It's never felt this good before.

"Ollie. Fuck. That feels amazing. I'm almost about to come already." Fuck it. There's no way I can hold on much longer, not with the feeling of his hand on my dick for the first time. My hips jerk up in a frantic pace with each of his strokes. I feel the orgasm travel down my spine, and my balls draw up. I grit my teeth and grab onto the bed sheets on either side of me.

"I'm coming!" It's a ragged exclamation, but my voice squeaks, actually fucking squeaks, when Oliver quickly shoves his mouth down on my cock, sucking me with so much force my eyes roll into the back of my head. I pulse in his mouth, and he swallows it all down.

"Mmm." He licks his lips. "I've never tasted cum before." His innocent statement is sexy as fuck, and my dick twitches with an aftershock.

"Oliver. . . that was. . . Wow."

"Same," he agrees.

CHAPTER SEVENTEEN
FINN

There's something hard digging into my hip, poking me, and I move my arm to brush it away. I expect to come into contact with hard plastic, maybe the TV remote. Instead, I brush hard *skin*—warm, velvety skin over steel—and wrap my hand around it, hearing a sleepy groan in response. It's like a shot of espresso directly into my veins, and my eyes instantly pop open, memories of last night flooding in. I can't believe how *good* it is with a guy.

I peek under the covers. Ollie is curled around me, still naked and tucked into my side. I'm naked too and sporting my own raging morning wood. His soft hand rests on my abdomen, nails painted neon blue for his birthday yesterday. I'm not sure what it says about me—and I really don't give a fuck—but seeing Oliver's smaller yet masculine hand, tipped with blue polish and wrapped around my cock last night really did it for me. I want to see it again. Feel him again. Fucking *taste* him again.

Ollie's deep breathing tells me he's still asleep, so I gingerly roll him onto his back and silently slip down the bed, underneath the sheets. He doesn't even stir, but he's about to.

I give him one long lick from base to tip and wait for a reaction. Nothing. Okay, I can do better than that.

Ollie still smells like sex and cum and sweat, and I fucking love it. I press my face to his groin, inhaling his addictive, musky scent. Before he can wake up to me smelling his junk like an absolute fucking weirdo, I swallow his dick and take him all the way to the back of my throat.

I don't know what I was expecting, but the quiet whimpering and moaning while he's still half asleep is turning me on exponentially. I can feel the precum leaking out of my own cock, smearing all over the silk sheets beneath me. I try not to rut against the bed, but it proves a difficult task because my dick is so fucking hard right now it's almost painful. I hollow my cheeks and suck harder, his whines and twitches spurring me on.

His breathing picks up, and I feel the sheet lift. I don't stop my punishing pace, still sucking him furiously, but I peer up, and we make eye contact. As soon as my eyes lock onto his baby blues, he comes with a strangled gasp—spurting load after load into the back of my throat—and I swallow it all down.

I crawl back up the sheets and pop my head out like nothing happened.

"Morning," I say and give him a peck on the mouth before flopping back down on my side of the bed.

Hah. My side of the bed. My brain apparently thinks we're an old married couple. What the fuck is wrong with me? Am I obsessed? Fuck, might be.

"Finn," he breathes out. "What was that for?"

I shrug. "Do I need a reason to suck your cock?"

His cheeks pinken. "No, definitely not. You never need a

reason. No reasons needed here. Just a dick available to suck any time of the day."

An unexpected laugh bursts from me, which seems to happen a lot more lately, and I shake my head at him, tucking my unruly strands behind my ears.

"Okay, noted. It's currently open season on Oliver's dick. Got it."

His pink cheeks turn crimson, but he smiles wide, showcasing the dimples I love so much. "What about you? Can I return the favor?" He nods to the giant tent in the sheets.

I glance at the harsh red numbers of my alarm clock to check the time. "Shit! We need to be at school in thirty minutes!" I exclaim, whipping the bedding off and heading for my bathroom. I must have shut the alarm off during my orgasm-induced slumber.

"I'll just tug one out in the shower real quick. You can make it up to me tonight." I wink before shutting the door behind me, leaving him naked and strung out in my bed. Just the way I like him.

The day goes by in a blur. It's getting harder and harder to keep my hands off Oliver at school. I have to keep reminding myself that he doesn't need the added stress of something like this getting out, and neither do I. I know Ollie left some bad things behind, and I have the nagging suspicion that it had to do with him being gay. But I can hardly push him to open up when I haven't.

We're walking to the cars after school with Jared and Ethan, discussing our plans for the weekend. It's still too cold for flag football, and there's supposed to be more snow on Sunday, too. "We should have a chill Saturday at my place and just play video games. No Eric, though," I say.

"Fucking right, bro," Ethan chimes in. "What the hell has crawled up his ass? It's like he's got some kind of passive-aggressive hard-on for Oliver or something."

"Yeah, except it's not so passive, is it? You saw him slam the shit out of Oliver on day one," Jared adds.

"Hello? Guys? Standing right here," Ollie says as he waves his hand between them.

Ethan smiles. "Sorry, dude."

Jared scrubs a hand across the top of his buzzed head, eyes contemplative. "Danny won't come if Eric does, so let's not tell him."

We all agree and pull our phones out to start a group chat, minus Eric.

"Shit. I must have left my phone in my gym locker. I'll be right back." Before I can stop him, Ollie jogs off, back toward the gym.

Ten minutes later, the three of us are still standing next to Jared's matte black Challenger, rubbing our arms for warmth as the frigid February air pummels us.

Ollie comes hustling down the sidewalk that runs parallel to the student lot, his messenger bag flopping against his hip. He's about halfway to us when Eric zooms past in his lifted Ford truck, way faster than anyone has any business going in a school parking lot. I swear he swerves slightly because he perfectly hits a big, slushy mud puddle.

It happens in slow motion. The freezing cold, muddy water arches up in a tidal wave before it slams down with the force of a thousand frozen icicles straight into Oliver.

The shock and force knock him off his feet and into the wet, snowy grass. Eric doesn't even stop—just drives by, out of the front gate, like he didn't almost perpetrate a hit-and-run.

The three of us drop our bags and take off across the lot. I'm out of breath by the time I get there, lungs seizing from the cold, but Ollie is already up, flinging mud and ice off his hands and arms.

"Jesus *fucking* Christ!" he shouts, shaking his now wet and shaggy blond head. More mud and ice fly off. He's fucking soaked from head to toe, and it's thirty-five degrees out. He may as well have jumped in fucking Lake Michigan.

"Let's go!" I shout at all three of them. "We need to get him warm and dry, right fucking now!"

Don't they know hypothermia is fucking real?

Like I will it into motion, Ollie's teeth start to chatter.

"Shit," Jared and Ethan say in unison.

Ethan grabs Ollie's bag while Jared and I help rush his shaking body over to my Jeep.

I toss my keys to Ethan. "Crank the heat up." I can't even think about the fact that someone else will be driving; I need to focus on Oliver. He's more important. I shut the part of my brain down that's freaking out right now. I can only handle one catastrophe at a time.

Jared opens the backseat, and I sit Ollie down, peeling his soaked pea coat off first. I climb in after him, and Jared hops in the passenger seat.

"My place," I rumble. Ethan listens, leaving Jared's car behind at the academy.

"Finn. . . y-you're. . . o-ver. . . react. . . t-ting," he stutters between chattering teeth.

"Uh-huh. Sounds like it." I hate to be sarcastic, but it's time to get a move on it. I rummage through my gym bag and pull out a hand towel, tossing it to him so he can dry his face and hair.

"Take your hoodie off."

Ollie huffs out a disgruntled breath but listens. His fingers tremble and slip on the hem, so I brush them aside. "Move, let me."

I glance at my friends in the front seat, but they're not paying attention. It's just us right now. I swiftly lift his sweatshirt and T-shirt, stripping them from his body. I bite my lip. *Shit*. Now is not the time to think about his tight abs and hard little nipples that practically beg me to suck on them to warm them up.

Ollie doesn't miss the appreciative stare I'm giving his body and stutters a half-frozen chuckle. I toss my puffy coat over his lap and shake the inappropriately timed thoughts from my mind and go for the waistband of his sweatpants.

"Finn. . ." He squirms and glances at the front seat before looking back down and lifting his butt up so I can slide his sweatpants down. I take his tiny gym shorts and boxer briefs, too. It's all soaked through. I take my own sweatshirt off and slip it over his head, then pull out my plaid uniform pants and hand them over.

"They'll be too big, but put them on."

Lastly, I make him bundle up in my winter coat, beanie, and gloves.

It only takes fifteen minutes to get home, and the Jeep has warmed up considerably, but Ollie's still shivering violently. I rub the hand towel over his head, trying to dry his wet hair more.

"Ethan, can you start a fire? Jared, hot chocolate for everyone. I'm going to run upstairs for blankets and a change of clothes."

"Finn, I'm w-warm now. I'm more w-worried about my st-stuff."

"Yeah, well, I'm more worried about you," I bite back. "I

can buy you more stuff. I can't buy another you." I realize I've shown more cards than I'd like with that single statement. At least Ethan and Jared were off doing shit and didn't hear. I purposely don't look at him. Instead, I turn around and jog upstairs to get us a warm change of clothes.

We don't normally hang out in the formal living room, but it has the largest fireplace. When I return downstairs, Ethan already has it loaded with logs and a fire blazing high. I haven't fully stepped into the room and can feel the toasty heat from here. Ollie is on the couch where I left him, huddled under the small throw blanket we keep there for decoration. I set down a neatly folded pile of clean boxers, thick wool socks, a thermal, and a new pair of sweats.

"You can wash the mud out of your hair later. We just need to get you warmed up first." I nod to the small hallway bathroom between the living room and kitchen. "Go change."

He gathers the clothes and stumbles on shaky legs toward the bathroom. I grab his hand. "Hey, you got it?" I don't need to elaborate. I'm asking if I need to figure out a way to sneak in with him and help without Ethan or Jared seeing.

"I'm good, bro," he replies and shuffles along.

Ten minutes later, we're all sitting on the big couch, squished together and nearly sweating under the weight of the down comforter that Jared dragged in from the downstairs guest room. Ollie is in the middle, and we're all cuddling him in a big puppy pile, sipping our hot chocolate, as Ethan flips through my Netflix list. I kept him on the other side of Jared, not touching Ollie. I know he's cool, but after that little flirty moment last week, he doesn't need to be touching what's mine.

Fuck. There I go again with the possessive thoughts.

I feel around under the comforter until I find Ollie's now warm hand and lace our fingers together, resting them on my thigh.

Ethan presses play on *All American*, one of my favorite football shows, and we start it from the beginning of season one.

"What's for dinner?" Ethan enquires, and I snort because it sounds like he's asking his mother.

"Leftover pizza," I deadpan. I'm not fucking cooking for them.

Ethan's pretty easygoing, so he just chuckles and says, "Fine with me."

Leftover deep dish it is.

CHAPTER EIGHTEEN

FINN

"Fuck. I thought they'd never leave," I say, nuzzling Ollie's neck as we lie in my bed listening to Kid Cudi—the smooth lyrics of "Mr. Rager" infiltrate my mood and relax me. A couple of hours after dinner, the guys called an Uber and left to retrieve Jared's car from school. I thanked them again and promised fresh pizza and beer this weekend. And now, I don't want to do shit but lie here in bed with Ollie.

"I want to hold you," I blurt. Pretty sure I just handed in my man card saying that, but it's true. I just want to cuddle. And I've *never* wanted to cuddle with anyone in my entire fucking life. But seeing Ollie hurt again. . . it hasn't been a good day for me, and I need a fucking hug.

"Come here." I grab Ollie by the waist and roll us so that I'm flat on my back and he's on top of me.

He lets out a cute little *oof* and braces his forearms on either side of my head, holding most of his weight off of me. "I'll squish you," he says, and I snort.

"You won't fucking squish me, now lie down." Our

bodies line up perfectly. I can wrap my arms around him and tuck his head right under my chin, so I do just that.

"I wanted to hop in my Jeep and chase Eric down," I confess, squeezing him tighter to me. "He could have fucking hit you. *Killed* you." I close my eyes and breathe deep, shoving the awful memories of my past back down where they belong. When I open my eyes again, Ollie is peering up at me—worry clouding his bright gaze.

He reaches up with soft fingers and traces the scar along my cheekbone. "Finn. I'm okay." I turn my head, clenching my jaw, and his hand falls away. He sees too much sometimes.

Ollie places his warm palm on my cheek, steering my gaze back to his. "It's okay to let people in, Finn. It's okay to let *me* in."

I swallow the lump in my throat, hugging him tighter when he lays his head back down on my chest. I rest my chin on him again, smelling his clean hair and the sandalwood and honeysuckle shampoo he loves to use.

It turns out I don't have a choice but to let him in more. Tonight's the night. The universe must have willed it.

"Finn, wake up!"

I bolt upright, my eyes automatically scanning the darkness, searching for the threat. Slivers of moonlight permeate the blinds, guiding my frantic gaze around the otherwise pitch-black room.

"Hey, it's me," Ollie whispers, rubbing my back, now sticky with sweat. I deflate, flopping back down. There's no threat. Except for the one to my sanity.

I must have had another nightmare.

I scrub my hands over my face and take deep breaths until my heaving chest settles. Yesterday brought up too much bad shit. My mind is fighting against me now.

I don't even want to know what I was doing that woke Ollie up. It could be any number of things. Crying. Sobbing. Screaming. Struggling against invisible restraints. That's always a fun one.

Goddammit.

Sometimes I feel like I'm still stuck upside down in the passenger seat, struggling to get free. I should have been more careful about sleeping in the same bed as him. Such a fucking idiot. Of course it was only a matter of time before this happened.

"Finn, stop. Please. Just talk to me." I don't even realize I'm still roughly rubbing my hands over my face and head, having a complete mental breakdown in front of the one person I need to be strong for. I drop my arms to my sides and groan.

"You don't have to be so strong all the time, you know? It's okay to be hurt, to be vulnerable. Isn't that what you told me that first day, Finn? Hmm?"

I swear to God, it's like he can read my fucking mind.

"Talk to me. Please," he begs.

My thoughts are so heavy they're weighing me down, trying to pull me under. I have to get this off my chest.

"My mom's dead because of me. That's why my dad hates me, too."

I figure that about summarizes things.

"Finn. . . no. You can't possibly think that." He grabs my hand and curls onto his side, eyes roving over my face while I gaze at nothing on the ceiling. I can't look at him while I tell him the worst part of my life.

"Finn?"

"Yeah?"

"What did you mean when you said your dad hates you too? Who else do you think hates you?"

I freeze. *Shit*. Did I really say that?

"Um. No one. Didn't mean anything by it."

"Come on. Just be honest with me, and I'll do the same. It's only fair."

That has me perking up a bit and becoming slightly more agreeable.

"I guess. . ."

"Yes?"

"I guess I just hate me, too. That's who. Me. I hate myself for letting her die. Being the reason she was there, on that highway, on that day, and that late at night. Distracting her with jokes and football talk. We were on our way home from winning the state championship. She's dead because of me. Dad hates me, and he has every fucking right to." My voice doesn't crack, which I'm proud of.

"Finn. It was an *accident*. It was *not* your fault."

"Yeah, I know it was a drunk driver. But I distracted her, Oliver. I did that. And she died because of it."

The truth hangs in the air between us, heavy and suffocating.

"Wyatt, look at me."

My attention snaps to him at his use of my real name. His eyes seem to glow under the light of the moon, and he looks ethereal and otherworldly, half cast in shadow.

"Listen to me. I don't know if you've had therapy or what, but that is absolutely one hundred percent not your fault. You're beating yourself up over something out of your control—*hurting* yourself, *punishing* yourself. You need to talk to your dad. You can't keep skirting around the issue and burying it deep down. There is *no* fucking way he blames you, no matter how much of a dick he is."

"You don't know him like I do. Haven't spent the last fifteen months being ignored, abandoned, and *controlled*." I grit my teeth at that last one because it's the worst for me. It's fucked me up, too. I can admit that. I need control. *Everywhere*. In a vehicle. Around other people. And apparently in the bedroom, too.

"Promise me you'll at least talk to him sometime soon?"

"Maybe," I grunt, just to move on from the topic of my dad and our fucked up relationship.

My dad is toxic. *I'm* toxic.

These bright and hopeful and *good* people. We're going to taint them, destroy that good in them—it's only a matter of time. Vivian and Oliver should have never come here.

"You and your mom shouldn't have come here."

He rears his head back like I've slapped him and sucks in a sharp breath of air.

I hurry to explain myself. "You and your mom. . . you're full of light and positivity and happiness. This house. It died right along with my mom. You shouldn't have come here. We'll only bring you down. And you don't deserve that. Vivian doesn't deserve that."

"Wyatt, listen to me right fucking now. You. Are. Wrong. It's quite the opposite, actually. You're not bringing us down. We're going to bring you up, adding positivity and spreading the sunshine, brother." He cheeses real big, and his white teeth shine in the moonlight.

"Did you not see the change in your dad? Because I did. Talk to him, okay? For me?" he asks.

I sigh, knowing I'll give in. Anything for him. "I'll try to find the right time," I concede.

"Thanks, Finn." Ollie scoots over and snuggles into my

side. "You're a good person, okay? I've never met anyone who's ever. . . taken care of me the way you do. Or had my back. Or kissed my face off, or. . . other things."

I chuckle at his rambling. "Thank you for seeing me better than I can see myself, Ollie." I squeeze him to my side and kiss his soft hair.

"It's your turn to share now," I tell him.

His pain is hiding in the shadow of his eyes, but I've seen it. Recognized it. Fucking *felt* it. And I'm not letting him get away without spilling his own guts.

"Tell me what happened to you, Cali Boy."

CHAPTER NINETEEN
OLIVER

It's still dark in Finn's room, but the light from the moon peeks through the gaps in the blinds, allowing me to see his face. Neither of us has turned a lamp on. I think we both feel more comfortable spilling our deepest secrets in the relative safety of the dark. We're lying together on Finn's bed, and I'm curled around him as usual. I already agreed to share my own fucked up past, so here goes nothing.

"Fair enough," I say, trying to gather my thoughts and figure out exactly where I want to start this pathetic story.

"So, I know you've overheard some things from my mom, and I've let a few things slip as well. But basically, at the start of this year, I decided I'd had enough of hiding and staying in the closet. I wanted a boyfriend. I wanted to have my first kiss." I smile because Finn gave me the best first kiss I could have ever hoped for.

"I came out to my mom first, and you know her. She was amazing and supportive and encouraging. It went perfectly, and I think I got a false sense of security from that, automatically assuming that all of my friends would react the same way. I mean, they were supposed to be my best friends and care about me, you know?" I use my index finger to chip away at the polish on my thumb, my left hand tucked tightly between Finn's body and mine.

"The first weekend after school started, we all got together at my best friend Micah's beachfront cottage. We always met at his place to surf together since he had beach access in his backyard." Finn grabs my fidgeting hand and rubs soothing circles on the back of it with his thumb, encouraging me to continue.

"I couldn't work up the courage until after we were done surfing. I spent hours on the water trying to have fun, but I was silently freaking out the whole time. It sucked. Anyway, we had just slipped out of our trunks and rinsed off in Micah's outdoor shower. Something we always did, no big deal. It's not like we checked each other out or anything, and we'd all been friends and surfing buddies since grade school."

I know I'm rambling, but I still don't understand exactly why they acted the way they did.

"We were in his kitchen, towels wrapped around our waists. And okay, in hindsight, maybe that wasn't the best idea. Maybe I should have waited until we were clothed, but by that point, the anxiety was riding me hard, and I needed to get it out."

I sigh, knowing I've yet to tell the hard parts. "They laughed. Thought I was joking. When they realized I wasn't, the humor on their faces vanished and morphed into shock, then anger. I can still remember what Micah said to me, word for word. My best friend since third grade."

"What'd he say?" Finn rumbles.

"I thought I knew you. But you've been a liar and a fag

this whole time. All those times you saw me naked. Slept in my bed. Did you like it? God! That's fucking sick, dude! Get out of my house."

"*Jesus Christ*. Ollie, that's a really fucked up thing to remember word for word."

"I can't help it. It's seared into my memory for all time. There's no erasing it, no forgetting it. Micah was my *best friend*. And he dropped me so fast my head spun from the shock. I couldn't even defend myself. I just grabbed my bag and stumbled out to my car, completely numb. Drove home in a fucking beach towel."

"Fuck Micah," Finn says, and I agree.

"Yeah, fuck Micah," I sniffle. My eyes sting, but I blink away the wetness.

"Seriously, Oliver, don't waste another tear on those fuckboys, okay? Please don't cry. They don't deserve you."

"I'm not," I protest, sniffling some more. "It's just really hard to repeat all of this, and I want to be done talking about it. So yeah, after I came out, it was like a switch was flipped in them. They did a complete one-eighty. Turned cruel and callous overnight. By the time I made it to school Monday morning—with puffy, bloodshot eyes—the damage was done. They'd *outed* me to everyone. And not just outed me, they spread lies about me. Made up all this stuff about me checking them out for years and trying to put the moves on them. Just all of this utterly ridiculous, homophobic bullshit. Of course there were a few sympathizers; it's not like I was the only gay kid at school. But I *was* the only gay *popular* kid."

I close my eyes and tell myself I'm away from them now. And I have Finn, and he'd never let anyone treat me that way again. It helps, so I continue.

"For an entire semester, I took their abuse, constantly.

Every. Fucking. Day." I don't get into the specifics of every horrible slur thrown my way or the half dozen times I was shoved to the ground for accidentally grazing one of them in the cramped hallways between classes. He doesn't need every pitiful detail. It'll only further my embarrassment.

Finn lets go of my hand, pulling me on top of him again and tucking my head under his chin. "Fuck, Ollie, how are you so strong?" He squeezes the nape of my neck, and I relax slightly.

"Just because I wear it well doesn't mean it's not weighing me down. I've just decided to smile instead of cry. I changed my phone number and deleted my social media. I cut off all contact with my old life back in Marlo Bay. It sucks because I loved my town, but I didn't love the homophobia and hate. I can only hope that maybe one day they'll realize what they did to their *supposed* best friend was disgusting and cruel. And you know, karma's a bitch and all that."

"That would have never happened to you if I was there. I'd have kicked all their asses."

I grin into his neck. "I know you would have, Finn." And then I press a gentle kiss to his Adam's apple. Ever my protector, and I fucking love it.

Both of us are dragging ass this morning after our impromptu therapy session in the middle of the night. But I also feel lighter because of it, and I'm grateful there aren't any secrets between us anymore. Finn isn't too tired to confront Eric, though. As soon as we park the Jeep, he's hopping out and storming over to Eric's truck, where he's hanging out with Hazel.

"Why'd you do that, cunt?"

Okay. Looks like we're throwing out C-words first thing in the morning.

"What?" Eric laughs, a puff of breath escaping his thin lips and dispersing into the frozen air around us.

"You know what you did yesterday, you stupid fucking coward."

"Wyatt, please. It's a bit early to be tossing around such crass words," Hazel chimes in, even though no one was talking to her.

"Mind your business." He doesn't even glance at her, and I know it pisses her off when her nostrils flare in outrage.

"I don't know what you're talking about, dude," Eric says, playing innocent like always.

"Bullshit. You swerved into that massive puddle just as Ollie was walking by. You drenched him in icy water and knocked him off the sidewalk. You could have hit him or someone else, driving like that in a fucking school parking lot."

"Just because you have issues with vehicles, doesn't mean the rest of us do. You're overreacting. I didn't do shit."

Oh fuck.

I glance from Eric to Finn and back again. This dude is seriously fucking stupid if he thinks he can say something like that and get away scot-free. Finn clenches his fists and steps forward, but I throw my arm out, halting his momentum. He can't get suspended or expelled; that would leave me here, all alone.

Hazel decides to stay in the conversation, inserting her own special brand of venom. "Yeah, Finn. Did you ever tell Oliver about your issues with cars? Or have you just forbidden him to drive?"

She doesn't wait for an answer, just keeps spewing her vitriol. "Oliver, I tried to warn you on day one about him. To watch out for his anger and violent behavior." She sidles closer to me and rests her blood-red talons on the sleeve of my puffy winter coat. Thanks to the other clown in front of me, my peacoat is destined for a trip to the dry cleaner.

"He hasn't hurt you, has he?" She whispers loud enough for Eric and Finn to hear, and it's full of fake concern. I slip my arm out from under her hand. I'm done with her shit.

"I'm not even going to acknowledge that absurd question with an answer. You've been cold-hearted and hateful since I first met you. Telling me Finn's personal business and lying about him. Trying to make him look bad when it only makes you look like a raging, psycho bitch."

I cross my arms and stare them down, taking a play from Finn's book. "Fuck you, Hazel. And fuck you, Eric. Stay the fuck away from us, you miserable cunts."

Guess it really is a C-word kind of morning.

Finn and I turn on our heels in unison and march to Preston Hall. That felt good—actually, it felt fucking amazing.

"Sorry I didn't tell you that Hazel warned me about you on the first day of school. We had only just met, but I already knew her words were lies. I could tell she was bitter, maybe an ex-girlfriend or something. I didn't want to push you to talk about anything personal when we didn't even know each other yet—"

"Ollie." Finn cuts me off. "It's fine, seriously. I know that bitch is poison, and you've only ever had kindness in your heart. Don't even sweat it."

Finn wraps his arm around my shoulder, even though we're at school, as we walk up the main sidewalk to Preston

Hall. I side-eye the people around me, but no one's really paying attention. Guess we just look like two bros.

"Thanks for stopping me from knocking Eric out," Finn says as we stand by our lockers, organizing our books for the day. "There's something else I should probably tell you about why it's so important that I don't get expelled."

I stare at him, not sure what else he's been hiding.

"If I don't graduate from Lake View, my dad gets control of my trust fund until I'm twenty-five. So, I absolutely cannot get expelled. I'm almost free from being under his thumb. I have my money now, but I have to graduate to keep control of it."

"A trust fund?" I echo because, um, *what*? That is some super fancy rich kid shit. I obviously knew Gabe was wealthy; I mean, look at his house. It's barely even a house, more like a mansion. But I didn't know Finn had his own money. That definitely explains a lot of things that have happened in the past two weeks.

"It's probably reason number two why he hates me. I have more money than him."

I choke on my own spit. "*More* money? Then your *dad*?"

"Yeah, my trust fund is from my mom's side of the family. She never flaunted it, but she came from old money. Dad is new money. Everything he has and everything he's become, he made happen for himself. And *that*, I do respect. But it doesn't change the fact that I know he's salty because I have more money than him. More than he ever *could* have, too."

"Jesus, Finn. Are you a millionaire or something?"

"About fifty times over," he says smugly.

Holy. Fucking. Shit.

I'm a sugar baby.

CHAPTER TWENTY

FINN

After that startling revelation this morning, I'm surprised and happy to find Oliver acting like nothing has changed. I mean, it's a lot to take in, and it's kind of human nature to act differently when you find out something like that. But I'm still just me, and it's a relief that he's still just Oliver. I never tell people about my trust fund. Anyone who has ever found out about the money acts differently. I don't want their fake respect; I need real loyalty in my life. And it looks like I've found that with Ollie.

God. He is something else.

I watch him as we walk to the cafeteria from our lockers. His nails are still neon blue from his birthday, and now he has several silver rings adorning his fingers and thumbs. He clutches at the crossbody strap of his messenger bag as we walk. His white dress shirt and navy blazer fit him perfectly, and his plaid slacks are tailored in a slim, lean fit, hugging his tight little ass and legs snuggly. His nose ring is silver today, and his hair is coiffed to perfection, tall on top with the sides still shaved low. His features are delicate yet masculine, and his lips are full and pouty.

He catches me looking, and a huge smile graces his doll-like face. He's smiling so wide I think I can see every fucking tooth in his mouth—even his molars. And the dimples. . . *fuck*. . . the dimples get me every damn time.

"What?" I grumble.

"Nothing," he says, then glances around. "Just happy," he whispers and links his pinky finger with mine for two seconds before quickly dropping it.

I want to hold his hand so badly, but instead, I shove mine into my tight ass pants pockets as best I can. I probably look awkward and ridiculous, but if I don't put my hands somewhere else, I might touch him. He's too tempting to me.

We get to the cafeteria and take our normal seats. Bethany is sitting with us again today. She doesn't hang out with many of the girls at the academy. She gets along better with the guys since she's not snobby like most of the bratty rich girls here. Hazel Bell being the worst.

Eric is still at the end of the table, and it's starting to piss me off that Trace is still acting buddy-buddy with him, even though Eric has always treated his brother like shit. I scan the cafeteria for Jayden and see him sitting with his own sophomore friends today.

Good.

Eric's an opportunistic predator and always finds the weak, separating them from the group and attacking. I don't understand how we were ever friends, but I just need to try and distance myself at this point. He's not worth losing fifty million dollars. I tell myself that whenever my cold stare meets his jealous eyes, green with envy.

Why? Why are you so jealous, Eric?

Bethany interrupts my internal ramblings with her chipper voice. "My cousin, Alyssa, has the hookup at the newest spa opening downtown if anyone wants to go tomorrow. Before they even have their grand opening." Does she not realize she's talking to a table of guys?

"Looks like Oliver needs a new manicure. He might go with you," Eric sneers from the end of the lunch table.

Before I can even respond or blow up, Oliver handles himself for the second time in a few hours. "Nah. Sorry, Bethany. I'm busy tomorrow. We're having a guys' day at our place. Last weekend before the parents get home, you know." Then he whips his searing gaze to the end of the table where fuckface is sitting. "And you're not invited."

Hah! It may be petty, but that was funny as fuck. I snort out a laugh instead of storming down there and losing control of my inheritance with one unsatisfying hit.

Thank you, Oliver. Again.

There's a pause—everyone is silent, unmoving. My eyes dart around the group, weighing the energy to see how they might react. They don't want Eric there either, but we planned to be a little more subtle about it and not tell the dude flat out.

Ethan is the first to break the silence as a booming laugh explodes out of him. "Damn, dude, that was cold," he hiccups. The rest of the table erupts into laughs, and even stoic Danny quirks a smile. Eric turns beet red, which fucking serves him right. A little embarrassment is nothing compared to the shit he's said and done to Ollie.

"Fuck all of you," Eric grumbles and grabs his lunch tray, storming away.

Can't help myself. "That's right! Walk away, fuckface!" I shout across the cafeteria, and everyone stops talking and turns in unison to stare at me.

Nosy fuckers. I just turn back around and take another bite of my chicken Caesar wrap; like five hundred people aren't boring holes into the back of my head right now.

Jared sighs dramatically. "You do realize you probably just made things ten times worse, right, Finn? You too, Oliver."

"Yeah, well, he can't keep treating me like garbage. I'm not going to be bullied by him anymore."

I squeeze Ollie's thigh under the table in support. Proud of him for standing up for himself. We can deal with any consequences together. I won't allow Eric to hurt him.

We're finally switching to a new sport after nearly two weeks of racquetball. And thankfully, it's basketball. That means the girls will be on one side of the gym, and the guys will be on the other. I was not looking forward to spending the entire class with Hazel after Ollie called her and Eric cunts this morning. She insinuated that I've hurt him. Put my hands on him. Makes me fucking sick, and I don't care to see or speak to the bitch ever again. Maybe I should take Bethany up on her long-standing offer to kick Hazel's ass.

Danny, Ollie, and I run drills with two other kids from class—setting up cones and working on hand-eye coordination, which seems to be Coach Donavan's theme for the semester. I put thoughts of Hazel and Eric out of my mind and concentrate on getting through the rest of class. Just a little while longer, and I can take Ollie home and make him come some more.

Coach blows his whistle. "Finnegan! Chase!" My eyes snap to his, and he motions us over. "Collect the cones and take them down to the storage room. I'm going to have everyone run through a few layups, then call it an early day. You boys can head home after you put the equipment up." He slaps me on the shoulder, and we scuttle away, ready to get the fuck out of here.

"Start stacking the cones, and I'll grab the bags." I jog to the back of the gym, and then we load the cones up and sling the bags over our shoulders. We practically sprint downstairs to the locker room, opening the storage room and tossing the mesh bags inside. We hurry to our area of the locker room and grab our belongings.

"I'm kinda sweaty. I'm gonna put a clean shirt on first," Ollie says before whipping his gray gym shirt over his head. But he just stands there, in the middle of the room, shirtless and sporting a giant erection in his tiny gym shorts. I start to have a filthy fantasy that needs to come to life.

I stalk toward Ollie and roughly slam my mouth against his, walking him backward until he's pressed against the cold metal bank of lockers. We have ten minutes tops before the rest of the class finishes up and comes in to shower or leave for the day. I rub my greedy hands all over his bare torso, pinching and tweaking his nipples just how I know he likes it. He moans into my mouth and thrusts his hips forward. I chuckle into his mouth. "So impatient."

"Hurry, Finn, I need to come. *Please*."

We could easily head home and pick this right back up, but neither of us can wait. I need this now, too. We've both realized how good it actually is with a guy, and we're needy as fuck.

I pull his shorts down and then my own, bending my knees slightly so our dicks rub against each other. We groan at the contact, looking down at them lined side by side. I hold my hand out and spit into it, then look directly into his eyes. His pupils are so blown that I can only see a tiny ring of blue. “Spit,” I command, and he obeys.

I reach down and take both of our cocks into my hand and start to jerk us off together. The wet squelches echoing throughout the empty locker room are obscene. “I’m not gonna last,” I grit out, not stopping the punishing pace on our dicks.

“Me neither, that’s the point,” he pants as he kisses down my neck and bites me right where my shoulder meets.

My dick pulses, and I nearly blow my load from the slight sting of pain. We both fuck my hand, chasing our orgasms. The feel of his dick rubbing against my own, sticky with our combined spit, is so fucking hot and so fucking *filthy*.

I reach around with my free hand and grab his bare ass. I slip my fingers between his crease and graze his tight hole. I’ve barely even touched him, but he instantly seizes up, shouting out my name as hot spurts of cum shoot out of his dick and onto my own. He slumps against the lockers, completely spent.

I continue to jack myself off with the extra lube of his cum. It’s so wet and slippery and just *wrong* that my nuts draw up after a few strokes, and I shoot my load all over Oliver’s stomach, smearing it in with the tip of my dick for good measure.

Oliver still hasn’t moved; he’s completely blissed out. I chuckle at the dopey smile on his face.

“Let’s go, Cali Boy, before they catch us with our pants down, covered in jizz.”

He barks out a laugh and straightens up, looking down at my cum still on his stomach and his little shorts stuck around his knees.

"Catch!" I toss him an extra hand towel, and he quickly wipes up and pulls his shorts back up.

We put our academy sweats over our gym clothes, and right as we're slipping our sneakers back on, the door bangs open, and loud chattering filters in. I snatch our bags so we can slip out the side exit before anyone sees.

We're laughing and running, high from the orgasms, what we just did, and the fact that it's Friday. And once again, we have no parents home.

We hop in my Jeep and buckle up. I place my hand on the gear and look over at Oliver, a wicked grin on my face. He's beaming right back, eyes shining, face flushed.

"I'm not fucking done with you yet, Cali Boy," I tell him and then put my arm behind his headrest and reverse out of the spot in one fluid move.

I can't wait to get home and show my stepbrother all the perverse things running through my mind right now.

CHAPTER TWENTY-ONE
OLIVER

"I couldn't help but notice you liked it when I touched your tight little asshole earlier today. Didn't you?" Finn whispers his filthy words directly into my ear and nibbles on the lobe, making me shiver. It's ten o'clock on a Friday night, but we aren't going out. It's Netflix and chill time in Finn's room.

I can't stop the gasp that escapes my lips as I grind my hard dick more forcefully into his, hoping he can take that as his answer. I don't think I'm quite ready to admit it out loud, but the slight caress of Finn's fingertips against my hole instantly made me come.

"Fuck, Ollie." He presses his forehead to mine and pauses for a second—I think we're both trying to calm down before we blow our loads. I'm panting and worked up, and the anticipation of what's to come causes my dick to throb painfully in my jeans.

"I need these off. *Now,*" Finn growls, adjusting the straining erection that's probably digging into his zipper, just like mine is.

He's already shirtless—his defined muscles ripple under my touch. He stands up and shucks his jeans. His hard cock bobs out, a bead of precum glistening at his slit. I guess he was going commando under there. I lean back on my elbows and stare at his thick cock jutting straight out at me. His tip is angry, red, and swollen. I want to suck on it, take him all the way to the back of my throat until I'm gagging and choking on it. I want him to *fuck* me with it. But not tonight. Tonight, I want his fingers on me—*in me*. I unzip and peel off my jeans and boxers, pulling my T-shirt over my head with one hand behind my back.

He climbs on the bed and crawls toward me—slinking up my body—slipping his tongue into my mouth and fucking me with it while he blindly reaches into his bedside table for lube. He gives me one last peck before he sits back on his heels and uncaps the bottle, squirting a generous amount onto his fingers. The possessive way his dark eyes stare at me makes my skin prickle, and I shudder.

"Bend your knees and spread your legs apart for me." My cheeks burn, but I do as he says.

Finn teases the rim of my ass with his cool, slick finger and applies the slightest pressure as he continues to rub slow circles. He pushes my bent knees further apart, opening me up to him. "Just relax. It's gonna feel good, Ollie."

I love it when he calls me Ollie, so my body instantly loosens and his finger slips in.

I squeeze my eyes shut and make an embarrassingly high-pitched squeak at the strange intrusion.

That feels *weird*.

"You okay?" he asks softly, looking up at me from between my legs, his midnight blue eyes sparkling with concern. I bite my lip and nod, unable to form words. It burns slightly, but I don't want him to stop. Finn starts to move his finger in and out and leans down to take my dick into his mouth. I relax at the contact and groan. It's so warm and wet. . . and the *suction*. Fuck, the suction is amazing.

"Oh fuck, oh fuck, that feels so good!" I cry out, thrusting my hips and pushing my cock further into his mouth.

Finn slips his finger out and adds another, curving them upward. My body jolts as he hits that never before touched sweet spot inside of me, and I cry out. His fingers continue to move in and out, rubbing and stroking me until I'm trembling. "*Ohmyfuckingfuck*," I whine.

How is he so fucking good at this? The fact that he has complete control over my body right now has my dick swelling even more in his mouth.

Shit, I'm not gonna last long.

My internal thoughts cease when Finn adds a third finger, stretching me wider. The intense feeling has me fisting the sheets and curling my toes. I'm completely pliant in his hands as he swallows my cock whole and continues fucking me with his fingers, stretching me and scissoring them every other time.

He licks down my shaft and gently sucks on my balls. "Here," he pants, clearly just as worked up as I am, "put your feet flat on my shoulders and pull your knees back."

"Oh, *God*. . ." This new angle is so deep and penetrating. I feel like I could come right now even though he's not even touching my dick.

"Just imagine this is my thick cock splitting you in two, Ollie. I'm going to fuck you hard, but you need to be ready for it first."

Finn picks up his pace and nails my new favorite spot on every thrust. “Ungh. . . oh fuck!” He keeps licking and sucking my balls into his mouth, and I can feel the precum dripping from my dick. “Finn, I’m gonna come, don’t stop. . . don’t stop,” I pant out as I fist the sheets harder and fuck myself on his fingers, hitting deep and hard each time. I’m a writhing mess, but I don’t care. It feels like he’s touching my dick from the inside. The erotic thought has my orgasm racing down my spine and through my ass.

“I’m coming. . . Finn. . . *oh God.* . . Finn!” I moan his name as hot jets of cum spurt out of my dick and land on my abdomen. My cock just keeps pulsing, and it feels like I’m never going to stop coming as Finn rides out my orgasm with me and fucks me slower and slower until he pulls his fingers out altogether.

“Holy shit, you just came hands-free. That was the hottest fucking thing I’ve ever seen in my life.” He’s in awe, but I’m too tired to open my eyes.

“Mhm,” I agree. Because I did. And fuck, was it amazing.

“How was it?” he asks, and I can hear the cocky grin in his voice.

“Life-altering,” I say simply, and his booming laughter makes my stomach flutter. I love it when he’s happy. . . I think I love *him.*

My smile falters for a second, but I cover it up quickly. I can’t tell him; I can’t ruin things. He’s my stepbrother, and our parents will be home soon. We’ve also barely known each other for two weeks—that is way, *way* too soon to say “*I love you.*”

I open my eyes when I hear the tell-tale sound of jerking off. I’m too tired to reciprocate or move, so I just lie there naked, with my legs still spread and cum on my stomach.

"Ollie, you look so fucking sexy right now. So thoroughly fucked. I'm gonna come all over this tight ass," he grits out, and his dirty talk has me perking up a bit.

He pushes my knees back again and jacks off against my lubed-up hole. I'm still slightly loose and open from the hard finger fucking I just took. His cock is bumping up against my entrance, and my dick is starting to get hard again. I have the urge to push against him and get it over with. He wants to take this slow, like I first asked him to, and so he doesn't hurt me. But after everything we've done the past few days, I just want him to fuck me already.

After a few more pumps, I look up and make eye contact with Finn as he grits his teeth and restrains himself from pushing forward as he comes, shooting ropes of jizz all over my ass. I watch, fascinated, as he scoops up his cum and shoves it into me with two fingers.

"Uhh," I grunt at the intrusion.

He leans forward and gives me a searing kiss, still fucking me leisurely with his own cum. "Sleep with me inside you," he whispers against my lips. "It won't be long now." His promise has a chill running down my spine, and I shiver.

God, I'm so ready for it.

Finn pulls the comforter over us and spoons me, not caring that our combined cum is *everywhere*. Oh well, sounds like a problem for future us.

The guys came over on Saturday, and we pigged out on junk food, pizza, and beer. It was fun hanging out with a big group of guys again, but it still makes me wonder how they'd react if I came out to them. Not sure I'll ever feel comfortable doing that again. I mean, straight people don't have to announce they're straight. Why the fuck should I?

The rest of the weekend passes in a blur of kisses, blow jobs, and making each other come as many times as we can.

Finally, it's Sunday night, and the knowledge that we have to return to the real world tomorrow morning sucks major balls.

"I wish our parents weren't coming back on Tuesday already," I confess, my head on Finn's chest as we lounge in his bed, finally watching *Squid Game*.

"Don't get me wrong, I can't wait to see my mom. But I'm not looking forward to having to hide this from anyone." At least our parent's bedroom is on the other side of the house, so we should be able to sneak into each other's rooms late at night. But now that I've had his fingers in my ass, I already want more. Guess I went from never-been-kissed virgin to cock slut pretty fast.

"Yeah. I like the house to ourselves, too," Finn agrees, kissing the top of my head and rubbing his face against my hair. "We'll just have to be more stealthy, maybe get walkie-talkies or something."

"Let's do it!" I burst out laughing because that would be fucking epic. "*Blow jobs at twenty-three hundred hours. My room. Over and out*," I say, in my best radio voice.

"Copy," he replies. "Or we could just text."

"True," I agree. "Ooo, like a booty call!"

"Come here, you dork." Finn pulls me on top of him, cuddling my body to his. I give him my full weight, not worried I'll squish him anymore.

"We still have one more day," he whispers. "Now go to sleep." He wraps his big arms snuggly around me, and I settle in, content as I drift off to sleep.

He's right. We still have one more day, and I intend to make the absolute *best* of it.

CHAPTER TWENTY-TWO
FINN

It's Monday after school, and Oliver is in his new art studio, standing on a ladder in his tight little boxer briefs—the black ones with little yellow ducks all over them. And it looks like his nails are sunshine yellow to match.

Fuck. I'm hard again.

I swear I can't get enough of him. It's like I was never even straight at all. I'm so fucking horny, all the time. I'm practically insatiable and was popping spontaneous boners all day at school. It was really inconvenient, especially in those tiny ass gym shorts.

I went searching for Ollie to ask him what we're doing for dinner on our last night before the 'rents return, but now I'm distracted by the sight before me. He's painting abstract shapes on the wall in shades of gold and magenta. Colorful paints haphazardly swoosh across his naked torso, and I can't help but zero in on those two glorious ass dimples. I stalk over to him, roughly grabbing his hips to ensure he doesn't fall, and kiss each one.

He pulls out an earbud and peers down over his shoulder at me, raising a single brow.

"You painting a mural in your underwear?" I ask the obvious.

"Yep," he says, wiping his cheek and smearing more magenta paint across it. "I decided to do an acrylic mural as my art project."

"That's ambitious, dude. What's it gonna be?"

He starts to climb down, and I keep a tight hold on his hips, guiding him. He sets his tray of paint and brushes down, cleaning up while he talks.

"Well, the theme is extremely general and open for interpretation, but the project centers around the idea of *Home* and what it means to each of us."

"And what does home mean to you, Cali Boy?" I can't take my eyes off him, strutting around half naked, covered in paint. It's fucking turning me on. I swear to God, he does this to me on purpose. But I can't even call him a tease with how many times I've come in the past few days.

"No matter where I go or live, there will always be a sunrise and a sunset—and they will always be beautiful." A blush rises in his cheeks. "I guess that's why a sunset represents home for me. I'm painting the sunset from my new bedroom window."

He feels at home here. With me. My heart swells, and I stride over to him. I grab the brushes from his hand and toss them carelessly onto the table. I spin him around and slam my mouth on his, keeping a grip on his shoulders and walking him backward until he bumps the wall.

"You feel at home with me?" I ask gruffly, grabbing him through his boxers to possessively massage his junk. In contrast, I kiss him tenderly, making his cock harden.

"Yes," he pants. "I've never felt more safe in my life. I'm happy here, with you."

His energy is vibrant. Radiant. Buzzing with positivity and light. And I just can't get enough.

"I love you," I blurt with zero fucking finesse.

We both freeze. My eyes bulge, and Ollie's mouth drops open. And I still have his dick in my hand.

"I mean. . . can we. . . um. . . Let's pretend I didn't just say that," I settle on, once again flustered by this angel-faced boy in front of me.

His mouth morphs from shock to mischief—a grin curling his lips and making his dimples pop. "Uh uh. No fucking way. You can't take that back."

I groan and cover my face with my hands, I can feel the heat settling in my cheeks, and I *hate* blushing.

Warm, soft hands grasp my wrists and tug them away from my face. "I think I've loved you since that very first night when you wrapped my ribs and took care of me."

His own confession wipes any lingering embarrassment away. What does it matter that we've only known each other for a couple of weeks if we both feel the same way? We've been through our own versions of hell and found comfort in each other—found love. There's no shame in that.

"Fuck, Cali Boy. I love you so fucking much." I kiss him deeply, caressing his mouth with my tongue. I slip my hand under the waistband of his boxers and grasp onto his hard length. "Let's go to my room. I need you again. Need to show you how much I love you." My voice is deep and raspy, and I feel animalistic, like I need to stake my claim.

Ollie groans. "I need to shower first. I'm covered in paint."

"Leave it. It's fucking hot," I admit, and he pulls back,

eyes bouncing between mine. He must find what he's looking for because he grabs my hand and tugs me down the hallway and into my room.

He slams the door and spins around, leaning against it and biting his lip. Then he slips his thumbs into his underwear and slowly pulls them down, stepping out and kicking them away.

Seeing his naked body makes my stomach flutter and cave in like a punch to the gut. The soft glow of the bedside lamp illuminates his golden skin and artfully disheveled hair. His lean muscles and toned abs stand out in artistic relief. He's a work of art, and I tell him as much.

"You're a fucking masterpiece." I run my hand languorously down his stomach, and his abs constrict under my touch. I grab his hand and lead him to my bed, pushing him down. He falls back, hard cock bobbing, golden skin covered in brilliant splashes of color.

"Finn," Oliver moans out. "I wanna fuck your mouth."

His body quivers, and he fists the sheets as I kiss down his chest and run my tongue along his sexy as fuck oblique muscles. I give him a little of what he wants and lick his cock from root to tip, swirling my tongue as I go. I get to the top and suck him down, deep throating him for a few strokes before popping off.

"And I wanna fuck your ass." I smirk up at him, hovering just beside his glistening erection. He tenses slightly since we haven't taken that step yet.

"O-okay," he stutters.

I crawl up his body and cup his cheek. "Hey, if you're not ready, there's no rush. I just. . . I just want to be close to you," I confess, tucking wayward strands of hair behind my ears.

"I'm ready. I want that too—want you."

My lip curls up on one side, and then I'm kissing all over his body, stopping to bite and suck on each of his nipples. Then I plunder his mouth, not once touching his cock, just teasing him. Working him up. I've never liked kissing before, not until Oliver. I could make out with him all day, like the horny teenagers we are. Our tongues tangle, dueling for dominance. I lick deep into his mouth, savoring his flavor.

I sit back on my heels, pull my T-shirt over my head, then slip out of my boxers. We're both naked and staring at each other. Oliver's eyes are burning me from the inside out, my stomach is anxious, and I'm so fucking turned on. "I've never done this before," I whisper. "Anal, I mean," I amend, clarifying what I meant. He knows I've never been with a guy.

Ollie reaches up and laces our fingers together. "Me neither, Finn. And that's what makes it so beautiful. It'll be good no matter what. Because it's you, it's *us*."

"You're right. It's just us, our pleasure, and however many times I can make you come before you pass out." His gaze darkens at my tempting words. They're almost a challenge.

"I'm pretty sure the pleasure is limitless when it comes to you and me," Ollie rasps out, and I have to agree.

"Yeah, because my boyfriend is sexy as fuck, and I get hard when you so much as glance at me."

"Boyfriend?" he asks in an unusually high pitch, and I realize what I just said. But it doesn't worry me or freak me out. It feels exactly fucking right.

My boyfriend.

"Yeah, my boyfriend. Does that work for you?"

"Fuck yeah, it does!" And then we pounce on each

other. It's a tangle of limbs and lips as we kiss, grope, and grind all over each other.

It takes strength, but I pull away, sitting up. Ollie follows after me with kiss-swollen lips, looking for more. "Lie back," I say, pushing him down. I reach over and grab the lube, squirting some on my fingers. Ollie knows what to do now and bends his knees, spreading his legs wide, offering himself to me. I slowly press in one, then two fingers, curving them up to rub his sweet spot.

"Ungh. . . yes. . . there," he moans, writhing on my fingers. I scissor them, opening him up and getting him ready to take my cock. I add a third finger, and his hips arch off the bed.

"Oh, fuck!" He throws an arm over his eyes and moans while I physically shake his body with the force of my finger fucking.

Without stopping my punishing pace, I push his knees even further back so they're touching his chest.

"Hold your knees back," I demand in a gruff voice, and he complies, gripping his thighs under the bend of his knees and pulling them back. His ass is completely exposed and vulnerable to me. That erotic thought nearly pushes me over the edge, and I haven't even been touched yet.

"I'm gonna come," Ollie warns, seconds before he shoots his release all over his stomach while I continue to pound his ass with my fingers. He goes limp, completely drained, and I gently remove my fingers. I scoot further up the bed, positioning myself between his spread thighs, right at his opening.

"Ready for me to be inside you, Cali Boy?" I breathe out, punctuating my dirty words with a press of my hips. His breath hitches when he feels my hard erection pressing into him.

He spreads his legs wider and peers up at me with hooded eyes. "Answer enough?"

I line myself up and push forward slowly, but I meet resistance, even after prepping him.

"You need to loosen up. Take a deep breath and relax your muscles on the exhale."

I try again when he releases his breath, but he clenches his ass again, and I don't want to hurt him.

"It's too big. I can't do it," he whines.

"It's not, and you can. Just need to get it in a little further past the head, and it'll feel good."

I caress his chest and abdomen—tweaking his nipples, massaging him, relaxing him—while pushing very slowly and very carefully into his tight body.

"That's it. Just relax and let me in."

My cockhead finally slips past the tight ring of muscle, causing his breath to hitch.

"You okay?" I murmur into his soft hair, pausing my intrusion so he can adjust.

He just nods his head into my neck and remains frozen. I push in more, inch by inch, until I bottom out fully.

Fuuuuck, that feels good. I can't believe I'm actually inside him right now.

I stay still, waiting until he's ready for me to move. I grit my teeth. "Shit, you're tight. I'm not gonna last long."

"So full. Move. Now," he moans out wantonly, wrapping his legs around me and digging his heels into my bare ass.

I pull almost all the way out, only leaving the tip inside, then surge forward. Ollie's breath hitches, like I'm physically forcing the air out of his lungs on every thrust, which I guess I probably am.

He looks like a fucking work of art taking my cock like

this—head thrown back, body still splashed with bright colors of paint.

Again and again, I pound into him, angling my hips just right. The noises Ollie starts to make are primal and obscene. He's moaning and grunting so loud, we're lucky it's only us in the house.

"Don't stop. It feels so fucking good. Right there, right there!"

Holy shit, he's vocal, and that's hot as fuck. I'm about to come, and it sounds like he is too, but I'm not ready for this to be over. So I pull out, making Ollie whimper in protest.

"*Oh God*, I'm so empty," he whines and pulls at his hair, looking like he might cry.

I grab his hips. "Flip over, hurry." Ollie rolls to his stomach, staying flat, but spreading his legs and arching his ass up. I climb between his thighs and quickly squirt more lube on his open hole, easily slipping back in. I can hit his prostate on every thrust in this position.

"Oh yes, fuuuck, fill me up, Finn. Fucking. Fill. Me. Up."

Jesus, he has a filthy mouth. I push my weight down on top of him, keeping him flat, while I nibble on his ear and punish his tight little hole. Wet squelches and the sound of skin slapping against skin fill my bedroom. Add in the moans and dirty talk, and it sounds like a straight-up porno.

"So. . . fucking. . . tight. Your hole is squeezing me like a vice. Milking me. You gonna make me come, Cali Boy?"

He groans into the pillow and spreads his legs wider, bending his knees and digging his heels into my sides. I grind the base of my dick against his ass, trying to get in as far as I can, and he goes absolutely crazy, bucking back against me. He's going to be so sore tomorrow, but he is fucking wild during sex, and I love it.

I don't stop pounding into his ass as I grab his hips and pull him up until he's on all fours. I stare down at my thick cock disappearing into his body over and over. His hole is stretched into a wide circle, taking all of me, and I can't look away from the erotic sight. I rub his ass cheeks, squeezing and caressing them as I continue to pound into him.

"I'm 'bout to come, touch me," he pleads, and I reach around with one hand, keeping a possessive grip on his hip with the other. I grab his leaking cock, jacking him off in unison with my thrusts. My thick rod spears into him relentlessly, and I make sure to hit his prostate on every stroke.

Soon, he's coming on a ragged shout. "*Finnn*!"

I don't stop fucking him, dragging his orgasm out as long as I can while he pulses rhythmically around my cock. It feels fucking amazing, and soon, I'm following right behind him.

Draped over his back, I bite down on the nape of his neck, shoving myself in and unloading deep inside of him. He yelps at the sting of my bite, but his ass is still pulsing around me in little aftershocks, so I know he likes it.

Ollie collapses, completely spent, and my softening dick slips out of him. I roll off the bed and pad over to my en-suite, knowing I need to clean him up before he falls asleep. I'm only gone for two minutes, but he's already snoring softly—face down on the bed, lying in his own cum, while mine drips out of his ass. What a fucking sight he makes right now.

I press a tender kiss in between his shoulder blades. "I fucking love you so goddamn much. Let me clean you up, yeah?"

"Mmhm," he mumbles. "Was so good. In a. . . cum coma."

I snort but proceed to wipe my jizz from his puffy, red hole. *Shit.* He asked for it, but I hope he's not too sore tomorrow. Maybe I should have been a little gentler. I toss the washcloth into the hamper and grab another, wiping away the paint splashes on his back, then rolling him over to finish his front. I use the last washcloth to clean up his softening dick. I can't really do anything about the wet spot he's lying in, but we need to get up and eat dinner in a little while anyway. I'll change the sheets then.

When we're both relatively clean, I slip under the covers and pull my boyfriend to my chest.

The word feels foreign yet right.

Boyfriend.

I have a boyfriend.

And I just fucked the shit out of him.

CHAPTER TWENTY-THREE
OLIVER

I roll over and stretch my limbs, wincing at the soreness in my ass. The sun is just starting to rise, but it's still mostly dark out. Too early to be up, but now that I am, I can't go back to sleep. Because what we did last night? *Wow.* Utterly mind-blowing. I am definitely a bottom—I already want his dick again. I crashed hard last night, and now I feel completely rested.

I swing my legs over the side of the bed and sit up, hissing out a breath.

Sonofabitch.

He really fucked me good. I smile at the memory of losing my virginity to Finn last night. It was fucking amazing, and I'll gladly pay the price today.

Finn stirs, reaching out for me, fingers trailing softly down my spine. "Hey, you okay?"

"Yeah. I'm just up for the day. Gonna take a bath and soak my sore ass," I joke.

Finn sits up, blinking his eyes awake. His eyebrows furrow, and his tone turns serious. "What's wrong? Did I hurt you?"

I chuckle. "No, no. It's nothing I didn't beg for. I like it anyway—the soreness. It'll remind me of what we did. All day long." I pad across the room and flip the bathroom light on. "Go back to sleep. I'm just gonna put my earbuds in and relax in the tub."

I should probably be embarrassed by how I acted like a complete slut last night, but I'm not. Finn's grip turned more possessive and more intense as I begged him to fuck me harder. It was wild and untamed. Nothing holding us back and nothing between us. I felt invincible, and I think I'm now addicted to Finn's cock.

After nearly an hour-long soak, I feel a lot better and less tender. I shuffle out of the bathroom in just my towel, but Finn is already dressed and ready for school, waiting on the edge of the bed for me.

"Aww, I was hoping for a quickie before school. It's our last chance before our parents get home," I say, trying to entice him.

"Not a chance, Sunshine. I know for a fact that your ass needs time to heal after what we did last night. You took a pounding, dude," he smirks, tucking his shaggy dark locks behind one ear. The teasing and lopsided grin make my stomach swoosh low, and I *accidentally* drop my towel.

Oh. Whoops.

"You little fucking tease," Finn laughs out.

"I'm already hard. Please, Finn. It'll take like two seconds," I whine, throwing a pout in for good measure.

He reaches out with both hands and grasps my hips, squeezing possessively. My hard cock is straining toward his mouth, like a magnet pulling me in. He opens his mouth and ducks his head slightly, licking me underneath and swirling his tongue around my crown. I tip my head back and groan. It feels fucking amazing having his mouth on me.

Finn slips off the bed and kneels in front of me, peering up. "You need to be quick, or we'll be late." And then he slams his mouth down on my cock, nearly swallowing me whole. A few bobs of his head later, and I'm coming down his throat, my dick throbbing and pulsing against his tongue. He pops off and swirls his tongue along my slit, lapping up every last drop. I shudder, sensitive from release.

He casually stands like he didn't just give me the beej of the century and simply says, "Go get dressed. Time to leave." And then he's strolling out of the bedroom, probably off to eat whatever bowl of sugary cereal he's into today.

I blink, willing my limbs to move. I think my brain has gone to mush.

Mom texted around lunchtime that she and Gabe would be at the house when we got home from school. I'm so excited to see her; I can't remember the last time we've been apart this long. Maybe surfing camp the summer before freshman year.

"Mom?" I shout, crossing through the mudroom and tossing my messenger bag by the stairs. I'll take it up later.

"Ollie! In the kitchen, honey!" I pick up my pace and stroll down the hallway, following the delicious aromas to the kitchen. Mom is standing in front of the stove, stirring what smells like chicken enchilada soup. She looks amazing —her skin is glowing, and her tan is darker than mine. Her freckles stand out more, and she looks even younger, fresh-faced.

She beams at me, setting the stirring spoon down and engulfing me in her tiny motherly hug. I breathe in her familiar rosewater scent and relax, pulling away. "Mom, you look amazing. You're like. . . glowing," I say, no other way to describe it.

She just giggles. "It's the sun and all the salt water—does amazing things for your skin, you know this."

I do know. I get a pang of longing for California when she mentions sun and saltwater. I lived those two things every day for the first seventeen years of my life. But not even the perfect wave could have made me stay. And now I'm happier than I ever thought I could be, thanks to the grumpy boy standing behind me. Mom sees him and ushers him in for his own enthusiastic hello.

"You just got back. You didn't have to cook, Mom."

"Oh, it's nothing. We were gone for so long, and after just moving here. I wanted us all to sit down again and catch up on what's been happening in each other's lives for the past two weeks. We're a family, and I'd like to make that a priority."

I side-eye Finn and clear my throat awkwardly. She really doesn't want to know what's been going on here the past two weeks. I blush slightly just thinking about it.

"Well, it smells great, Mom. Thank you." I kiss the top of her head and peer over at Finn. Guess we're back to playing pretend. We're just two friendly stepbrothers. Nothing to see here, folks. Move along.

Dinner is a little awkward. We never had time to settle into a comfortability before our parents flew off on their honeymoon to Aruba. But it seems to have been what everyone needed because the Gabe I saw at family dinner before their trip and the Gabe sitting before me now, smiling and asking me how the academy has been and how I like my classes, are like two different people. It's a little unsettling, and I can tell that Finn feels the same way by the furrow in his brow every time Gabe says something nice.

Mom and Gabe tell us all about their trip and everything they did and saw in Aruba while we stuff our faces with chicken enchilada soup and spicy beef empanadas. Finn and I skip over all of the Eric and Hazel bullshit and, of course, our new relationship, instead telling them how well I've adjusted to my new life at the academy with Finn.

"Have you thought about where you want to have your birthday party? I still feel terrible that I missed such an important one."

I groan internally. I don't want to have this conversation on her first night back. I know she's going to push for a party, but she doesn't understand any of the bullshit that's been happening with Eric and Hazel. A party is the last thing I want.

"Mom. You saw Grandma's paintings around the house but haven't seen my art studio yet. I don't need a party. Finn, Gabe, and you. . . you've all given me more than enough to make my eighteenth birthday feel special and memorable. I really don't want anything else. This dinner right now, some of my favorite foods, it's enough of a birthday dinner as I need. Okay?" I stare into her aquamarine eyes, so similar to mine, and try to convey that I don't want her pushing this.

She sighs. "Alright, sweetie. But I *do* have a suitcase full of gifts for you boys." And her giant grin springs back to life, popping her dimples, and she looks even younger like this. I flick my gaze over to Gabe. He's a good-looking guy, a distinguished older gentleman, but damn he got lucky snagging my mom.

"And you, young man." She points a dainty pink nail at Finn. "You are such a kind, thoughtful soul. Gabe, you raised this one right."

Finn blushes under her compliments, and it's extremely endearing.

"I want a full tour of the paintings around the house. And Ollie, I'd love to see your art studio, as long as there's nothing super secret going on in there," she teases, knowing I've always been super private about my art, never hanging it up or displaying it. The mural I'm working on for school is the first thing I've done that I can't hide. It's nerve-wracking, but I've been pushing so many of my own boundaries lately. What's one more, I guess.

Finn nods in agreement, and I agree to show her later.

"So, I made churros for dessert. Finn, can you help me carry everything in?"

That has me squinting my eyes with suspicion. She never needs help carrying anything. She was a waitress for years, and she juggles, *actually juggles*, for fuck's sake. I keep my mouth shut and continue discussing how I've been adapting to the change in weather with Gabe.

Casually discussing the weather with Gabe.

Huh. Who woulda thought?

My mom must really have some kind of magic happy dust because he's. . . not the same. I cringe when I think about the fact that they were on their *honeymoon*, and he was probably releasing some long overdue tension.

Ugh.

Fucking gross.

CHAPTER TWENTY-FOUR
FINN

"Finn, can you help me carry everything in?" Vivian peers across the table at me, aquamarine eyes soft and warm.

"Um, sure." My voice sounds gravelly, even to my own ears.

I follow her into the kitchen and stand stiffly by the refrigerator, waiting for her instruction. She pulls a sheet pan of churros out of the warming tray and places it on a hot pad. She turns around and leans against the counter, looking so small and young in her fluffy socks, leggings, and oversized cable-knit sweater. It feels weird that she's my stepmother, Ollie's *mom*. With no make-up on, she barely looks older than us.

"I just wanted to ask you something. When Oliver wasn't around." She shuffles around, and her awkwardness makes me feel uncomfortable. "So. . . you boys had a nice time without us? No issues? It's just, he wouldn't tell me if anything did happen or if anyone wasn't being. . . nice to him." She smiles sadly. "I'm not sure what he's told you about California, but I worry about him." She doesn't know he told me everything—probably more than he's ever told her.

My cheeks burn as her inquisitive eyes bore into me, and inappropriate thoughts pour into my brain, unbidden.

I fucked her son last night.

Took his virginity.

He had his dick in my mouth, then I had mine in his ass.

Fuck.

I clear my throat awkwardly. "There's nothing to worry about, Vivian. Honestly. It was chill." I smile, trying to reinforce my words.

She seems to accept my answer and gives me a little hug. "Thanks for watching out for him. I knew I could count on you."

Why do her words make me feel. . . *guilty*?

Maybe it's because I fucked him so hard he has a sore asshole. And now, he's sitting at the table with my dad. Probably squirming in his seat.

She reaches into the cabinets and struggles to grab the small plates on the top shelf. I step up next to her and easily get them down because of my height.

"Thanks!" she chirps, setting them out and dishing up two churros per plate.

"Ollie will probably want three," I tell her like she hasn't raised him for the past eighteen years.

She just laughs and agrees with me. "You're probably right." She adds a third to his plate and mine. "I can't help but notice how close you two have grown. And quite quickly, hmm?"

Is that a question? I feel like it's a question, and I can't disagree with her. Can't lie. She's never been anything but kind to me. "Yeah, he's. . . he's pretty awesome," I settle on, and it feels weak and lame. A cop-out. But I'm not ready to confess my undying love for Oliver to his mother. Not yet, at least.

"I think so, too," she says and winks at me. I don't want to read too much into that wink, but I feel like she's insinuating something.

Our little chat ends, and we take the dessert plates to the dining room. Ollie gives me a questioning stare, and I just mouth *'later'* to him.

By the time we finish dessert and more talking—*God, so much talking*—we've been sitting at the dinner table for two hours, and, sure enough, Oliver is starting to squirm in his seat. I bet his ass is starting to ache. I mean, shit. Mine is, too. I don't think I've ever sat at this table for this long in my life. I stretch my socked foot out diagonally under the table until I find his leg. I rub my foot up the inside of his thigh, pressing the ball of my foot into his groin. He chokes on a sip of water and clears his throat, pushing back from the table.

"Well, I don't know about you, Finn, but I have tons of homework to do. So yeah, I'm going to go do that. . . upstairs." He pushes his chair in. "Mom, thanks for dinner. It was delicious. Glad to see you both back safely." He doesn't wait for me, just turns and stalks out of the dining room, and I smirk. He's definitely going to try and get me to fuck him.

"You demanding a dicking down tonight, Cali Boy?"

I'm lounging on the bed, amused by his neediness, as he stands naked before me, pouting. He can't even pretend to hide it. I love it.

"I am."

"Well, you need to rest."

"I already did. It's been twenty-four hours."

"Well, you probably need more than that. Or did you already forget how hard I fucked you last night?"

He turns red at my words, even though he's standing in front of me in his birthday suit.

"I'm fine," he insists, continuing to protest.

"Then show me."

"W-what?" he sputters, and I'm getting some serious déjà vu from when I said the same thing about his ribs on day one.

"Your asshole. Let me see it. See if you're okay to fuck."

He huffs and tries to act all indignant, but his dick is getting harder and harder at my vulgar words, so I keep it up.

"On the bed, ass up."

"Finn—"

"I've seen it all before, Sunshine."

He groans but crawls up the bed anyway.

"Turn around."

"Finn—"

"Let. Me. See." I inject a thread of dominance into my tone to let him know how serious I am.

Ollie bites his lip and hesitates for a second before spinning around on all fours.

"Put your head down and spread your cheeks with both hands."

"*Oh God,*" he moans, spreading his ass apart so I can see all of him. He's a little red, but other than that, he looks fine. I run my finger through his crease, and he groans, pressing back against me.

"So needy," I praise. "You love my cock, don't you?"

"Yes. I do. I need it. Stretch me open, Finn."

I grab the lube from the bedside table and dribble some down his crack, rubbing it in with my fingers. I work one finger in, just teasing him. He lets go and props himself up on his forearms, hanging his head and moaning.

"More," he demands, and I add another finger, fucking him a few times before he tells me what to do again. "Two is enough."

"You'll take whatever I give you," I say, adding a third finger and continuing to fuck him until I think he's ready. I quickly stand and yank my sweats and underwear down, scrambling back to bed. I need to be inside him.

"I'm going to stretch you with my cock, now," I whisper, leaning over him and pushing in past the tight ring of muscle, all in one thrust.

Ollie yells out, squeezing the sheets, and my dick, in a death grip.

"Shh. . . we aren't home alone anymore," I whisper, easily gliding the rest of the way in. I curl around his back and cover his mouth with one hand as I pull out and slam back into him.

"Mmmf!" His muffled grunts and labored breathing are the sexiest things I've ever heard. He's so vocal, so responsive, so *wild*. I need him in my bed every day.

"You. Need. To. Be. Quiet." I punctuate each word with a hard thrust into his clenching ass. I let go of his mouth and grab hold of one hip while I rub his back and spine, caressing and just *feeling* him. I've never wanted to be so close to another person in my life. Being inside his body isn't enough. I want to be inside his soul.

I'm so fucking close. I reach around and squeeze his straining cock. "I'm gonna come, I'm gonna come," he chants.

I wrap an arm around his body, lifting him up and

bringing his back flush to my chest. I cover his mouth with my hand, not risking it, and continue to pump his dick in time with my thrusts. I fuck him relentlessly. With my dick and my hand. He's moaning and whimpering, his head leaning back against my shoulder. He's like Jell-O in my arms while I pound into his tight little hole. And then his dick is spurting, ass clenching, forcing my own orgasm from me. I bite Ollie's shoulder where it meets his neck to muffle my own release. This orgasm is so strong. It feels like it'll never end as I shoot load after load into Ollie, filling him up. My vision blacks out for a second before I pull out, and Ollie falls limp to the bed.

I spread his cheeks again because I'm a sick pervert and watch as my cum oozes out of him, his hole twitching at the emptiness.

A loud snore startles me, and I cannot believe this guy actually just fell asleep. I've spoiled him by cleaning him up after sex. Guess he's gonna expect it now. I smile and shake my head. I seriously love this dude.

CHAPTER TWENTY-FIVE
OLIVER

It's been a month since our parents returned from their honeymoon, and my mom is happier than I've ever seen her. I'm glad she's home, I missed her, but it's been hard for Finn and me to show any affection or find time to mess around. He says I'm too loud during sex, so we either have to wait until super late at night or just do quick blowies.

Gabe is still acting like a changed man. Finn says the fact that he's been home for dinner almost every night isn't normal. Not even from when he was growing up.

Eric and Hazel have backed off since we called them out a month ago. I still feel like I'm constantly watching my back around them, waiting for retaliation. Like I'm stuck in the eye of the storm and about to cross back into chaos soon.

It's mid-March, but the air is still chilly. The wind from the lake swirls around me and penetrates my thin blazer. I opted to leave my coat in my locker because it gets too hot lugging it around all day. I pick up my pace, trying to get to

Spanish class as quickly as possible. I push through the heavy double doors and take a detour to the restrooms.

"Have you even hit puberty yet? Look at your arms. You look like a skeleton, not even a shred of muscle." The cruel laugh and distraught whimper have me hastening my steps as I enter the bathroom in the back of Sable Hall.

I find Eric cornering a small freshman with curly black hair and wire-framed glasses. "Eric!" I bark, with more bite than maybe I should. They both turn toward the intruder. "What the fuck are you doing?" He's terrorizing the poor kid.

Eric backs off and lets the kid scamper away. He doesn't even look at me, just runs out of the bathroom, his wheeled briefcase bouncing behind him.

"Oh, you thought you could stop me?" Eric's manic laugh echoes off the spacious bathroom walls. "You're just a little pussy Cali boy. You can't do shit."

"Don't call me that." He doesn't get to taint my favorite nickname from Finn.

"Oh, I'm sorry. Did I hurt your feelings? Going to go cry to Daddy Finn? You've already turned all my friends against me, but I don't see Finn now, and he's not always around for backup. You think you're such hot fucking shit with Finn at your beck and call," he sneers.

I won't acknowledge that his words bother me, so I roll my eyes and huff out an annoyed breath, trying to convey my nonchalance. "Whatever, Eric. I'm going to class. See you there."

He stalks toward me from across the bathroom and crowds me by the door, getting right in my face. "The weather's going to be nice enough for football on Sunday. In the 50s. So you might want to have a stomach bug that day."

I bristle at his veiled threat and swallow thickly but don't acknowledge him. He backs up a step, and I slip free, immediately leaving. I keep walking until I turn a corner, knowing he can't see me when he comes out. I pause to take a deep breath and calm my shaking hands.

What the fuck is his problem with me?

I slip into my seat next to Bethany, far away from where I used to sit with Eric and Hazel that first week of school.

"You okay?" She leans over and whispers. "Your hands are shaking."

I glance down at my hands resting on my desk.

Oh. They *are* still trembling.

I quickly stuff my hands under my desk, tucking them under my thighs. "Just cold," I lie, and she gives me a concerned frown.

Señor Garcia starts the lesson, and I focus on his words, ignoring the uneasy feeling in my gut.

Other than Eric's threatening words, the rest of the day flies by without issue, and now it's Friday night. We've all agreed to go to the club with Bethany and a few of her cousins. Jared and the guys are all worked up and excited over meeting up with the girls, and Finn and I just make a joke out of it, playing along with who our 'type' is. Finn apparently likes blondes, and I go for the dark and mysterious brunette. It was hard to keep a straight face, but I'm pretty sure they bought it. Well, maybe everyone except Danny. I swear he sees and knows everything, yet he never spreads any gossip. I don't think we need to worry about him, even if he does suspect something.

"How do you get your hair so soft and fluffy anyway?"

Finn asks from where he's perched at the end of his bed, finger-combing his shaggy hair.

"What am I? A fucking pomeranian?" I laugh.

"Could be when you poof your hair up that much," he snickers.

"Ha ha." I stroll over to him and run my own fingers through his dark locks. "Let me do your hair tonight. Pleeease." I make sure to smile enough that my dimples pop out. And then I pout. That always does the job.

"Ugh. Okay, fine. Just don't make me look stupid."

I mock gasp. "I would never make my boyfriend look stupid. Besides, that's impossible for you. You're sexy no matter what." I'm laying it on thick, but it's true. "I'll be right back." I spin on my heel and run to my mom's bathroom to grab a hair tie. He's getting a man bun tonight.

Our parents are out to dinner, so I'm not worried about intruding when I slip into their bathroom. I flip the light on and walk over to the double sink, scanning the white marble countertop for a hair band.

My eyes stutter and do a double take, my brain unable to comprehend what it's seeing. There, lined up on the counter, are three pregnancy tests.

I step closer and peer down, my stomach rumbling with nerves.

Positive. Positive. Positive.

What. The. Fuck.

How is this possible?

Shit, I know how. And *gross.*

My mom's still in her thirties, but... *a baby*?

I'm going to have a sibling?

Oh, God... Finn and I are going to *share* a sibling.

This is fucked up. This is so, so fucked up. I run my

hands through my hair, messing up all the work I just did to make it perfect.

I abandon whatever I came here for and stumble backward, crashing into the door. I spin around and practically run from the room like it's a house of horrors and not a luxurious bathroom with a crystal chandelier.

When I get back to Finn's bedroom, I wander in on autopilot, plopping down at the end of the bed and staring at the floor.

"You okay, dude? You look like you just saw a ghost."

I can't hold it in. "My mom's pregnant."

"What!" he shouts, and I'm startled out of my daze.

"She. . . they're. . . we're going to have a sibling, Finn. *Together.*" I shudder because it makes me feel weird.

Finn combs his fingers through his hair and then grips his neck anxiously. "This is. . . not ideal," he says.

"Not ideal? Dude, this makes us even closer to being real brothers! There's going to be a brand new human being related to *both* of us! Now we *really* can't tell our parents about us. This is so fucked." I think I'm panicking. How is he not panicking?

"You know what, it all makes sense now," Finn says, still cool, calm, and collected while I'm having a major life crisis over here.

"What does?" I ask, tucking my hands into my armpits so I don't pick at my new purple nail polish.

"My dad. His complete change in behavior since he's been home. They must have been trying for a baby. No way was this an accident."

He's right. My mom would have never "accidentally" gotten pregnant with her new husband. She must have gone off birth control. They planned this. They wanted this.

"Fuck. I can't deal with this right now. I'm getting drunk tonight."

"Me too," Finn replies, and my mouth falls open, brows shooting up my forehead. I flick my wide eyes to his uncertain gaze.

"But. . . but you can't drive then."

"I know, Oliver. We can take an Uber."

"Really?" I know my smile is a little too big—a little too hopeful—but we haven't gone out drinking together, and I'm pumped.

"I think I'm ready to try. I can't keep living like this. I need to get over this irrational fear sooner or later, and you've brought me out of my comfort zone, so I figure it's time."

I launch myself at Finn, wrapping my arms around his neck and whispering into his ear, "I'm so proud of you."

CHAPTER TWENTY-SIX
OLIVER

The Uber ride to the club downtown went surprisingly well. Finn kept a death grip on my hand and told the driver to take the long way to avoid the highway. Even though it meant a longer time in the car, it's the best choice so he doesn't push himself too far, too soon. This is completely different from the time Ethan drove us home in a rush. Finn was in protector mode, focused on me and only me. This conscious decision is a big step for him.

"So you're positive I don't need a fake ID to drink?" I ask for the tenth time as we get closer to the drop-off point.

Finn just laughs. "No, dude, I told you. Bethany and her girl gang of cousins have the hookup everywhere. Just use your ID to get in at the door since you're eighteen. They won't mark our hands because we're meeting up with everyone out front first."

As we pull up to the front of the skyscraper, you wouldn't know there's a swanky nightclub at the top. It's super exclusive and not advertised at all. It doesn't even really have a name. They refer to it simply as The Spot, or so

Finn tells me. Either Bethany or, more likely, one of her cousins must have a *very special* relationship with the owner. I'm super excited to get up there and see what this place looks like.

We enter the lobby, the bright interior a startling contrast to the inky night outside, and I have to squint until my eyes adjust. Jared, Ethan, Danny, and Trace are standing with three girls who look a lot like Bethany—all gorgeous brunettes with tiny waists and big boobs. They're wearing flowy mini skirts and crop tops, like March in Chicago actually means it's spring break weather. It definitely isn't.

"Where's Bethany?" I whisper to Finn as we make our way over. And then I see her, strutting over from the reception desk near the back. Her long chestnut hair flows behind her like a silk curtain, and she's wearing high-waisted, skin-tight black pants with a lacy black crop top, showing a small amount of stomach and a massive amount of cleavage. Her stilettos are a glossy cherry red, as are her lips.

"Damn," I say out loud, and I can feel Finn's stare burning a hole into the side of my face while I gawk at Bethany.

"You like girls now or something?"

That makes me giggle. He's funny. "Nope. Still like dicks. But damn, she looks fucking killer in that. Like a fucking mafia princess or something."

Finn snorts at that. "Far from it. Her dad's a research scientist. A genius. Jayden practically worships him. He looks like he could be a character on *The Big Bang Theory*. No idea how he made *her*." He nods to the supermodel strutting down the invisible catwalk toward us.

We intercept Bethany, and she gives us each a tight squeeze, grabbing our hands. She pulls back to peer at Finn, and her eyes scan his face, ping-ponging as she tries to read the emotions he keeps so tightly locked up.

"How did it go?" she whispers, and I realize she knows he just pushed past his comfort zone by riding in someone else's car.

"Surprisingly. . . fine. We didn't take the highway, but it's progress," he admits shyly, and my heart soars. He's so fucking cute, and he's trying so hard. God, I want to blow him. Like right now. Again.

Bethany squeezes Finn one last time and then tugs us over to the group to introduce her cousins—Alyssa, Chloe, and Emmy. All three of them look like sisters, but I don't think any of them are. Finn said they're the only daughters of four very wealthy, very influential brothers in Chicago, all of whom have their own specialty. Bethany's dad is the mad scientist slash doctor slash genius of the group. I swear I wasn't far off when I called her a mafia princess; we are in Chicago, after all.

We check our coats with reception in the back, and I smooth any wrinkles from my black button-up. I decided to go less casual today in case they have a dress code, and, judging by everyone else's attire, I'm fucking glad I did. Finn didn't tell me much about this place, and it would have been really embarrassing to show up in holey jeans and an oversized flannel.

Yikes.

Finn and I are dressed similarly in black dress shirts and pants, but that's where it ends. I have thin silver pinstripes running down my fitted slacks and a dark-purple skinny tie to match the suspenders I'm sporting. And do you even have to ask? Yes, my nails are a deep plum to accentuate. My black patent leather dress boots and silver nose hoop complete my look, and I feel pretty good about myself. Finn couldn't take his eyes or hands off me before we left the house, and I'm kind of hoping they don't have a black light at this club.

Bethany does a double take at my outfit and squeals, clapping and doing a little tap dance in her Louboutins. "Yasss! Oliver, this outfit is everything! You took a risk, honey, but it works!"

She grabs her three cousins, who all proceed to gush over how good I look. They seem nice but are already drunk and giggly, so I'm relieved when they go back to hanging on the guys.

"Okay, let's take two elevators. Press 'P,' and it'll take you to the top," Alyssa states. She seems like the ringleader and a little older, maybe nineteen or twenty. She twirls on the spot, and her skirt nearly flares out enough to show her ass. The other three girls step in after her and Trace darts forward like a ninja.

"Later, suckers," he taunts and slips in with the giggling girls as the elevator doors close.

"He's definitely going for Alyssa," Ethan laments. "Dammit, she's the one I had my eye on. Hot older chick. Bet she's good in bed."

We all step into the second elevator, and I press the penthouse button. Looks like we're going fifty floors up.

"Dibs on Emmy!" Jared shouts.

"Chloe." Danny swoops in quickly and quietly with his claim before Ethan can even open his mouth.

"Aw, dudes, seriously?" Ethan crosses his arms and leans against the mirrored wall. "How you gonna do me like that? You know I'm not gonna hook up with Bethany. Now I have to try and pull someone random, and that takes so much more effort."

Finn shakes his head at Ethan's whining.

"What? You guys aren't annoyed they called dibs before the night even starts? Now the three of us have to be each other's wingmen, I guess. Okay, we can do this. I mean, Ollie, you're looking snazzy as fuck."

Ah, shit.

I just wanted to chill and drink with Finn in a cool atmosphere, soak in the vibes, and not deal with straight people drama or being a wingman. I don't even think I could be one if I tried.

Luckily, Finn saves me. "Nah, dude, we're chilling tonight. Not trying to pick anyone up."

"Lame. But I got this. You'll see."

Jared and Danny laugh at our outrageous and horny-as-fuck friend as the elevator doors finally open.

We meet up with the rest of the group, and Trace's arm is already slung over Alyssa's shoulder. Her long, straight ponytail sits high on her head and swings in front of me like a pendulum as we walk toward the entrance of The Spot.

It's dim up here, much darker than the bright lobby below. The unassuming wooden door could be the back entrance to any fancy restaurant downtown.

It's as easy as Finn said it would be. We show our IDs to the wide-neck dude standing there, even though most of us are just eighteen, and walk right in.

We head down the long, dark hallway, retro sconces lining the brick walls. They cast a golden glow, illuminating our path to the next, more antique-looking door. It's thick, wooden, and distressed—with antique black hinges, an ornate door knob, and a roaring lion's head for a door knocker.

Alyssa steps forward and does some kind of strange arrangement of knocks and taps, and ten seconds later, the door slowly opens inward.

Holy. Shit.

This isn't a club. This is a fucking speakeasy. A real-life underground Chicago speakeasy. And when I say underground, I mean figuratively, I know we're fifty floors up, thank you.

There are intimate, dark wooden tables with candlelight and soft pendulum lighting above. The chairs are large wingbacks, upholstered in a buttery soft brown leather.

Soft jazz plays from a live band, the small stage tucked against the left side of the room. There are booths and couches, which are a retro red velvet that I love. They look like the one Finn got me for my art studio. This place screams of wealth, indulgence, and hedonism. It feels like a blast from the past, and I am vibing with it—even my outfit is.

The bar is a glossy mahogany and spans the entire width of the back wall, and the barstools are the same chocolate brown leather as the wingback chairs. The massive chandeliers shine golden, complimenting the red glow of the gothic-looking sconces.

It's chill and relaxing, and I can't wait to see what specialty drinks they offer.

"Let's get drinks first," Alyssa declares, and we grab seats at the bar. The music is low, and so is the noise. There are only a handful of other people clustered around tables, and most of them are much older than us.

I peruse the specialty cocktail menu and decide on a pomegranate and mint gin cocktail. It's crisp and refreshing and goes down smoothly. It's a quality drink, and I'm a little worried about how trashed I could potentially get on these. Finn goes for a classic gin and tonic.

"I'll be right back. I need to go say hello to someone,"

Alyssa says and then slips into the back, Trace frowning after her.

Ethan is next to me at the bar, sipping his scotch and scanning the room behind us, probably looking for a potential target. He doesn't really need a wingman anyway. He's completely charming, and his charcoal gray suit fits him impeccably. His black hair nearly shines blue under the crystal chandeliers, and his dark brown eyes are so expressive they can grab anyone's attention.

His eyes lock onto someone across the room, but I can't tell who he's looking at.

"Excuse me, gentleman." And then he's gone, slinking into the darkness.

We chat about school and find out more about the girls. Emmy and Chloe are seniors in a neighboring town, and Alyssa is twenty and a sophomore at Northwestern.

Alyssa comes back not even fifteen minutes later, which seems to have appeased Trace—he's back to being all over her. Danny and Jared have their targets under their arms, too. And Bethany is her usual chatty self, holding a deep conversation at the bar with an older woman with white hair, both of them sipping red wine.

Finn takes a deep, relieved breath. "Well, they all seem occupied now. Let's duck out to the rooftop bar. They have tons of heaters, so it won't be cold."

"No way. They have a rooftop bar?" I sound incredulous to my own ears. "That's fucking sick."

CHAPTER TWENTY-SEVEN

OLIVER

We grab our drinks and open the narrow wooden door that has steps leading up to the roof. It has the same brick walls and retro sconces as the entrance hallway, carrying the theme to the roof.

When we open the top door and step out, I'm speechless. My fingers twitch and dance against my pants, dying to paint the amazing view in front of me. Fairy lights hang in artful loops across half of the roof, and there's a long wall of fire pits with tables scattered everywhere. A glass bar sits on each end of the space, and the rest of downtown Chicago looms above us even though we're fifty floors up. It's magical, and I feel transported into a different time and place. Finn steps close so our sides touch and subtly links our pinkies together so no one can see.

"Come on. Let's go sit in that corner. No one's over there, and it has a couple of heaters."

We settle onto a soft gray couch and motion to the waiter for two more drinks.

"Want anything to eat?" Finn asks.

"No, thanks. I'm good. I don't feel like asking about their allergy information, anyway."

"If you're hungry, I'll ask. You shouldn't drink that much gin if your stomach is empty."

I love how he's always so thoughtful and tries to take care of me. My stomach swoops low, and I fidget a little bit. Thinking about big, tough, broody Finn being sweet to me gets my dick hard. And it really can't get hard in these tight dress pants on a rooftop bar in the middle of downtown Chicago. I mean, yeah, it's dark up here, but it's not *that* dark.

"I'm fine, really. Thanks, though."

Our new drinks arrive, and we lean back against the comfortable cushion, taking in the city before us. The railings are glass, giving us an unobstructed view.

"This concrete jungle is so different from California, but I love it. My fingers are itching to paint this right now," I confess.

He pulls his phone out and takes a few photos of our view.

"So you can paint it later."

God, he's thoughtful.

I grab the phone from him and flip the camera, taking a few selfies. They're really good even though Finn isn't smiling. He has his sexy smolder going on with his dark hair loose and shaggy. He's fucking hot.

Finn scoots a little closer, and our thighs press together. It's torture not being able to touch him or kiss him like I want to. It's fun being out and about, but while we're keeping our relationship on the down low, I think I'd rather just be at home. With Finn. Doing whatever we feel like and not worrying about who's watching.

I down my second drink.

"Whoa, dude, slow down. Those are way stronger than you think. Probably stronger than Bethany's party punch. If you keep it up, you'll be flat on your ass before you know it."

I crane my neck around and motion for the bartender's attention, holding my empty glass up. He promptly brings another over, and I think pomegranate is my new favorite flavor.

Finn grabs the drink from my mouth, causing a few droplets to dribble down my chin. "Hey! What the hell, dude?"

"I said you can't fucking chug those. This is your third in less than an hour. You have to pace."

I huff out an annoyed breath. "Yeah, well, quit rubbing up on me, looking so hot, and I wouldn't have to try and drink my horniness away."

Shit, I think I'm already drunk.

"Look down," I whisper and subtly press my hips up into the air, showing him the bulge snaking down my leg, trapped in the tight confines of my dress pants.

His eyes dart up and glance around at our surroundings frantically.

"Dude, stop. Or I'm going to get hard, too," he hisses, and I can't help but laugh.

I grab my drink back from him and hold it over my lap, trying to cover my obvious erection.

"You're too horny to take anywhere," he chastises, and I giggle more. I never used to be like this.

My phone vibrates in my front pocket, and it startles the shit out of me. "Oh fuck!" I jerk forward and nearly spill my drink all over my crotch. I quickly set it down on the end table. That would have been an easy way to ruin the night.

"That just vibrated against my dick," I chuckle, and Finn cracks a grin, shaking his head.

"It tickled."

Finn snorts. "Bet you liked it."

"Maybe," I tease, wagging my eyebrows and standing up to slide my phone out of my pocket. I open my texts and see a message from Bethany. "Beth says for me to get my dapper self down there, right now. She wants to dance."

"To jazz?" Finn questions and I agree because how the hell do you dance to jazz? But I'm definitely down to try.

"Let's find out." I send a quick text back to meet us at the bar by the rooftop entrance, and then I chug my third drink before Finn can stop me.

"Ollie. . ." he growls, and his deep blue depths are storming.

"Chill. I'm fine, okay?" I blink—very slowly—and Finn narrows his eyes at me.

"Come on," I say, nodding my head toward the stairs to go back inside.

"No more. Have some water next."

"Fine," I agree. "I'll have a bottle of water after I dance, *or whatever*, with Bethany."

Finn accepts my answer, and we go downstairs to the rest of our group. Everyone's coupled up and sitting farther down the bar. I can see that Beth is a little left out, and now I feel bad.

"Evening, gorgeous," I purr, as I slink onto the barstool next to her. Finn stands sentry behind us. "Can I buy you a drink?"

"Oh. Well, hello there. Aren't you just absolutely dashing?"

"Positively rakish," I agree and give her a sly grin, playing this little game until she quits.

"I'll accept that drink, but only if you'll dance with a girl first, hmm?" She holds her dainty hand out, palm down and wrist limp. I take it like a gentleman and place a soft peck on top.

That does it, and she can't keep the charade up, bursting into a fit of classic Bethany giggles. A few older men around us turn to stare at her, but she doesn't pay them any mind.

"Finn, you don't mind if I borrow your brother, do you? Promise I won't molest him too much." Her aquamarine eyes sparkle under the golden lighting of the bar, bringing out the flecks of yellow in them.

Finn doesn't answer, just takes a seat, keeping his back to the bar, so he can watch what we're about to get up to. I give him a little wink—or at least what feels like a wink to my drunken brain—and let Bethany drag me toward the small stage where four guys are still playing slow, soft jazz.

She lets go of my hand and crooks a finger at the saxophonist. He leans over far enough that she can whisper into his ear, his long dark beard skimming the top of her cleavage. He nods and says something to his bandmates as Beth drags me over to the empty space in front of the stage.

The slow jazz fades away, and they start a loud, fast-paced song that sounds like it's from the fifties or something. I don't have the slightest clue how Bethany expects us to dance to this.

"What is this?" I shout into her ear. She's starting to bounce a little and find her groove.

"Swing music. It's easy. Just be ready to dip me and follow my cues!"

I'm not sure I believe her when she says *it's easy*, but I'll give it a go. I'm feeling loose and nimble. I shake my arms out and tap dance in place.

Yeah, I have no idea why either.

Bethany grabs my hand and guides it to the middle of her back, my palm grazing the bare skin between her pants and lacy crop top. Then, she rests her hand on my upper shoulder and grasps my other hand tightly, jutting it out to the side.

"Okay, we're just gonna do a bunch of triple steps, toss in a few dips, and see where it goes!"

Um, say what?

She must read the confusion on my face because she tips her head back and belts out a laugh that rings clear across the space. "Three little hops. Now come on, just follow me."

I keep my eyes down and my arm out while I watch Bethany's shiny red stilettos. I stumble along for a few beats, but I've always been light on my feet, so it doesn't take long to get the rhythm down.

Soon, we're flying around the space—laughing, twirling, and I've even successfully dipped her a few times. We're floating around the room as if we've practiced together a million other times. I don't know if anyone's watching, we're moving too fast, but I'm having so much fun, I don't give a shit if they are.

All this spinning makes me dizzy, and I'm caught off guard when Bethany tries to do one of those jumping straddle moves. I lose my balance and fall flat on my ass, Bethany landing in my lap, straddling me.

Oof.

A peal of laughter pours from her cherry-red lips, and she just sits on me in the middle of the small dance floor—that's not really a dance floor. Soon my own drunken laughter is joining hers.

As I get myself under control again, I hear Bethany giggle. "Hey, Finny."

I peer over my right shoulder and see Finn standing there, arms crossed and glowering.

He didn't like it?

And then I cast my gaze around the rest of the room, realizing we've gained the attention of just about every man in this place.

The music abruptly switches back to slow jazz, and I can almost hear the awkward record scratch.

Finn reaches down and gently pulls Bethany to her feet. He clasps my forearm in his and lifts me, leaning in to whisper into my ear. "They aren't just looking at her, Oliver. You two put on quite the show. You trying to get me hard again, Cali Boy?"

Oh. Oops.

"Let's get some fresh air. You need that water. Both of you," Finn states.

"I'm going to the ladies' room," Bethany counters with pink cheeks and glassy eyes.

"We'll walk you to your cousins then. There are too many eyes on you right now, and I'm not leaving you alone."

"Aw, thanks, Finny," she coos and squeezes herself between us, linking arms and prancing toward our group.

All the guys—minus Ethan—catch up with us on the roof later, leaving the girls to their bathroom break.

"It's going to be really nice on Sunday. We should play football," Jared says, and I get a nervous feeling in my gut, remembering Eric's words from earlier.

"You might want to have a stomach bug that day."

Not exactly a threat, but enough to make me feel weird

about it. I don't want to ruin the night or start drama, so I don't speak up. Instead, I settle my nerves with a fifth... or maybe sixth pomegranate gin.

My vision is starting to blur around the edges, and I blink heavily, squinting at a dark corner on the opposite side of the building from us.

"Ethan?" I somewhat slur, and everyone looks at me, then follows my gaze to the couch in the corner.

"Am I super wasted and hallucinating too, or are we all seeing this?" Trace asks.

A tall blond man, maybe in his mid-twenties, cradles Ethan's face while they kiss hungrily in the dark corner.

"Huh," is all I can manage in my current state. He's been flirty, yes, but I didn't expect him to have his tongue down a man's throat like that.

"Don't get any ideas. You're *mine*, Cali Boy," Finn whispers into my ear. I squint up at him, but he doesn't look shocked. Like at all. Maybe he knew about Ethan.

"Don't worry, he's not broody enough for me," I tease.

Everyone else is too busy staring at their apparently bisexual friend to notice us making *'come fuck me'* eyes at each other.

CHAPTER TWENTY-EIGHT

FINN

We left the club, or as Ollie obsessively called it, the *speakeasy*, and took another Uber home, passing out after two failed hand jobs and one half-attempted blow job. It's embarrassing, really; we're eighteen. We should never be too drunk to get off. I tried to tell him the drinks were too strong, but apparently, pomegranate is the nectar of the gods, and he couldn't withstand its siren's call. Well, that's what drunk Ollie told me Friday night. He's obsessed with the place—and that drink—and already wants to go back. I may have to meet this elusive owner and offer some kind of deal... or bribe... so we don't have to rely on Alyssa or Bethany to come here anymore.

The revelation about Ethan wasn't really a revelation to Bethany, Jared, or me, and Beth's cousins don't know him well enough to care one way or another. So that really left the shock for Trace and Danny, and I guess Oliver, too. I'm not too surprised he didn't give a fuck and came out abruptly like that. Ethan's always been the more wild and free kind of friend, doing or saying what he feels, when he feels it. Spontaneous, you could call him.

Ollie and I both slept Saturday away, and our parents didn't bother us, knowing that we're working on some of our final projects. I texted Ethan later in the day to make sure he was okay and remembered everything. He was fine, as usual. It's hard to phase him. He said he didn't even think about it. He met someone he clicked with and just went for it, and *that* I can definitely understand.

And now it's Sunday. It's the first day since January that's been somewhat dry and barely warm enough for us to play flag football, and I am pumped. Definitely not pumped that Eric is here, but he seems to have mellowed out, and we don't speak anyway. Just because we're playing football doesn't mean that has to change.

I put the Jeep in park and hop out. The scent of damp earth and wood smoke from nearby chimneys fills my nose as the crisp wind whips my hair around my head. I pull my beanie out of my pocket and slip it over my hair, taming the unruly strands. I should probably just give in to the man bun like Oliver tells me to.

"Smells like it might actually snow one last time," I say.

"Yeah, it's a bit cold to be playing football," Ollie complains, even though it was way colder the day we played back in January.

"Don't act like you weren't just as excited as me to see the forecast," I retort.

Oliver just chuckles. "Yeah, yeah, point taken."

We make it to the picnic tables where the guys are standing, Jayden too. We say hello and drop our bags, starting to stretch. Eric is quiet, but I still give him a slight head nod. No reason to start the game on a bad foot.

Oliver breaks away from Eric, and Jared spots his opening. He lets the ball go in one fluid movement, and Ollie jumps into the air, not stopping his forward momentum. He catches the ball and lands perfectly on his feet like a fucking house cat. Gliding down the field gracefully, his lithe form weaves in and out of the guys on the other team like he's figure skating. The agility this kid has is insane. Must be from all the surfing. I can't help but feel proud of how he's taken to most of my friends and to football. He's a natural athlete, that's for sure.

By the end of the game, Oliver once again kept all of his flags and scored the most touchdowns. And once again, Eric is salty. It's fucking hilarious that this surfer boy from California moves to the Midwest and completely sweeps the floor with these guys who have been playing football since they could walk.

"Good game, boys, good game," Jared says per usual. Eric just mumbles something about how it used to be, but I ignore him. I don't know why he's acting like such a little bitch lately.

We jog in place and stretch out our sore muscles, cooling down before heading to the two picnic tables where Jared set up the drink cooler. We've worked up a sweat, so it's not too chilly to have a quick lunch outside. I grab a red Gatorade and toss a blue one to Oliver, smirking. His lip curls up on one end, clearly remembering the first day we met and my embarrassing confession. He unscrews the cap and takes a few swigs, keeping eye contact as his Adam's apple bobs with the force of swallowing. His tongue darts out to lick the tiny blue droplet from his lip, and I've never wanted to be a drop of Gatorade so fucking bad in my life. He knows he's teasing me as his eyes sparkle with mirth when I try to subtly adjust the growing bulge in my pants.

The little shit.

"Yo, Oliver, your turkey swiss is in the separate blue cooler in the backseat," Jared shouts. "My mom bought the bread you told me about, so you're all good, man, I promise."

I completely trust Jared, so I don't question it. Don't even think twice about it.

"Thanks, Jared," Oliver says as he walks toward the truck to retrieve his lunch, but Eric cuts him off with a palm to the chest. I clench my fists and stand, ready to intervene. I don't like Eric touching him.

At all.

"I'll grab it, man. I gotta go get the big one anyway." He smiles, but it seems a little strained.

"Okay, thanks," Oliver mumbles, and I plop back down, motioning for him to sit beside me on the bench.

Eric comes back a few minutes later with the two coolers and sets them down on the table. I grab the little blue one and hand it to Oliver.

We all dig into our lunches, laughing about how Mr. Rattler accidentally farted in class on Wednesday when he bent down to pick up the dry erase marker he dropped. Ethan is nearly in tears trying to recount the story to everyone else. Just like he was the day it happened.

Poor guy. He's never gonna live that shit down.

Oliver clears his throat next to me, and I glance over at him. He's opening and closing his fist like he's squeezing an invisible stress ball.

"You okay?" I murmur softly.

"Yeah. . . I just. . ." He grimaces and rubs the base of his throat.

"What? What's wrong?" My eyes scan his face, darting all around and cataloging everything.

"I dunno. I feel kind of strange. Like anxious, maybe? And my fingers feel kind of tingly."

I hold his Gatorade out to him. "Here, take another drink. Maybe you're low on electrolytes or something. And put my gloves on," I say, pulling them from my front hoodie pocket and plopping them down on the weathered table. "Your fingers are probably just cold."

He's still clenching his fist repeatedly but stops to look up at me, eyebrows drawing together and creasing in the center. "Huh?" he asks, looking completely confused.

I sit up straighter and set the drink down, concerned by his strange behavior.

He clears his throat again and then coughs, gaining the attention of the other guys.

I place my hand on his back and rub in slow, soothing circles. "Oliver, what's the matter?" I whisper urgently, trying not to panic. His breaths are starting to pick up speed, and he's damn near hyperventilating.

Is he having a panic attack or something?

"What's happening?" Jared sounds worried, but I ignore him for now.

Oliver sways in his seat, collapsing into me like he can't even hold himself up anymore.

"Shit, Ollie!" I scoop him up and carefully lay him on the ground. Everyone is talking over one another, and I can't think straight.

"Shut the fuck up, you idiots! Jared, call 911, *now*!" I bark out.

"Oliver, try and breathe, *please*. Just keep looking at me, focus on my voice."

I try to infuse confidence into my tone that I'm definitely not feeling, but I need to stay as calm as possible so he doesn't freak out. I grab Oliver's hand and squeeze. "You're okay, baby. Stay calm. Help is coming."

His wheezing is getting worse.

"What's wrong with him?" I vaguely hear Jared's yelling, but I can't focus on anyone other than my boyfriend right now.

"Finn! They're asking what's wrong with him!" Jared shouts, his voice cracking with distress.

I press my fist to my mouth, trying not to lose it. "I don't know! *I don't fucking know!*"

Oliver's just lying there, staring back at me with panic-stricken eyes. His chest heaves with the exertion of trying to breathe. My eyes burn with unshed tears as I fight the torrent of emotions swirling around inside of me right now.

The color drains from his face, his skin goes deathly pale, and his smaller hand grows cold and clammy.

Fuck, fuck, fuck!

His lips are turning blue and a little puffy, and he's clawing at his throat while his mouth gasps for air like a fish out of water. Bile churns in my stomach, and my throat aches with emotion. I feel completely helpless and useless seeing him like this, just waiting for someone else to come save *my* brother.

I see a droplet land on my gray hoodie and seep into the fibers, darkening the color. I glance at the overcast sky, but there aren't any storm clouds. Another drop plops on my chest.

It's not raining.

I'm crying.

I grab Oliver's other hand before he breaks the skin on his neck and his whole body thrashes against me. It looks like he's having a seizure, and the anguish drilling a hole into my heart is all-consuming.

God, please, I can't lose him, too.

"Oliver. . ." I sob, turning my head to wipe my snotty nose on my shoulder.

"Help is coming. Just hang in there, *pleease.*"

This is bringing up way too many memories I've fought hard to bury, and I'm about to lose my goddamn mind. The despair is trying to claw its way to the surface, ripping strips of flesh from my insides and shredding my heart on its frenzied ascent.

I lift my head to the sky and roar, "Fuuuck!"

This helpless feeling is turning into anger, and I try not to lash out at my friend when I demand, "Where the fuck are they, Jare?!"

The guys are huddled behind me, hovering around Jared's phone with grim expressions on their faces. Jayden is crying while Trace hugs him to his side.

"They're three minutes out," Jared says, voice trembling.

Oliver stops flailing, and I whip my head around to stare down at him. His eyes flutter, and he's not struggling anymore. His arms go limp in my grasp. I place them on the ground and gently cup his face with my palms as I lean forward. "Hey, hey, Ollie. Keep looking at me, just keep looking at me," I choke out, emotion clogging my throat as I try not to crumble.

Then his eyes roll to the back of his head, and his lids flicker shut.

No.

No!

"Oliver!"

"*Ollie!*" I bend over and place my ear to his chest.

I'm not sure he's breathing. If he is, it's too shallow to notice.

Oh God, oh fuck. This can't happen.

I pull my hair hard, nearly ripping the strands from my scalp. Three minutes is too fucking long!

And then it clicks like a lightbulb.

The EpiPen. The fucking EpiPen!

I sprint over to the bench and desperately rifle through Oliver's backpack until my fingers graze the distinctive shape of the large plastic tube, and I yank it out. I quickly scan the three easy steps as I dash back to him.

I uncap the top of the pen with my teeth and spit it out as I jam the orange tip directly into his thigh, straight through his pants, until I hear the click.

The effect is swift, and I've never been so fucking grateful in my entire life when I hear that first wheezing inhale. Then another. Every strangled breath he takes has me silently thanking God for listening to my desperate prayers.

Ollie's eyes flicker open—wide and terrified and nearly bulging out of their sockets.

"Hey, hey, you're okay." I grab his hand, and his frantic eyes flit to mine. "Shh. Just focus on breathing. I'm here. I've got you." I brush his hair off his forehead and maneuver him so that his back is to my front and he's sitting between my legs. I gently guide him to rest against me and keep my palm over his heart. Partly to soothe him and partly to reassure myself that he's actually breathing.

"Easy there, Cali Boy. Just take slow, easy breaths. Paramedics should be here any minute."

I know he can't respond right now, but I continue to whisper reassurances into his ear until EMS arrives. I don't give a fuck that all my friends are standing there watching.

I stand there numbly as the paramedics work on Oliver. I'm trying to process what the *fuck* just happened.

There's a heavy feeling in my stomach, and the sounds around me seem to go in and out as I watch my boyfriend *suffer*.

". . . he's in shock, yeah, I know. Well, try and get him to talk."

A woman in her mid-thirties with a kind face and slick blonde ponytail places her hand tenderly on my shoulder to try and get my attention.

"Do you know what he's allergic to?"

"Uh. . ." My brain does not want to work right now.

"You used the EpiPen, right? He went into anaphylaxis, and it's the only thing that saved him. *You* saved him."

What?

I thought I was using the shot to jump-start his system until help arrived. I rub my forehead, and I'm starting to get a headache from the stress.

"Peanuts, but he didn't eat. . ." I trail off as my brain catches up to my words, and my furious eyes seek out Jared.

He must read my mind because he instantly holds his hands up in surrender. "I swear to God, Finn, I would *never* do that. My *mom* would never do that. You've *got* to believe me!" He's damn near tears, but I'm already far past that point, so I don't give a fuck about his feelings, even if he is my oldest friend.

"Finn!" Ethan comes jogging over as the paramedics lift my stepbrother onto the stretcher after stabilizing him.

He's carrying a plastic baggie with a partially eaten sandwich in it. *Oliver's* partially eaten sandwich.

"I went back to see what Oliver ate and look," Ethan

proceeds to open the baggie and take off the top layer of bread. There, smeared right on top of the cheese, is a tiny streak of peanut butter. He probably couldn't even taste it.

I feel my face heat up until I'm sure it's as red as the sirens on top of the ambulance. I slowly and methodically turn around to face my other friends.

I'm about to commit murder. In front of the police, no less.

Eric immediately averts his eyes and stuffs his hands in his pocket.

My eye twitches from the repressed anger I'm feeling and the strong need to *maim*. This motherfucker has been jealous of Oliver since day one, but to try and *kill* him?

I fucking erupt.

I stalk toward Eric like the prey he's about to become and snatch him up by the front of his shirt. I yank so hard I hear his shirt rip as I drag him up to my face, centimeters apart.

"You tried to kill my brother?" I ask calmly through a clenched jaw.

Eric opens his mouth to answer, but I don't even give him a chance. I use my leverage on his shirt to abruptly shove him back a step while I cock my other fist back and swing full force into the side of his face. I hear a sickening crunch, and I don't know if I just broke his face or my hand. I can't feel a thing with all the adrenaline coursing through my system.

He cries out and slumps to the ground when I let go. Jared pulls me back in a bear hug as I lunge toward Eric again.

"You think I'm fucking playing right now?! Test me. Fucking test me, Eric! I dare you!"

It's only because of Jared's whispered words that I stop.

"Finn, calm down. Let us handle this coward. Oliver needs you."

I glance over to see Oliver with his eyes closed and an oxygen mask over his nose and mouth. They already have an IV going.

Eric is sobbing on the ground in front of me, clutching the side of his face as blood trickles from the split in his eyebrow. "I'm sorry, Finn. It was supposed to be a joke. I just thought he'd break out into hives or something."

I curl my lip and bare my teeth in disgust at him. "You're fucking dead to me, and you better believe we'll be pressing charges. If you *ever* even look at my brother again, I'll make sure Jared's not around next time I come for you."

He just gulps at that and stares down at his feet, clearly ashamed and worried.

A policeman and paramedic stalk toward us from the other side of the ambulance; thankfully, they somehow missed me punching Eric in the face.

Jared nudges me and murmurs, "I got this."

"Yeah, we've got the evidence." Ethan holds the baggie up. "I'm sure you can give your statement later, but we'll get it started. Just go be with Ollie."

Jared intercepts the police officer and lets the paramedic continue toward the rest of us. "Are any of you family? Someone can ride to the hospital with him."

"He's my brother," I say confidently as I step forward and climb into the back of the ambulance, leaving all the bullshit behind and focusing on what's important.

Oliver.

CHAPTER TWENTY-NINE

FINN

I brush Oliver's tangled golden locks away from his face and press my lips to his forehead. He looks so small and fragile, lying in the sterile hospital bed with all these tubes and wires hooked up to him. I squeeze his hand, leaning in to whisper into his ear, "I love you, baby." They said he might be able to hear me, that his body's resting, but talking to him may help him come to.

I need to see those beautiful blue eyes again. To know he's actually okay.

A throat clears from the doorway, and I flick my tired gaze over there.

Well, I guess the cat is out of the fucking bag now.

My friends probably know, Vivian definitely knows, and my dad—fuck him, I don't give a shit. The lie I always tell myself tastes sour on my tongue and churns in my stomach when I swallow it.

It's not about the angry vein ticking in Dad's temple as he stares at our joined hands from the hospital room doorway. It's about Ollie. It's about making sure this fucking amazing ray of light in all our lives wakes up and is *okay*. I fucking *need* him to be okay.

Vivian bursts into the room past my father and gently takes Ollie's other hand, careful of the IV. "Oh my God. My baby," she sobs with a hand over her mouth. My dad strides over and pulls a chair for Viv, gently guiding her to sit down. She looks a little unsteady.

"What happened?" Her tear-streaked face looks to me for answers. She doesn't mean physically—I know the doctor already spoke to them about his medical condition. Dad would have had the full report, too, doctor to doctor. Even if it's only to look good in front of his wife.

Nope, she means the *how* and the *why*. The hard part. The part that even I don't have all the answers to. But I can speculate.

I explain to them how *Eric fuckface Carson* has had it out for Oliver since day one. His jealousy over our friendship and Oliver melding into the group seamlessly, pushing him out. I even tell them what happened two days before they left for their honeymoon at flag football. And then, about the icy puddle at school. I can apologize to Oliver for not keeping those secrets later. This is serious, and we need to, at the very least, get a restraining order against Eric. He's clearly unhinged and needs help controlling himself.

Vivian is in tears, and Dad is livid by the time I finish. I've never seen him turn such a vibrant shade of red before. If the situation wasn't so dire, I might laugh. But then again, he looks like he really *does* care. Like he wants to be the one to murder Eric himself. I'm a little taken aback because it's more than he did for me when I was in the hospital and needed him. But I'm glad another person is standing behind Oliver right now, so I shove those thoughts to the back of my mind.

Retelling what happened and seeing the anguish on Vivian's face causes me to shift uncomfortably in my chair. The pain of nearly losing Ollie reverberates in my chest and sends a shock wave of chills across my entire body.

Vivian is sobbing, and Dad crouches in front of her, taking her hands in his own. "Sweetheart, look at me."

I try to give their moment some privacy, but it's hard in this room, and I'm not willing to leave Ollie's side.

"Oliver will be okay. Trust me. His body is resting after the massive adrenaline crash, and he'll wake when he's ready. They had to give him more epinephrine after the initial shot, so he's exhausted. He's on antihistamines, oxygen, and IV fluids to increase his blood pressure. He's in good hands," Dad assures her. "As for this other boy. *Eric*," he sneers, glancing at me, and for once, I agree with his tone as I bite back my own growl.

"I'm going to call Hank."

Hank is Dad's best golfing buddy. I wouldn't say best friend because all they do is golf together. I'm convinced he's incapable of nurturing anything beyond that. Well, until Vivian. I can admit that he treats her right.

Hank O'Brien is a top detective with the CPD, and even though we're in the suburbs, he can still help. He'll push anything through the system, for anyone, for the right favor. Dad doesn't need to explain further to me. There will be a restraining order by tomorrow and a warrant for Eric's arrest by Wednesday. And the evil side of me hopes it happens at school and I'm there to watch.

"Dad, can I talk to you outside for a second?" I flick my eyes to the door, indicating we should step outside, away from Oliver and Vivian. I don't think she even notices when we leave. She's just sitting there clutching Ollie's hand and whispering to him. Probably a lot like I was when they first walked in.

I close the door behind us and tell him more about what happened after the ambulance arrived.

"I don't think it'll be an issue, but I punched Eric in the face." I hold my hand up—bruised and swollen. "Might have broken my hand."

Dad's brows furrow, and he gently grabs my hand in his, squeezing it lightly. "That hurt?"

I shake my head.

"That?"

"Not really. Just sore." I feel like I'm ten years old again, and it's the last time Dad gave a shit about me falling off my bike and getting hurt.

"Ice it, but it just looks bruised, maybe sprained."

"Yeah, I'm not too worried about myself at the moment. Just Ollie," I admit.

"You two are close." It's a statement, neither a question nor an accusation.

I meet his onyx eyes head-on. "We are. But I'm not discussing this right now."

His jaw muscles clench hard, but he just nods his head once. I'm relieved he's dropping it.

"Is Eric hurt at all? Do we need to be prepared for him to press charges against you?"

"I mean, I split his shit open," I say unrepentant.

Dad sighs. "His shit?"

I nod, swiping my finger across my eyebrow to indicate where.

"I hope that won't hurt our case, but it should be pretty cut and dry."

"I'm so fucking mad at myself that I didn't see something like this coming, Dad!" I slam my fist against the concrete wall and hiss, "Fuck!"

The nurses at the station stand up questioningly. They must see the pain reflecting in my eyes and turn away, sitting back down to give us privacy.

"Hey, hey. Wyatt, look at me. Don't do that. It wasn't in your control. You can't beat yourself up over it. Physically or mentally."

Is he consoling me?

Fuck, this is too weird and too similar to the conversation we should have had about Mom's death and the accident.

I pinch the bridge of my nose and squeeze my eyes shut. Nope. Can't do it. One tragedy at a time.

"You said the boys all gave their statements at the scene? And you even have the sandwich?"

I take a deep breath and compose myself before opening my eyes again. "Yeah, Ethan had it. And Eric confessed to all of us."

"Alright, I'm going to have Hank come to the hospital and get your statement. I don't want you going to the precinct like you're the criminal."

"Thanks, Dad," I say, and I actually mean it. He nods to me and pulls out his phone before I slip back into the room to be with Oliver.

CHAPTER THIRTY
OLIVER

My mind is foggy, and my body feels weightless, but I can't open my eyes. I vaguely register a squeeze to my hand and the soft murmurs whispering across the dark oblivion I'm floating in, but I can't respond. I move my arms like I'm swimming, desperately trying to paddle my way to the surface.

To Finn.

To my *home.*

The sounds are getting louder, and my heart is pounding in my chest, thrashing against my rib cage.

Beep. Beep. Beep.

"Shhh. Baby, you're okay. I'm here." Another squeeze, but I still can't open my eyes. I'm drifting in this vast emptiness, and I'm just so, so tired. The sound of Finn's deep voice soothes me, and I let go, falling back into the darkness.

The next time I rouse, the gentle beep of my own heartbeat pulls me from my slumber. The harsh scents of plastic, bleach, and *hospital* fill my nose as I lift my hand to scratch at the itch on my face. My fingers touch plastic tubing, which I follow to my nose.

Oxygen.

What the fuck happened?

Something tugs at my hand, and I look down to see an IV taped to the top. *An IV?* I sit up too fast, and the world spins. I think I might be sick.

"Whoa, whoa. You're as white as a sheet, Ollie. Lie back down." Finn eases me back and grabs the hand control to incline the bed instead. The whirring of the bed's gears fills my head, and I close my eyes as another wave of dizziness washes over me.

"Water," I croak out. My mouth and throat feel dry and sore. I still haven't opened my eyes back up, but I hear Finn rustling around, and then a cool thumb caresses my bottom lip. I open my mouth on instinct, and Finn places the straw on my tongue. I greedily gulp down mouthful after mouthful of cool water, soothing my aching throat.

Finn pulls the cup away. "Okay, that's probably enough for now."

"Tell me," I rasp out. The water helped some, but I still don't feel good. And then I find out why. Finn tells me everything, and I can't even imagine the fear or panic he would have been feeling at that moment. He wouldn't have known it was my allergy; the food was supposed to be safe. But his quick thinking literally saved my life.

I owe Wyatt Finnegan my whole entire life.

"They're not sure if you actually stopped breathing or if your airways just swelled so much it appeared that way, so you have to stay overnight."

"Stopped breathing!" I shout because. . . *what the actual fuck*!

"Yes. Ollie, it was. . ." He closes his eyes and takes a

deep breath. When he opens them again, they're glistening with so much emotion that I feel my own eyes well up.

"It was bad. I thought you were going to die. I thought I was going to watch the only other person I've ever truly loved die right in front of me, *again*." His whole body shudders.

"I should have thought of your allergy sooner. I'm such an idiot."

"Finn, you saved me. Come here, please." I scoot over in the small hospital bed and pull the sheets back, patting the space next to me. I probably stink, but I need a hug, and I think he does too.

Finn slips his sneakers off and climbs into bed next to me, careful not to pull on any of the wires and tubes connected to me.

"How long have I been out?" My voice sounds weak, and my lungs *feel* weak.

"About four hours."

"Where's my mom?"

"They got here not long after the ambulance, and I just convinced her to take a break and grab something to eat. She's probably going to be mad at me for that, now that you've woken up while she was gone."

I snicker and then cough. Fuck, my lungs feel wheezy.

Finn presses the nurse's button. "They said you would need to do some breathing treatments when you woke up," he explains. "You need to do them right away. I can't ever see you like that again, dude." He curls on his side and lays his head on my shoulder. He seems so small and vulnerable right now, so completely unlike *my* Finn. And it's breaking my fucking heart.

He kisses my neck quickly and then hops out of bed

when we hear the nurse's cart rolling down the hallway. He's back in his chair before she even turns the corner.

"Well, hello there, Mr. Chase. It's so good to finally get to meet you. I'm Sarah, and I'll be your nurse until seven tonight. Then the lovely Rachel will be with you until the morning." Sarah seems young, probably right out of nursing school. She has baby pink scrubs and platinum blonde hair pulled back into a low bun. Her hazel eyes are kind when she asks if I'm ready for my treatment.

Twenty minutes later, she leaves after taking all of my vitals and telling me to order dinner. But I'm not really hungry for hospital food.

Mom rushes in immediately after Sarah leaves, and suddenly I feel completely exhausted. "Baby!" she coos. "Thank God you're awake! Are you okay? What do you need?" She pushes the hair off of my forehead.

I'm too tired to talk, and somehow Finn just knows this, so he answers for me. "He just had an albuterol nebulizer treatment, so he's supposed to rest his lungs right now and eat something, too."

"Oh, okay, good. I have a package of your favorite cookies in my purse if you're starving right now, honey?" I nod and eat the entire box before immediately passing out again.

The next time I woke up, Gabe was there. He was really concerned and helpful—doting on my mother and me while Finn's narrowed gaze followed him around the room. He still hasn't talked to his dad. I know it, or he would have told me. It'd be good for him, if he could just take the leap. Especially after what we found out the other day.

I ate a proper dinner, albeit a hospital meal, and then slept soundly through the entire night. I was released the next morning and was home by nine am.

I'm currently tucked in bed after a fresh shower. My mouth and tongue are still a little swollen, and my thigh aches from where Finn jammed the EpiPen in, but other than that, I feel okay.

Finn sneaks in after taking his own shower and ensuring our parents that everything would be fine. He's going to be the one staying home from school to take care of me. Gabe already has surgeries planned, and those patients need him more than I do. My mom has the entire week blocked out for event planning. She now runs a charity for heart research, which she and Gabe set up on their *honeymoon*. My mom has always worked, and now that she doesn't have to, I'm not surprised that she couldn't even take a full week off before starting something new.

Finn climbs into my bed and spoons me, tugging my back to his front. "Just like old times," he murmurs. "No parents at home."

I thrust my ass out to him and rub it along his dick. He groans and pulls back. "Cali Boy, we shouldn't. You just got out of the hospital, for fuck's sake. I feel like I'd be taking advantage of you or some shit."

I roll over and prop myself up on one elbow. "You wouldn't be. I can't kiss or use my mouth right now, but there's nothing wrong with my ass," I tease, and then I get a little more serious. "I just want to feel close to you."

Finn pushes me to my back and buries his face in my neck. "I'll have to kiss and suck on your body instead then." I shiver at his words and reach down under the covers to slip my boxers off.

Yeah, no shame. I'm getting some.

Finn whips the covers back and gazes at my naked body. My dick twitches and gets hard from his stare alone. My whole being shudders as Finn runs his rough hands up my bare torso, *appreciating* me. *Loving* me.

"Finn," I whine and thrust my hips up.

"Not yet," he says, rolling me over onto my stomach.

"I want to try something new."

"Something new?" I repeat. He's already fucked me; what else could he want to do?

"Yeah. You're gonna fucking love it, trust me. Just relax and let me make you feel good. Forget about everything except for the feel of my mouth on you."

"Mouth?" I repeat again, like a talking parrot. And then my ass cheeks are spread and a warm, wet tongue is lapping at my hole.

"Oh fuuuuuck," I pant, moaning and squirming. I spread my legs and arch my back, thrusting my ass up. Again, no fucking shame at this point. He can do *anything* to me, and I'll love it.

He licks me from my balls to my asshole and back again, teasing me. He spreads my cheeks wider and circles me with the tip of his tongue, adding pressure ever so slightly until he pushes in and starts to fuck me with it.

"Finn. *Holy fucking shit.* Oh my God, I'm not going to last." He just keeps licking and probing, and *fuck*. . . how have we not done this yet? He pulls his tongue out, and I whine pitifully.

"On your knees, ass up." The sound of a bottle of lube opening seems to echo around the otherwise quiet room.

I obey, immediately crawling up to my hands and knees. He presses down between my shoulder blades, forcing me to keep my top half on the bed and my ass in the air, completely exposed. He nudges my knees further apart, and I groan at the stretch, burying my face in the bed. This is so embarrassing, yet it's turning me on so fucking much.

"Fuck. Touch me, please."

Cool liquid drips down my crack, over my hole, and down to my balls. I can hear him squirt more on his fingers, then he's pressing in with one. I reach under to grab my aching cock because I need some stimulation, but Finn pushes my hand away.

"No. I don't want you to come yet."

I whimper but don't reach to touch myself again. Finn adds a second finger, pumping in and out of me. He curls them down and hits that spot again, and I cry out. "Right there, oh fuck!" Finn immediately uncrooks his fingers. "Hey—" I protest, but he just cuts me off.

"Not yet." And then he's shoving a third finger in me, and I'm so full, so fucking full, but I need more—I need his cock. And I need to be close to him.

"Fuck me. *Now,*" I demand. Finn slips his fingers out and pauses.

"What? Finn, please." I'm being needy as fuck right now, but I don't care. I almost died yesterday.

"I'm just staring at your gaping hole. Just waiting for my cock. It's the sexiest thing I've ever seen in my entire life."

Guess this just reinforces the fact that Finn likes to *look* at me—it's definitely not the first time he's done it.

And fucking hell does it turn me on.

My moan dies in my throat when he pushes into me. I'm so open and relaxed that his head easily slips past the tight ring of muscle, and then he's sliding all the way in until my ass is pressed against his pelvis and our balls are touching.

I arch my back even more. "You've teased me enough, you moody asshole, now fuck me. I want to feel you."

Finn listens and starts pounding into me. My breath hitches on every thrust as I'm pushed into the headboard. I reach one arm out and brace against it while keeping my shoulders down and ass up. This new leverage allows me to push back against Finn's cock, and we start a punishing pace. I'm going to be sore tomorrow, and I can't fucking wait.

Finn reaches around and bands his arm around my torso, pulling me up so that we're both on our knees as he continues to fuck me relentlessly. His arms are wrapped so tight around me while he fucks into me; it feels like the world's filthiest hug. He suctions his mouth to my neck, and I writhe against his cock. He's going to leave a mark. He's claiming me. I tilt my head, welcoming it. One hand slides up to my nipples and begins tugging on them, while the other slides lower and fists my weeping cock. I'm so close.

"Come with me," I moan out seconds before I'm nutting all over my sheets and Finn's hand. My ass clenches around Finn, causing his hips to stutter and then surge forward, deep inside me. I can feel his dick pulsing, filling me with his cum, and I grind against him.

He hisses and pulls out. "Shit, that's sensitive."

I fall forward, back to my hands and knees.

"Don't move."

I stay with my ass in the air. I can feel my hole loose and open, still pulsing and dripping with Finn's cum. His rough hands caress my cheeks—pushing them together, then spreading them apart again. More of his jizz oozes out and down my balls, dripping to the bed.

"I want to see this every fucking day for the rest of my

life," he confesses and then leaves for the bathroom, returning with a warm washcloth to clean me up. I'm too shattered to feel embarrassed. That was rough and hot, and I want to do it again. But I almost died yesterday, so instead, I yawn and lay my head back on my pillow.

"Nap time?" Finn questions.

"Yes, but first, I want you to do something for me."

"Okay. . ." He sounds unsure.

"Talk to your dad tonight. Life's too short, and anything can happen. I know I don't need to tell you that, but it's true. Just do it for me. You already said you would. Please."

"Okay, Cali Boy, I promise. Now just rest. I'm worried I wore you out."

"No, you just put me back to sleep. That's a good thing." I'm smiling as I drift off to sleep with my stepbrother and the love of my life next to me.

CHAPTER THIRTY-ONE
FINN

"You're a doctor, Dad. A *surgeon*." I pace across his office while he watches me with his hands steepled in front of his chin.

Back and forth. Back and forth.

I ambushed my dad when he got home late tonight. Oliver crashed early, around nine pm. Now it's an hour later, and I'm making good on the promise I made him earlier.

"Yet, you didn't give a single fuck about me or my injuries after the accident." I glance at him, and his jaw is tight. I don't give him a chance to interrupt and continue on with what I need to get off my chest. I'm tired of these feelings eating away at my insides.

"You didn't rush to me in the ER. You didn't scrub in for my surgery. You didn't care how I felt after I watched Mom die right in front of me!" I shout as I lean forward in his face and slam my bruised fist down on his desk. The human heart-shaped glass paperweight teeters precariously on top of a stack of papers but doesn't fall.

"You didn't take me to any doctor appointments afterward. You didn't check on my wounds. You didn't do anything a good doctor does for his patient, let alone what a dad does for his son who nearly died." I ease out of his face and turn around, raking my hands through my messy hair.

"I get that Mom died, and it was my fault. But. . . what the fuck is *wrong* with you?" My voice cracks on the last word because it hurts to let this out.

It hurts like hell.

"I was only sixteen," I add quietly.

His oversized desk chair squeaks against the marble floor before I feel his tight embrace wrap around me from behind.

"Son. . ."

I try to shrug him off, but he's taller and stronger than me. He hugs me tighter as I continue to struggle. "Lemme go," I grit out, refusing to show any more weakness in front of him.

"No. Wyatt. Just stop for a second. Can I talk now?"

I huff out a breath and stop trying to wrench myself free. He grips my shoulders and spins me around to face him.

"Is that truly what you think?"

I scowl. "What are you talking about, Dad? I stated facts. *Fucking facts!*"

He winces and slumps his shoulders, looking defeated. "Yes. Right. I meant the part where you think I blame you for your mother's death."

I clench my jaw and look off to the side, squinting my eyes to examine the oil painting of an eighteenth century merchant ship that's hung there since I can remember. I wonder if Oliver has seen this one.

"Look at me, Son." I begrudgingly comply and turn my head to face him.

"Believe me when I say I *never* blamed you. I've never, not even once, thought it was your fault. It was a drunk driver, Wyatt. Driving on the wrong side of the highway. At night. No headlights until seconds before impact. . . need I go on? It was *not* your fault."

My heart starts to race, and my hands feel cold and clammy. Maybe Ollie was right, and he really doesn't blame me. "Then why have you treated me with such callous indifference for over a year? Why were you egging me on when Vivian first moved in? Calling her my mother. *Why?*" I let the emotion I always try to keep hidden shine through my eyes and bleed into my voice. I see the moment it hits him. The regret that he was a shitty father, a shitty doctor, and a shitty husband.

"I'm so sorry, Wyatt. I know it's not enough. And will probably *never* be enough. But I can't change the past, only the future, and I promise you I will, Son. I shouldn't have let things go on like this for so long. And I never should have allowed you to feel like that. Never should have said such cruel words to you. I had a talk with Vivian in Aruba. It was a wake-up call. She helped me realize how I treated you—how I spoke to you at our first family dinner—was completely unacceptable. I've been meaning to have this conversation with you for a while now, Wyatt. It tears me up inside that you've been blaming yourself this whole time. I had no idea. Your mother would be absolutely furious with me." His onyx eyes glisten with unshed tears.

I have to interrupt him because it really *was* my fault. "I'm the only reason she was driving that late on the highway. She came to see me play. And then right before. . ." I sniff. "I distracted her by laughing and joking. You see, Dad?

She wouldn't have even been there if it weren't for me!" My chin quivers, and I fucking hate it. I try to look away, but Dad grabs my cheeks between his rough palms and forces me to keep my eyes on him.

"Stop it. Right now. If it was anyone's fault besides that drunk son of a bitch that hit you, it was mine. I should have been there. Driving my wife, supporting my son. You should have been on the activity bus with your teammates. I let my career consume me your entire childhood, and then, after your mother passed, I let my grief consume me and neglect you."

I don't let him off that easily. I shake out of his grip and walk over to the desk, perching on the edge and forcing him to turn around to face me.

"I know Vivian's pregnant," I reveal. His eyes widen and dart to mine—his eyebrows nearly touching his hairline.

"How?"

"Doesn't matter. You need to change, Dad. Be the father to this baby that he or she deserves. Because you weren't it for me. You were never there, and then even worse, for the past year, you've made me fucking loathe myself. I had no one, Dad, no one!" I squeeze the edge of the desk so hard, I feel like my fingernails might rip off. I close my eyes for a minute, unable to stop the torment from leaking out of my chest. The beast is waking up, and he's hungry again. Hungry for more pain. So I shove it down to keep the monster at bay.

A sharp intake of breath filters in from the hallway, and I peer around Dad as he turns to see what kind of audience we have for our very private moment. And it's no surprise. Vivian is standing there clutching Oliver's arm with one hand and covering her mouth with the other. I don't need to look at Oliver to know pity and empathy are shimmering in his blue depths.

Well, this conversation is definitely over now. I stand up and march to the door.

"Wyatt, wait."

I won't wait. I'm done for the day and at my emotional limit.

I slip past Vivian and Oliver without making eye contact and power walk to my room. I need some alone time. To decompress and sift through that entire fucked up yet enlightening conversation we just had. I close my bedroom door behind me and lock it, flopping face down on my bed and groaning into my pillow.

What a clusterfuck this situation is.

There's a soft knock at my door, and I already know it's Ollie. I climb out of bed and answer the door. "You shouldn't be out of bed, Oliver," I chastise.

"I'm feeling a lot better. I needed to get out of bed for a little while. Mom and I made root beer floats. That's what we were going to tell you."

Now I feel even shittier that they overheard my outburst, and I stormed past them when they were just offering dessert. Vivian's pregnant, and Oliver nearly died. They don't need to deal with my traumatic past on top of it.

I sigh and tug him into my room. "Come here. You need to lie down." I steer him toward my bed that's already rumpled from where I was just tossing and turning. "I'm sorry. I shouldn't have shut you out like that." I help him into bed, walk around, and climb into the other side.

"It's okay. I know that had to have been a hard conversation, and I wanted to give you time to process. But now I'm here and hoping you'll talk to me."

How can I deny him when he's so genuine and so fucking polite? He was basically assaulted yesterday and nearly *died*, but he's worried about me and my issues.

God, I love him.

I tell him how my dad insists he doesn't blame me and never has, but the damage is done, and I'm fucked up because of it. I also apologize for letting it slip that I know Vivian is pregnant. I'm sure he wanted to have a private talk with his mother about something that big.

"It's fine. I talked to my mom and Gabe after you stormed off." He looks a little sheepish, but I'm really grateful he handled this one on his own. Feelings and babies and all that are not my jam.

"They're so excited for this baby, and I insisted we're happy for them too. No hard feelings whatsoever." He looks up at the ceiling, breaking eye contact. "I hope that's okay. It's just, there's no changing it, so what's the point of being anything but happy about it?"

"Dude, you are like pure fucking sunshine sometimes. Come here." I grab the nape of his neck and squeeze, pulling him to me. I press my mouth to his and kiss him reverently. "I love you. Thank you for handling that."

"Love you, too."

It still feels surreal, yet so good to hear those words from his lips. I lean forward to kiss them again.

CHAPTER THIRTY-TWO
FINN

"Bethany and the guys have been blowing up my phone since Sunday, worried about you," I tell Ollie as we veg out on our favorite overstuffed leather couches in the theater room. It's early Tuesday afternoon, and we're staying home another day to give his body more time to recover. And if he's staying home, you better believe I am too.

"Ugh. I haven't even looked at my phone since before all this shit happened," he grouses.

I slide my phone out of my pocket and check my notifications. "Ethan literally called me seven times in a row, which is not normal."

"Call him then. You're not interrupting anything." He waves his hand toward the TV where we have Food Network playing in the background.

I open my phone and click Ethan's name, calling him back.

"Dude! Finally! Switch to FaceTime! Hurry!"

"What? Why?" I do it anyway, and Ethan's large, beaming smile fills the screen.

"Ollie! Bro, you there? How are you?"

Ollie leans his head into view. "Hey, Ethan. I'm fine, just taking advantage of a good excuse to stay home from school." Playing it cool like always.

"Well, you shoulda been here today. The police just got here, and I think they're coming for Eric!" There's a manic gleam in his eye, and he might just be as sadistically satisfied by this as me.

"I wanted you guys to have front row seats," he whispers conspiratorially into the phone.

He flips the camera so we're looking at the Mall inside Preston Hall. A few students are milling about, but everyone is probably in the cafeteria.

"Are you hiding behind a corner like a creeper?" I snort.

"Shh! Watch!" The glee in his voice is fucking hilarious.

Two uniformed police officers drag a protesting Eric from the cafeteria and across the Mall.

"It was just a joke! I didn't mean to hurt him! I didn't know it was that bad, I swear! It wasn't even my idea! Hazel, she—"

"Kid. Stop talking," the burly officer with the beer gut says, cutting off whatever Eric was about to say to implicate Hazel. "You're only making things worse for yourself. I'd advise you to keep your mouth shut until you call your parents and they call their lawyer."

Eric huffs an indignant breath and hangs his head as the officers steer him through the gathering crowd with a firm grip on each elbow. His hands are bound with zip ties behind his back; luckily, no one sees where Ethan is hiding. They pass by, but our view is jostled around and goes dark for a second. I see a bunch of. . . leaves? Then the camera is in focus again, Eric is being folded into the back of a police cruiser, and they take off.

The camera flips, and Ethan grins, a twig sticking out of his thick raven locks.

"Dude, are you in a bush now?" Ollie snorts out.

"Fucking right I am. Did you want to miss that? Cuz I sure as hell didn't."

"You could have just recorded it and sent it later," I deadpan. But yeah, that was pretty fucking satisfying to watch. Even more than when I split his eyebrow.

"Nah. I don't need that kind of negativity stored on my phone. Bad karma. Besides, it was more exciting to see it live. Right?" He wiggles his eyebrows like an idiot, and I can't help but laugh.

"It *was* pretty satisfying," Ollie agrees.

"Hey, Ethan. Can you rally the troops and come over to our place after school? I don't feel like texting everyone separately. I'd rather just say what I need to say once."

"Yep, I got you, man. I need to get to class, but I'll see you guys later. Rest up, Ollie." And then he ends the call.

"What do you need to say to everyone, Finn?" There's a nervousness to his tone that tells me he already knows.

"Besides the fact that they all want to see you up and well again—because they do. You were on the ground, unresponsive last time they saw you. Jayden was a mess—"

"Shit." Ollie pinches the bridge of his nose. "I should have at least texted Jay back. Fuck, he's only fifteen. I wish he didn't have to see that. I wish none of them had to see that."

"I know, dude. Let's just make sure that *never* fucking happens again." I stretch my arm along the back of the couch, and Ollie cuddles into my side.

"So besides them wanting to see you, we need to talk to them. . . about us."

"What? No!" He sits up fast and stares at me with wild

eyes. “Don’t, Finn. Please. Not on top of everything else. I can’t deal with more.”

I tenderly cup his face in my palms. “Ollie, it'll be fine; trust me on this. I know I let you down, let you get hurt by Eric, *again*. And I hate myself for that. But these are my best friends. Everyone already knows Ethan is bi after the club, and no one gives a shit. They aren’t going to react badly. I swear to God.” I know he’s been traumatized by his past, I *know* this, but it’s not going to happen again.

“Okay, first of all. What Eric did—all of the times—was never your fault. You couldn’t have stopped any of it. The tackle, the puddle, the allergy. Completely out of your control. What you did do was help me, take care of me, fucking *save* me. So none of that, okay? And second, why does it have to happen right now? *Today*.”

I sigh. “Because. . . I lost my shit at the park, and I’m pretty sure it was obvious to everyone that I care about you a little more than as just a brother. I’ve had my suspicions that Danny knows for quite some time.”

“Shit. I got that vibe from Danny, too.”

“He saw me checking you out in the locker room on the first fucking day,” I admit, and a lopsided grin tugs at his full lips.

“And I’d rather tell them in the privacy of our own home where no one can overhear. They won’t out us. I promise you that, Oliver.”

May as well bite the bullet and tell him all of it. “I think my dad knows, too. He saw me in the hospital with you and then said something about how close we are. We probably need to prepare for another family dinner soon. One where everyone lays *all* their cards on the table.”

For being a brand new family, we sure do have some serious fucking topics to discuss.

"Fuck my life," he groans and flops back against the couch.

I check the security tablet by the front door and see all six of my closest friends standing there. It's Tuesday afternoon, and the whole gang's here to check on Ollie and hear whatever I have to say. I take a deep breath, knowing they won't judge us, but still feeling uneasy.

I open the front door, and they all file into the foyer. Bethany slips in first, a giant teddy bear clutched to her chest.

"Where is my sweet baby? I need to see him right now!" Bethany exclaims, emphasizing her demand with a stomp of her Jimmy Choos.

Ollie steps into view down the hallway and gives a little wave.

"You could have texted me back! I just wanted to know how you were doing!" Bethany shouts down the hallway to him, and he quickly comes over to us.

"Yeah, me too," Jayden says, sniffling. "I thought you died there on the ground, right in front of me. You looked dead." He pushes his glasses down and wipes at his eyes quickly.

Ollie pulls Jayden into a fierce embrace, squeezing him tightly. "Hey, I'm sorry, Jay. I just needed some time to come back to myself." Then he grabs Bethany into the same hug. "Sorry, Beth," he whispers and lets go. "I haven't had friends who care like that in a while."

"Are you guys really making the kid who almost died apologize? Get out of here with that." Trace strolls in, dapping us both up. "Ollie, it's good to see you up on your feet, bro. Don't listen to them. You can take time for yourself to unplug. People do it all the time, and they don't even need a near-death experience as an excuse."

Jared, Ethan, and Danny bring up the rear, following us all to the kitchen where we congregate around the island and the fruit and veggie trays Ollie put out.

Jared's been oddly quiet. He didn't text me much beyond making sure Ollie woke up and was okay. He clears his throat now and blurts out, "Can I just say something real quick? Ollie, I am so sorry. I feel so fucking guilty. Even my mom does. It was my responsibility to make sure your food was safe, and I failed."

Shit. I had no idea he felt like this. I wouldn't wish that on anyone because I know how it feels.

Before I can speak up, Ollie interjects. "Please don't do that. I've had enough of people blaming themselves." He pauses and eyes me purposely, then continues, "It was no one's fault except Eric's. No one could have anticipated he'd do something like that."

"Well, it may be Hazel's fault, too," Ethan adds. "I heard Eric snitched at the station, and it's not looking good for either of them."

We all sit quietly for a minute and let that sink in while we munch on our snacks.

I reach under the island and grab Ollie's hand. "There's something else I wanted to tell you while you're all here." I squeeze his hand for reassurance and just dive in head first. "Ollie. . . he's not just my stepbrother. He's my. . . boyfriend."

There's a beat of silence.

Or two.

"So, you're gay now?" Ethan asks. Fair enough question, I suppose.

"I don't think so. I just like Oliver," I answer truthfully.

"Huh," he says. "That's cool, bro. I'm just glad to see you happy again, honestly."

A chorus of agreement rings around me, and I feel a little choked up by it.

"I already knew," Danny chimes in, confirming what we both suspected. "And I agree with Ethan. You haven't been happy for a long time, Finn. But you are now, and that's what matters to me."

"I have to admit I'm a little shocked," Trace says, then amends his statement, "but totally cool with it, of course."

"I'm with Trace." Jared looks pretty shocked, his green eyes blinking rapidly.

He's probably beating himself up over not knowing sooner as my best friend, so I try to ease his mind a little. He's tortured himself over the sandwich, just like I did, and I don't want him feeling like this, too.

"It just happened. These feelings came out of nowhere, just like Ollie, and they turned my life inside out in the best possible way. I'm done fighting my emotions; I can't keep doing it. I'm taking steps to tackle some of my other issues, too. And it's all thanks to Ollie."

Jayden is the last of the guys to say anything, which isn't surprising. He's a lot younger than us, so he isn't around quite as much. "I'm really happy for you, Finn. And it actually explains a lot. Like why you always stare at him in Stats class."

"Thanks, little dude, but I don't *stare,*" I chuckle.

"Hah. You totally stare at Oliver. I never knew it was like that, but hey, if you're happy, it doesn't matter who you choose to love."

"So you guys love each other?" Jared asks. There's no

judgment, just open curiosity, so I decide to be open back, but Ollie beats me to it.

"Yeah. We do."

Everyone lets that settle in, and I realize Bethany's been quiet, which is not normal. I scan the kitchen. Where the fuck is she?

My concerned gaze finds her sitting in the corner at the small table with tears streaming down her cheeks, still clutching the fluffy white teddy bear to her chest. Her eyes are bright from crying, so I hurry over and pull her into my chest, hugging her in a big, brotherly embrace. "What's wrong? Are you mad I didn't tell you sooner?"

"Oh gosh no, Finn!" She wipes her face against the soft fabric of my black hoodie like she's done since we were kids. "You've just been so sad for so long. And then Hazel treated you so vile that I'm just so beyond happy for you. To see you with life in your eyes again. It's amazing. And now I know why. I mean, my baby *is* special." She grasps Oliver's wrist and pulls him over for a group hug, giggling instead of crying now. We hug her back, squeezing her smaller body between us.

She slips away and grabs the teddy bear. "This is for you, Ollie. Sorry it has tears and maybe some snot on it now." She thrusts it at him, and he goes a little pink in the ears but takes it.

"That's sweet. Thanks, Beth," Ollie mumbles as he gives her a side hug.

Bethany knows I can hear her—I'm standing right next to them—but she whispers into Oliver's ear anyway. "Finn used to be a lot different. . . before. You're bringing him back to who that boy was. The boy I grew up with and have loved like a brother my entire life. And for that, I love *you*."

She embraces him tightly and sniffles some more, wiping her nose on *his* hoodie now.

Who the fuck does that?

"Ugh. Beth. That's really nice, but *yuck*!" He tries to squirm out of her grip for a second, then just laughs, giving up and hugging her back.

"Love you too, by the way," he murmurs and kisses the top of her head, resting an arm over her shoulders as she leans into him.

My heart skips a beat at their exchange, and I clear my throat, feeling uncomfortably emotional in front of all these people. I return to my spot by the stove and lean against the countertop, crossing my arms.

"We aren't telling anyone else, though, so just keep it between all of us. I know without a doubt that I can trust each of you with this secret. We just don't want the drama or the attention that something like this would stir up in high school. We want to get through the next couple of months, graduate, and live our lives. . . hopefully with all of you still as our friends."

Ollie decides to reveal a little more, which is a big step for him. I wasn't going to share his business, as that's his story to tell, not mine.

"When I came out to my best friends back in California, they turned against me and bullied me for an entire semester, so I was really nervous when Finn said we needed to talk to you about it. And that's another reason why we want to keep it on the down low at school."

Everyone says how sorry they are or how shitty that is for someone to do to their best friend, and warmth radiates throughout my chest. They are great friends, and I'm so proud of Ollie for stepping out of his comfort zone for me, just like I've stepped out of mine for him. It's helping us both grow and is another reason why this relationship is just so fucking *right.*

CHAPTER THIRTY-THREE
FINN

Going back to school on Wednesday was easier now that Eric's not there and all our friends have our backs. The rest of the academy found out what happened and rallied behind Oliver, welcoming him back with more gusto than they ever did in the first place over a month and a half ago. It feels fake as hell, but I'll take it over bullying any day.

Hazel wasn't at school, and I haven't heard from my dad yet, but I'm guessing there are new developments for him to update us with tonight. Eric snitched fast—before he even made it to the cop car. Just proves what a little bitch he is. Not that I give a shit. He did us a huge favor by taking the evil bitch down with him.

Now, it's Friday night, an hour before the dreaded family dinner, and Ollie and I are relaxing in my room. He's still recovering, so we took a half day yesterday when he started to drag around lunchtime. He snuggles into my side, resting his palm on my chest and sighing contentedly.

"You haven't repainted your nails yet," I observe. The doctors had to take his nail polish off at the hospital to monitor his oxygen levels properly, and it's the first time I've seen him without.

"Why? You miss it?" Big cerulean eyes peer up at me with a teasing glint.

"Yeah. I fucking do."

His grin widens, and he swings a leg over me, straddling my lap. I nuzzle my face into the crook of his neck and breathe in his clean, soapy scent.

"I love your nail polish. I love to see it on your fingers when they're wrapped around my cock, gripping me tightly," I growl, breathing deeply. "And I love your smell, and your hair, and your dimples. . . and your ass, too." I bite his neck, and he yelps.

I press my hand to his mouth, eyes boring into him. "Shh, or I won't fuck you."

He nods his head frantically, and I remove my hand. "It'll have to be quick. Your mom wants us down at six."

I grab the lube from my bedside drawer and hold it out to him. "Prep yourself."

"W-what?" he sputters, looking unsure and chewing on his bottom lip.

"Don't think about it, just do what feels good and get yourself ready for me."

The only layer between us is our thin boxers, so we remove those, and then our dicks are rutting against each other. It feels incredible.

Ollie squirts some lube into his hand and, still straddling me, leans forward with one arm braced on the bed. He reaches behind him and groans, his face contorting from hesitation to pure pleasure.

Fuck. It's so hot to see him working himself open. I just wish I had a different view. But there's time for that later.

"You're so sexy, baby. I can't wait to fuck you," I say, encouraging him to keep going. "Add another finger."

He closes his eyes and makes a strained face as he keeps fucking himself.

"Scissor them."

"Finnn. . . I can't. I'm going. . . to. . . come—" And then he does, his quiet whimpers making my own dick twitch. I need to be inside him, now. His sticky release coats my stomach, but I don't give a fuck.

I grab the lube and reach between us, slicking up my cock before he can even catch his breath. "Sit on me."

He whimpers and whines but gets up on his knees, balancing his hands on my chest and attempting to lower himself. I grab his hip with one hand and my rock-hard cock with the other, guiding him down. Once I slip past that initial ring, Ollie sits down with his full weight, impaling himself.

"Ungh! Oh, fuck! It's so deep like this!"

My abs tighten and ripple at his words. They make me feel animalistic, like some kind of caveman response was flipped, and my dick pulses for a beat inside him. He squeezes me back, and I groan.

"So. Fucking. Tight." I grit out. It's almost *too* tight.

"Bounce on me," I demand, and he does. He goes fucking wild, lifting up and slamming back down, impaling himself fully on my length each time.

"Finn! Oh God!" His forehead glistens from the strenuous activity, and I realize I'm making him do all the work.

I pull him down on top of me so we're chest to chest, his leftover jizz smearing between us.

"Just relax and let me fuck you," I breathe into his ear.

I band my arms tightly around him and piston my hips

in and out of him, starting slow at first, then picking up my pace until he's grunting from the force of every thrust.

"Shh. Don't scream," I warn. Then I bend my knees, angle my hips under him, and slam home, hitting that special spot deep inside him just right.

His breath hitches, but he stays quiet as I seal my mouth to his, stealing every exhale. I reach between us and stroke him twice before he's tightening around me and crying out as he comes again. I'm right behind him and spill myself deep inside of his spasming hole.

I rub his back gently as I pull my softening cock out of him, and he winces slightly, rolling off of me.

I grab his hand because we need to get a move on. "Let's go shower. There's no time to relax. We have a lot to get through at dinner."

"Ah fuck. Don't remind me. Just let me enjoy my orgasm for a minute longer."

I chuckle and pad to my bathroom, starting the shower and getting our towels out.

I'd take care of him for the rest of my life if he'd let me.

"Ollie, it's good to see you looking well, Son."

Son?

Now he's calling him "Son." I want to scoff, but he's been trying to be a better person since he got back from Aruba.

"Thanks, Gabe," Ollie says politely, and I swear to God he better call *me* Daddy before he *ever* calls my father Dad.

"Yes, sweetheart. You have a nice little flush to your cheeks now. You looked too pale in the hospital."

I pretend to scratch my upper lip, but I'm really trying

to hide the inappropriately timed grin threatening to tug at my lips. He's flushed all right. Back-to-back orgasms and rigorous sex will do that to a guy.

"Thanks, Mom. I feel a lot better," he mumbles, the tips of his ears turning bright red.

"Well, let's dig in while it's hot. I was too tired to cook with the new charity and the baby and all. So I hope takeout Italian sounds good to everyone."

It's the first time Vivian has brought up the pregnancy around me, and I know Ollie is side-eyeing me right now, hoping for a delicate response. We're sitting on the same side of the table this time, with Ollie's mom on the other side next to my dad.

"It sounds delicious, thanks, Vivian. I hope you haven't been too sick lately?"

There's a pause, and I think I may have surprised everyone.

"Oh, that's sweet. It hasn't been too bad this time around. Not like with this little monster." She smiles lovingly at Ollie, and my heart flutters with a painful longing for a brief second. "It's probably because he came out with a head full of golden curls. They say too much hair can give you indigestion."

"So we might have a bald baby?" Ollie asks, and we all chuckle.

"Maybe," she agrees, and everyone is more relaxed now, talking like a normal family, excited to welcome a new baby.

Move along, folks. Nothing dramatic is about to happen. Nope. Not at all. I just have to somehow come out with, *"Hey, Dad. Hey, Stepmommy. I'm fucking my stepbrother, and he's my boyfriend, too. Not sure if I'm gay, so don't ask. Neither of us is going to college right away either, if at all. And let's not forget to discuss dead mothers and attempted murderer ex-friends."*

Dad interrupts my spiraling thoughts, and I focus on the end of the mahogany table where he sits, elegantly slicing into the lasagna with his expert fucking surgeon hands.

"So, I wanted to go ahead and get the legal talk out of the way," Dad chimes in, serving Vivian and then himself a heaping slice of cheesy lasagna. The ricotta is spilling out of the sides, and my mouth waters for my own slice.

"Eric has implicated Hazel Bell. Even going as far as presenting text message proof that it was her idea. She was the mastermind—orchestrated the whole thing. None of the other sandwiches made by Jared's mother had peanut butter. She confirmed it. Eric brought a small, snack-size pouch of peanut butter for the specific, premeditated reason of triggering Oliver's food allergy. He acted recklessly and carelessly, and he nearly killed someone. If he were anyone else, he'd be in jail. But his parents, *both* of their parents, have money and connections, so it won't go to trial. But this will follow them for the rest of their lives, and I'm sure it will come with community service and fines and, as you know, expulsion. Lake View will not tolerate an attack on another student, even if it was off campus."

I quietly chew a breadstick as I let that sink in. I guess it works for me. "Ollie, how do you feel about that?" I ask.

"Does Hazel have a restraining order, too?"

"Yes," Dad replies.

"I guess I'm happy with that outcome. I definitely did not want anything to go to trial. I want to move on from it."

Me fucking too.

"It will not. Hank knows that no one wants that. It'll be settled before it ever gets that far. I'll handle everything with the lawyers. We shouldn't need anything from either of you besides the statement Wyatt already gave."

"Thanks, Dad." I can acknowledge that he came through when we needed him. Maybe he really will be here for this new baby. I fucking hope so.

We eat silently, enjoying the flavors of garlic and marinara in every bite. I'm stalling, but shit, I'm hungry.

I set my fork down. Time to get to it. Bite the bullet. Face the music. Leap into the breach.

"Ollie and I are together. He's my boyfriend."

There. Done.

I lean forward and grab the spatula, helping myself to a second slice. And then scooping another one onto Ollie's plate, too. I grab my fork and saw off a giant piece, shoveling it into my mouth.

"B-boyfriends?" Dad is the first to break the silence.

Huh. Guess he *didn't* know. Not exactly.

"Oh my goodness, boyfriends? I'm. . . I'm so happy for both of you! I knew you had chemistry, and I was pretty sure something might be going on, but I had no idea you were this serious. This will definitely complicate some things in your lives, but it's okay to be who you are and who you want to be with, honey." She reaches across the table and grabs ahold of my hand, squeezing.

"You've taken care of my son since day one, and I couldn't ever hope for someone better than you, Finn. I know you'll both treat each other right."

I feel the heat rise in my cheeks at her kind words, and I tuck my hair behind my ears, peering at Ollie next to me.

How is tonight going so well? This feels like a trick.

"I. . . I need a minute." My dad pushes away from the table, dropping his linen napkin on the table next to his half-eaten dinner.

Yeah, I thought so. Of course that was too fucking easy.

"Oh, Gabe—" Vivian tries to stop him, but he storms out of the dining room and down the hall to his office, shutting the door behind him. At least he didn't slam it.

I pick my fork back up and take another bite, feeling Oliver's gaze bore a hole into the side of my face.

I swallow my bite. "What?"

He rolls his eyes. But if a grown man wants to have a time out, then, by all means, have your fucking time out.

"I'll go talk to him. You two have done nothing wrong. You can't help who you love. And I know you love each other; I can see it in your eyes. He'll come around. We have a new little person linking us all." She rubs her non-existent bump and follows after Dad.

"That didn't go half bad, I suppose."

Ollie just snorts but doesn't disagree. We continue to eat in silence, waiting for Vivian to convince Dad to finish the conversation.

About ten minutes later, they both come back to the table. Pretty impressive of her, actually. Dad is stubborn as fuck, and that was fast.

He clears his throat before taking his seat again. "I apologize for walking out like that. I just wasn't expecting you to say *boyfriends*."

He turns his dark gaze on me. "I didn't know you were. . . gay, Wyatt."

He sounds like he can barely utter the word.

Whatever.

"I'm not. Not really. I just like Oliver." I tell him the same thing I told my friends—the truth.

Dad's dark brows crease in the center. "What does that mean?"

"It means he doesn't want or need a label," Ollie chimes

in, sticking up for me. I find his hand under the table and thread my fingers with his.

Dad rubs his forehead, like he's thinking way too hard about this. I can't help but laugh, his startled eyes whipping to mine.

"You're thinking way too hard about what it means, Dad. We're graduating soon, and I'll be moving out. Oliver too." I turn to Ollie and add, "If you want." Because we haven't talked about that yet, but I'm pretty sure he'll want to come with me.

"You know I'll gain full control of my money once I graduate, so I'm going to get my own place and work on starting my own business. And while we're airing it all out, I may as well tell you this, too. I didn't apply to any colleges like I said I did. I'm not going straight into more schooling. I have my own funding and a dream, and I'm chasing it. If I decide to go back to school once everything settles, I will. If I don't need to, then I won't. It's my life and my choice. Just like who I love."

There, I said it. It's all out there, and I feel better for it.

The dust hasn't even settled, and Ollie drops his own bomb. "I didn't apply anywhere either. Sorry, Mom. It's just with everything that happened last semester and then the cross-country move, I couldn't handle it. I'm taking a gap year, working on my art, but I do plan to go to school after that."

Vivian's mouth falls open, fingers touching her parted lips. "Oh, Oliver. Honey, you could have told me. I'm not going to lie; I'm a little shocked, but you know I'd understand. You have to do what's right for your mental health, and I'll always be your advocate."

"Will you be staying in Chicago?" Dad finally speaks up.

Vivian's turquoise eyes shimmer with hope as she peers across the table at me.

"My plan was to always get out."

Dad flinches at my words, and Vivian's face falls.

"But. . . things have changed." I reach over and squeeze the back of Ollie's neck, then rest my arm on the back of his chair.

"I have Oliver, and now this new little sibling on the way. I want to be in his or her life. So for now, yes, we're staying. Just moving to our own place. Together." I can't help but let my fingers trickle up the back of his neck and into his soft hair, scratching his scalp with my nails. Yes, our parents are watching, but I'm not doing anything inappropriate.

"See, Gabe. He is just the sweetest, most thoughtful boy, just like I've told you. This baby is so lucky to have you as a big brother. Both of you."

I swear this woman's blood type is sugar. I can't imagine her being anything but happy.

I direct my gaze to Dad, and he's staring at my hand caressing the back of Ollie's neck. He notices me watching and flicks his eyes to me, jaw ticking. He definitely doesn't want to *see* it. Even if he's going to act fine with it. Hmm. Oh well. I lightly rub the back of my knuckles across Ollie's neck, and he shivers.

Dad's nostrils flare, and he darts his eyes down to his now cold lasagna. A smug grin tugs at one side of my mouth. Hah. Too gay for him. This is going to be fucking great. I can't wait to push his boundaries, but that's probably enough for now, so I remove my arm before I give Ollie a hard-on at the family dinner table.

"Gabe, honey, do you mind grabbing the tiramisu from

the fridge? Then you boys can tell us all about your plans after graduation."

And that's how our night ends. Eating coffee-soaked sponge cake and telling our parents about our dreams of opening a car museum and exhibiting in galleries across the city.

Definitely could be worse.

CHAPTER THIRTY-FOUR
FINN

It's been over two months since Ollie nearly died, or should I say was nearly *murdered.* I didn't feel one ounce of sympathy when we came to school the week after Eric's arrest to find extremely unflattering mugshots of Hazel Bell—snotty red nose and all—taped to every locker in Preston Hall. No one took credit for it, and I normally wouldn't condone something like that, but the psychotic cunt plotted to murder my stepbrother. She can get everything that's coming to her. Eric too.

Dad was right in his prediction. There wasn't a trial, and Eric and Hazel's parents were able to miraculously reduce the serious felony charge of reckless conduct to a Class A misdemeanor.

I still feel like it should have been attempted murder, but seeing Hazel serve her community service picking up trash along the lake shore in a bright orange vest while the rest of us sunbathed was pretty goddamn satisfying. And knowing they can't come anywhere near Oliver for the next five years gives me peace of mind. They'll also be on probation for the next two years. They may not be in jail, but they fucked up their future. Eric and Hazel aren't graduating either. They got expelled and had to finish the year being homeschooled.

My dad really came through with his connections, handling everything with as little stress to Ollie as possible, which I appreciated.

Once the drama of Eric and Hazel's arrests faded to the background, the school year passed quickly and easily. We finished our exams, and Ollie presented his mural via video call from his art studio at home, creating a smaller replica with his beloved oil paints. The mural showed so well that it's being featured in a gallery downtown. They also want him to exhibit more.

Now that I know, with certainty, that my entire trust fund stays in my control, I've started looking at properties for my car museum. Ollie's been a great help and has a natural eye for design and aesthetics. He's going to be a huge asset in making this work, and I couldn't be more excited about it.

It's finally graduation day, and there was a time when it was all I yearned for. But things are so different now. I'm staying in Chicago, but we're moving out next week, ready to start our life together. If I could go back and tell sixteen-year-old Finn to just hang on, and things would get better. . . Well, never mind. I probably would have punched myself in the face.

"Oliver Walter Chase," the assistant headmaster calls, and there's booming applause and cheers from the entire arena. Everyone knows what happened to Ollie, what Eric and Hazel did, and they rallied behind him, showing him a crazy amount of support, even if it felt fake to start with.

I break the rules and stand from my spot a few rows back to cheer for my stepbrother *and boyfriend*—but that's still a secret from the people at this school. It's still only our closest friends who know about the relationship. Soon though, when we're out in the real world, we won't be hiding. We'll be living together and sharing a life together. And I can't fucking wait.

Ollie walks across the stage, accepting his diploma from the headmaster and flashing the crowd his award-winning dimples.

He's so goddamn sexy, even in a cap and gown. I wonder if he'll let me fuck him in it tonight. . .

A few rows later, it's my turn.

"Wyatt Carter Finnegan."

I can hear Vivian and my dad cheering, along with all of Bethany's cousins, who came to support her. I walk past Ollie, who's smiling so wide I can't help but return it and give him a little wink.

I accept my diploma and shake hands with the faculty on stage, smiling at everyone's genuine happiness for me.

There was a time when I thought the world hated me. But now, there's more love surrounding me than I've ever had in my entire life.

Ollie and I meet our parents in the middle of the quad for the obligatory graduation pics. The early evening sun is still bright, the day a perfectly comfortable temperature for early June. A startling change from the weather Ollie first showed up to.

"My boys!" Vivian screeches and jogs over to us, Dad hot on her heels. She's barely even showing, but my dad is ridiculously overprotective. He's even been to every single one of her doctor appointments. I think he has changed, but only time will tell for sure.

"I'm so proud of you both!" She stands on her tiptoes and wraps an arm around each of our necks, pulling us into a tight hug that we have to bend over for. We chuckle as she releases us.

Dad places a protective arm around her shoulders, "Congrats to you both. A noteworthy accomplishment for sure."

"Yes, it is! Let's take some photos." Vivian beams. Her golden hair, the same shade as Ollie's, is pulled back into a sleek fishtail braid, and she's wearing a beautiful, floor-length floral dress—looking every bit the California girl she is.

We take all variations of photos per Vivian's requests. Then Bethany and the guys show up, forcing us to take even more ridiculous photos, posing around the quad and the giant obelisk in the center.

The sun is beginning to cast its golden glow across the sprawling green lawn, threatening to call an end to the day's festivities, which is fine with me. This is our last night at home before we finally move out and get the privacy we so desperately needed since our parents returned from their honeymoon.

Oliver hasn't seen it, but I bought us a penthouse downtown. It's close to the location I've been looking at for my car museum and near the lake, too. The views are absolutely stunning, and I cannot wait to show him our new home.

"Let's head to dinner. I have a reservation for seven at the new steakhouse," Dad says.

"Sounds good. I'm ready to get out of this gown. It is hot as shit," Ollie says, and I agree.

Fuck this dress.

We shuffle through the revolving door and into the lobby of our new building. It's the morning after graduation and our long-awaited moving day. I don't have our parking pass for the underground garage yet, so I had to park at the meter on the street.

"This place is *amazing,* Finn," Ollie gushes, his eyes panning the stunning architecture surrounding us. It's a newer building, with floor-to-ceiling windows and stunning metal work, just like our penthouse. The gleaming white marble floors are veined with gold and sparkle under the sunlight. Lush, champagne-colored couches adorn a seating area with a white faux fur rug, and a giant flat-screen TV plays generic photos of the amenities offered. The young woman at the welcome desk, Jasmine, I think, gives us a little wave. We don't have to check in, ever. That penthouse apartment was *not* cheap.

"We have a private elevator, which opens to a small lounge before you get to our door. But the entire floor is ours, and no one else can access the elevator except us and our pre-approved cleaning service," I tell him.

His eyes bounce everywhere, and the adorable little smile on his lips makes me feel so satisfied that I can provide something like this for him.

"Should I carry you over the threshold?" I tease as we stroll the rest of the way through the lobby toward the back elevators.

Ollie chuckles at that and stops to hop on my back, wrapping his arms around my neck and pressing his cheek to mine. "No, but I'll take a piggyback ride. Now, mush!" he shouts, and I loop my arms under his legs to keep him up on my back. I shake my head and laugh at his antics, walking to the elevator.

There was a time not too long ago that I would have

freaked out about how this might look to outsiders. But now, I don't give a fuck because it's *exactly* how it looks.

This is my boyfriend, and we're in love.

The little old lady standing by the regular apartment elevators smiles kindly at us and waves, eyes twinkling like seeing our young love brings her joy.

I think we're going to be happy here.

Ollie reaches out and presses the only button available —a simple star. The doors immediately open, and I whisper into his ear that the code is his birth year backward.

Ollie reaches out and presses *four-zero-zero-two*, and the doors slide closed, taking us up thirty floors to our new place.

"Are you excited to see your new home, Cali Boy? I've heard the sunrise and sunset views are stunning."

"Hell yes!" He nuzzles his face into the crook of my neck, causing goosebumps to pebble across my skin.

I let go of a leg and reach into the front pocket of my jeans, pulling out our new house key. "Here." I open my palm, and Ollie plucks them from my hand.

The doors ping open, and we get our first glimpse of the lounge area outside our apartment. It's fully furnished by the building and looks like a replica of the downstairs lobby. It's luxurious and beautiful—not exactly to our taste, but that's okay. The inside is what matters.

I left it sparsely furnished—a bed, TVs, and an over-stuffed black leather couch. I purposely left it like this because my boyfriend is a fucking amazing artist, and I want his touch in our new home. I want color and life and fucking *sunshine* in this place.

"*Wow*. Dude. This is fucking sick. Look at the view!"

I smirk because he hasn't seen anything yet. These

windows are tiny compared to the floor-to-ceiling view he'll get once he opens that door.

"Let's go in." Ollie unlocks the door, and I step in, letting him slide down my back.

His mouth drops open, and his brilliant blue eyes practically glow. He turns in a slow semicircle, taking in the massive amount of open square footage and the view of the city, Lake Michigan glittering in the not-so-far distance.

"It's bare because I want you to paint it, decorate it, do whatever the fuck you want to it. Make it our home."

He spins around and launches himself at me. "This is more than I ever could have imagined for myself. I would have been happy in a one-bedroom apartment with you, but this. . . wow. Thank you."

I grunt out a "welcome" and show him the few pieces of furniture we do have.

"The bed's already made. I had the cleaning service stock the fridge and the bathroom, too."

I link my pinky with his and peer at him. "We don't have to go anywhere until we goddamn please. No school. No work. Just you and me."

I lead us to the bedroom, where our new king-size bed is set up in the middle of the room against the exposed brick wall. The ornate, dark wood bedposts, fluffy black comforter, and black silk pillowcases look like they're just waiting for debauchery.

I take a deep breath and face him, keeping our pinkies linked. "I want you to fuck me."

CHAPTER THIRTY-FIVE
OLIVER

"W-what?" I'm not sure I heard him right. He's been getting used to my fingers, but I figured he'd always strictly be a top.

"I want you to fuck me," he repeats.

"Are you sure?" Why the fuck am I asking this? I should be dragging him over to the bed and fucking him before he changes his mind. But I know this is more than just sex. This is about Finn dropping yet another safety net, and I need him to know it's alright to let go of the control. I'm going to make it so good for him.

"Positive. Now, let's christen our new bed," he says, tugging me toward the giant bed.

Finn glances over his shoulder at me and smirks. "What do you look so scared for?"

"I'm not. Just trying to decide how I want to take your ass," I lie. My stomach is in knots, and I'm starting to get nervous—I've never fucked anyone before.

His smirk stretches into a full-blown smile, and I think my heart may have literally just skipped a beat. "I trust you," he says, and I melt even more. He spins around and walks backward toward the bed, pulling me along and biting on his bottom lip.

Holy fuck, that's hot. I cannot wait to know what it feels like to be *inside* him.

Heaven. It's gonna be heaven.

When the back of his legs bump the bed, he pulls his T-shirt over his head and yanks his joggers and boxer briefs down in one go.

All my nerves vanish at the sight of his naked body, and I practically lunge at him. Our mouths meet and tongues tangle. I want him so badly, but I know I need to take this slow. Even slower than he did for me. This is something he never imagined for himself, and on top of that, his issues with control make this even more of a delicate situation.

His hands slide under my shirt, massaging and kneading my back as we explore each other's mouths. I lift my arms, and he pulls it over my head. Then we're chest to chest, and I love the feel of his skin on mine. He's a little taller than me, a lot broader than me, and his erection presses into my lower belly, deliciously taunting me.

After a few more minutes of kissing, I decide it's time for me to take over. I caress his face, cradling it in my palms as I flip the kiss from something wild to something tender. I trail my hands down the sides of his neck to his shoulders, squeezing and massaging the way he did me. Then I put slight pressure on his shoulders, urging him to sit at the end of the bed.

"Wait there."

I stroll to the bedside table, feeling Finn's lust-filled gaze tracking me the whole way. I grab my phone, connect to the Bluetooth, and press play on my newest Spotify playlist.

"Where Are You?" by Elvis Drew and Avivian flows through the speakers built into the walls, and the slow, seductive words fill the bedroom.

"Scoot up."

He listens.

I leave my basketball shorts on because I know they drive him wild and climb onto the bed toward him.

"Spread your legs."

Again, he listens, and I crawl between his thighs, licking one long stripe up his straining erection. He grips the sheets on either side of him and sucks in a sharp breath. I lick him again, and he groans deep from the back of his throat. I suck on his swollen tip and take him further, working the base with my hand. He cradles the back of my head and tries to guide me deeper, but I pop off his crown instead.

"Uh uh. Hands behind your head. I'm the one in control here."

He obeys, peering down his body at me with half-lidded eyes.

Oh. This is fun. I think I like this.

I continue working his cock with my mouth and hand, but his hips start to buck, so I stop.

"Fuuuck, don't stop. Ollie, you're killing me."

"You were about to come. Now bend your knees."

I grab the lube from the table and squirt some onto my fingers. I kiss him on the mouth, but he doesn't care that I was just sucking on his dick. He's eager and loving it. I reach down, still kissing him slowly, and find his hole. He's gotten used to this part and likes it.

I work in one, then two fingers, stretching and scissoring him open. His breathing picks up, and I suck in every moan. I love kissing him while he pants—there's something so primal and so fucking feral about it. Makes me feel untamed. I slowly pull away from his soft lips. The turbulent emotions roaring through me make me feel possessive and protective of this vulnerable boy below me.

I gaze down at him, propping myself up on a forearm. "Are you ready?"

"Fuck, yes. I need you."

My eyes bounce between his, and I find nothing but desire, love, and *hunger*. Not even a hint of fear or uncertainty.

I stay where I am, eyes locked on his midnight blue depths as I guide my aching cock to his entrance.

"I love you so fucking much," I say as I push into him. His breath hitches, and I pause for a second to let him adjust before sliding all the way in.

Holy fucking shit.

This feels. . . This feels like *everything*.

We're both frozen, staring at each other, in awe of the switch this relationship has just undergone.

"Move, Ollie," he finally croaks.

I snap out of my stupor and pull out, only leaving the tip inside before I slowly push back in. Three more times, and he's moaning and groaning, back arched against the bed, pulling his own hair as I languorously fuck him.

No. *Make love to him*. Because that's what we're doing right now. I love this man so fucking much, and I'm showing it to him right now.

"Ollie, *fuck*. So good."

"Look at me," I demand, not stopping my slow, deep thrusts.

His eyes pop open, and they're shimmering with so much emotion that my breath catches in my throat, and I nearly choke on my next words.

"You feel so amazing, Finn. I love you so much." I lean down and kiss him as slowly as I'm fucking him.

"Love. You. Too." He grunts out on each powerful thrust of my hips.

Changing my angle, I hit his prostate hard, and he cries out, grabbing the soft globes of my ass and making me fuck him deeper.

I finally decide to take it up a notch and pick up my pace.

"Gonna. Come," Finn grits out. "Don't stop."

I reach in between us, stroking him fast. Sweat drips from my brow and plops onto Finn's chest. I watch as it trickles down the hard grooves of his big, muscly body.

"*Fuuuck*! Ollie!" His ass clenches around me so hard that it instantly triggers my own orgasm, and we're coming together. His hot cum splashes against my stomach, and I fill him up with mine. It oozes out as I continue to fuck him until I'm soft and finally slip out.

I collapse onto the bed next to him. I just need a minute before I can clean us both up like Finn always does for me.

I roll onto my side, gazing at his strong profile while he breathes heavily, eyes closed.

"That was. . . shit, Finn, I don't even have words. Just. . . Thank you. For trusting me with that. And I kinda hope it wasn't just a one-time thing. Because feeling your tight ass griping me like that, knowing I was *inside* you, *fucking* you. Goddamn dude, I want to do that again."

Finn startles me when an abrupt laugh explodes out of him. "I think we can switch it up sometimes." He turns his head, and we lie there staring at each other. A million unspoken emotions pass between us. He's so beautiful I don't want to turn away.

We've both come so far from where we started not that many months ago. Some people may not agree, may not think it's right. But we love each other—help each other, *heal* each other—and there's nothing that could ever be wrong with that.

EPILOGUE
FINN

Four Years Later

"Fiiiiiinn!" I smile when I hear the cute little voice squealing my name down the hallway. Fiona runs into our parent's theater room, Ollie hot on her heels.

"I Princess Fiona!" She points to her other brother. "Ollie ogre!" I burst out laughing at that.

Ollie holds his hands up like claws and grunts as he shuffles with a limp and a hunched back. I bend over double where I'm standing by the wet bar and clutch at my stomach as I try to calm down enough to speak. "You're supposed to be Shrek, not Quasimodo," I say between laughs. Then, I mouth *'what the fuck'* to him because he looks kind of scary for a three-year-old girl, but FiFi loves it.

"Finn, help!" She clings to my legs and hides behind me, peeking around and squealing every time Ollie reaches for her with his weird, zombie-ogre-hunchback hands.

Our little FiFi is three years old and going on thirteen. I didn't know it was possible for someone so small to have so much sass, but here she is. She's a ball of fire with her dark brown hair, vibrant blue eyes, and adorable dimples, just like her mom and brother. She's going to be a heartbreaker, that's for sure.

We both gave Viv a hard time over the name she chose for our sister, Fiona Elise Finnegan, aka FiFi Finnegan. The alliteration was a bit much, but now, I couldn't imagine her being called anything else. It fits her perfectly. She's the princess of the family, and she knows it—my dad, Ollie, and I are completely wrapped around her little finger, and we aren't going anywhere.

Ollie and I decided to stay in Chicago permanently to stay present in our sister's life. We also have a beach house in San Diego, as well. You can take the boy out of Cali, but you definitely can't take the Cali out of the boy. I knew he missed it, especially surfing, so for his twenty-first birthday last year, I surprised him with a modest, beachfront property. It was pretty bare-bones, so we spent a lot of the summer out there, painting, remodeling, and decorating. And you better believe we have a sunset mural on one of our bedroom walls, right next to the floor-to-ceiling windows showcasing the real thing.

Sometimes, when the timing is just right and the lighting is dim, I can hardly tell between Ollie's painting and the actual sunset. He's perfected his skill since high school and only has one year left for his fine arts degree. I opted for business, just like Ollie suggested, and I have two years left. Oliver took a gap year and had his art featured in several prominent galleries throughout Chicago. I took an extra year beyond that, finalizing the last touches on my car museum and preparing for the grand opening. I found a great warehouse just an 'L' ride away from our penthouse.

Two million trust fund dollars later, my dream was finally ready.

Ollie helped design our logo and made sure everything stayed on brand during renovations—his biggest contribution being the splashes of paint and graffiti art all over the walls. It complements every car we showcase and ties in with the pops of color in all of the furniture. I couldn't have even dreamed of the success that I've achieved—*we've* achieved—because I could have never done it without Ollie.

Not only has the museum pulled in wealthy, older car enthusiasts, but also the younger, hip crowd. And I know the vibes that Oliver helped me pull off contribute to that. As do the *three* cars from various *Fast and Furious* movies. All of the guys and Bethany showed up to the grand opening to support us, and it was amazing.

There's one year left on the restraining orders against Eric and Hazel, but I'm not too worried about them trying to reach out. Last I heard, Eric was in NYC getting his master's, and Hazel was in Florida with a husband and a newborn.

"Finny! You be Donkey!"

Ollie cracks up at that. "Yeah, Finny. If I'm Shrek, you're definitely Donkey."

"I'll show you Donkey!" And then I'm chasing them both down the hallway, braying like a complete idiot.

"Mommy! Daddy! Help me!" Her squeals turn into high-pitched screams, and I know it's time to calm her down, but Viv intercepts her first.

"What's happening, Princess Fiona? Do I need to call the Queen's Royal Guard? Are these monsters bothering you?" She plays along like we always do, encouraging FiFi's imagination.

"Silly Mommy! It's just Ollie and Finny! See!" She points her tiny little finger at us repeatedly, and I chuckle, scooping her up and squeezing her tightly to me. She's my little miracle, and I know she's the reason there's been so much growth and healing between my dad and me these past four years.

"Want a snack, munchkin? I think the ogre's hungry since he couldn't eat the princess."

"Yeah, I'm famished," Ollie says, pretending to bite FiFi and making her squeal more.

"Your dad's in the kitchen. Let's head in there," Viv says, and we all follow her downstairs—FiFi still clinging to my neck like a little spider monkey. Vivian knows Ollie and I came over to talk to her and Dad about something.

We head to the black marble and dark wood kitchen that looks exactly the same as it did four years ago when we left. Dad's at the island, reading his newspaper and sipping his strong coffee.

"Boys. Good to see you," he says amicably.

"Dad."

"Gabe."

Vivian pulls out bowls of fruit, assorted bagels, and different flavored cream cheese. She quickly fixes a plate for FiFi and sets her up at her Minnie Mouse table with an iPad. She won't pay attention to a single word the adults say as long as she has her tablet.

"So, it's almost July, and we'll be heading back to California soon. We were wondering if FiFi could stay with us for a couple weeks? Just the three of us. I know you're both so busy and wouldn't be able to stay long."

"We just have so much fun with her and love her so much," Ollie adds.

Viv practically melts and clutches at her chest. "Oh

gosh, you boys. How did she get so lucky to have such amazing big brothers?"

They know they can trust us with her. We took shifts with them when she was a newborn, and I feel more like her father than her brother, anyway. And I know Ollie feels the same. I don't know if we'll have biological kids one day or adopt, but this little girl is a piece of both of us. There is something so incredibly special about that, and I feel like a puddle of goo every time I look at her sweet little face.

"Of course, we trust you to take her. She'll be so excited. Right, honey?"

My gaze darts to my dad, and I wait. We've never taken her for longer than a night, and that was just to our home in the city.

"Of course," he agrees, and an undiluted smile fills my face, tugging at my eyes.

"FiFi!" I call out, and her bright blue eyes, identical to Ollie's, peer over at me. Her cheeks are full of watermelon, and I smile at her cuteness. I make sure she swallows before I surprise her with the news.

"Want to go to the beach with us?"

"Eeeeee!" She jumps out of her chair, knocking over her bowl of fruit and spilling her juice all over the iPad.

"Oops! I sorry!"

My dad chuckles and adds, "But we're not responsible for any damages incurred."

"It's not a problem. She can do no wrong. I mean, have you seen those eyes? And those dimples?"

"Ollie. Those are *your* eyes and *your* dimples," I deadpan.

"Yeah, and they're killer, right?" He swoops his golden hair back and smiles wide, popping said dimples out. I just roll my eyes.

"I want to surf like Ollie!" FiFi shouts.

Our parents brought FiFi out for a week when we first finished renovations on the beach bungalow. She took to the ocean right away, just like her brother.

"You got it, munchkin." I scoop her up and let her sit on my lap, eating my food since she spilled hers.

The three other people around me stare at her with sweet, dopey smiles. She's made us all soft, but it isn't a bad thing. I'm looking forward to taking my two favorite people out of the city and relaxing for the next two weeks—building sand castles and boogie boarding in the shallows.

We don't have to worry about her understanding that we're a couple quite yet, she just sees her big brothers when she peers up at us with her innocent blue eyes. But when the time comes, we've decided we won't lie to her. We have nothing to hide, and we're not ashamed. Our parents have long accepted our relationship, and we've all undergone massive healing to become this happy, healthy, full-of-life family. We won't ever go back to the lies and hidden truths. This is a peace-loving Cali family now.

ACKNOWLEDGMENTS

Thank you so much for getting this far and finishing my first book! It seriously means so much to me. I really hope you love Finn and Ollie as much as I loved writing them. These boys will always have a special place in my heart. I'm sad to end their story but so excited to start my next. I plan to write a little bit of everything, so I hope you stick around for more sweet and spicy happily ever afters!

I'd also like to thank Elizabeth Dear—amazing author and supportive friend. Your encouragement and the fact that you stayed up past your bedtime to finish my book all in one night really gave me the push that I needed to do this thing!

Morgan—my beta reader, feral housewife, and one of the funniest people I've had the pleasure of getting to know. Your genuine excitement and positive feedback were so valuable, and I'm incredibly grateful for that.

Silver at Bitter Sage Designs absolutely killed the cover design. I mean, look at Ollie, you guys! It was such a fun and exciting process. You are truly talented, and I can't wait to work on more projects with your gorgeous designs.

And finally, I'd like to thank my editor Molly, with Novel Mechanic. As a new author, the idea of editing was a little daunting, but you made the process as painless as possible, and I really learned so much! I appreciate every single mark, thought, and comment.

ALSO BY CHARLI MEADOWS

The Loyal Boys

Cali Boy

Bad Boy

ABOUT THE AUTHOR

Charli Meadows is an obsessive reader, avid Bookstagrammer-turned PA, and now an author herself. Lover of all things romance, she plans to write a little bit of everything but make it sweet and spicy.

Living in North Carolina with her husband and young daughter, you can usually find Charli working her boring corporate job or at home playing video games. When she's not reading, writing, or daydreaming about books.

Subscribe to my newsletter! Join my Facebook Group!

Made in the USA
Middletown, DE
03 September 2023

37925698R00196